More cheers for Beth Groundwater's

A CLAIRE HANOVER MYSTERY SERIES

To Hell in a Handbasket

"Groundwater's second leaves the bunny slope behind, offering some genuine black-diamond thrills."—*Kirkus Reviews*

"An engrossing and entertaining mystery that keeps you reading until the final page."—Gumshoe.com

"The wait is over for the second title in the Claire Hanover Mystery series … Her page turning style is welcome to any reader looking for a great read."—*Fort Collins Coloradoan*

A Real Basket Case

An Agatha Award Finalist for Best First Novel

"A tense, exciting debut."   —*Kirkus Reviews*

"This will appeal to *Desperate Housewives* fans and those who like cozies with a bit of spice."   —*Booklist*

"*A Real Basket Case* and its author are a welcome addition to the mystery genre."   —*Crimespree Magazine*

"An enjoyable mystery . . . *A Real Basket Case* should not be missed."
                    —Romance Reviews Today, RomRevToday.com

"I really enjoyed this book. I can't wait to read the next!"
                    —Mystery Lovers Corner, SleuthEdit.com

"A clever, charming debut novel. Her well-crafted characters comprise a nicely balanced cast, and she does a good job incorporating a blend of humor and relationship drama into a deftly twisted plot with the kind of surprise ending guaranteed to satisfy. Quick-paced and well written with clear and comfortable prose, *A Real Basket Case* is a perfect afternoon read for cozy fans." —SpinetinglerMag.com

"A gutsy sleuth, a fast-paced plot, and intriguing characters that keep you guessing. *A Real Basket Case* is a real winner! Don't miss it."
—Maggie Sefton, *New York Times* bestselling author of the Knitting Mystery series

"A crackling good novel with the kind of twists and turns that make roller coaster rides so scary and so much fun!"
—Margaret Coel, *New York Times* bestselling author of the Wind River Mysteries

"An impressive debut! Groundwater brings new meaning to the term menopausal in this flawlessly crafted mystery. Her gutsy, power surging heroine keeps the pressure on until the final chapter."
—Kathy Brandt, author of the Underwater Investigation series

"Like one of Claire's baskets, Beth Groundwater has put together the perfect mixture of humor, thrills, and mystery. A terrific debut!"
—Christine Goff, author of the Birdwatcher's Mystery series

To Hell in a Handbasket

To Ellie,
Enjoy Claire's wild ride!

BETH GROUNDWATER

To Hell in a Handbasket

A CLAIRE
HANOVER
MYSTERY

Beth Groundwater

MIDNIGHT INK
WOODBURY, MINNESOTA

MIDNIGHT INK™

Previously published in 2009 by Five Star Publishing, an imprint of Gale/Cengage.

First Midnight Ink Edition
First Printing, 2012

Book design by Donna Burch
Cover design by Kevin R. Brown
Cover illustration © Glenn Gustafson
Editing by Connie Hill

Midnight Ink, an imprint of Llewellyn Worldwide Ltd.

Library of Congress Cataloging-in-Publication Data

Groundwater, Beth.
  To hell in a handbasket : a Claire Hanover mystery / by Beth Groundwater. —1st Midnight Ink ed.
       p.   cm. — (A Claire Hanover mystery; 2)
  "Previously published in 2009 by Five Star Publishing, an imprint of Gale/Cengage"—T.p. verso.
  ISBN 978-0-7387-2702-8
1. Ski resorts—Colorado—Fiction. 2. Murder—Investigation—Fiction.
3. Breckenridge (Colo.)—Fiction. I. Title.
  PS3607.R677T6   2012
  813'.6—dc23   2012021942

Midnight Ink
Llewellyn Worldwide Ltd.
2143 Wooddale Drive
Woodbury, MN 55125-2989
www.midnightinkbooks.com

To Breckenridge, Colorado, my new hometown,
for welcoming my husband and me with open arms.

ACKNOWLEDGMENTS

First I'd like to thank those who helped me with background research for this book. Derek Woodman, Undersheriff of the Summit County Sheriff's Office, answered numerous questions, gave me a tour of their facility, and had one of his patrol officers model their uniform for me. Also, Wally Lind and Don Lewis of the crimescenewriter "Crime Scene Questions for Writers" Yahoo! group gave me excellent feedback on the plausibility of various scenarios for citizen involvement in police investigations. Hopefully, I didn't stretch reality too far for you, fellas.

Also, I want to thank Gail Westwood and other staff at the Breckenridge Nordic Center for answering questions about their snowshoe trails and equipment, and the staff at Tiger Run Tours for giving my family a great time on our "research" snowmobile ride. Thanks to Robert I. Friedman, author of *Red Mafiya: How the Russian Mob Has Invaded America*, for a fascinating and useful resource.

I owe huge thanks to my writing critique group (Robert Spiller, William Mason, Barbara Nickless, and Maria Faulconer) for their insightful feedback on this manuscript. Thanks to editor Denise Dietz and the other professionals at Tekno Books and Five Star Publishing who worked on the 2009 hardcover edition of *To Hell in a Handbasket*. Many thanks to the professionals at Midnight Ink who worked on this edition and make all of my books look good—and thus make me look good: acquisition editor Terri Bischoff, senior editor Connie Hill, and cover designer Kevin R. Brown. (Purple is my favorite color!) And special thanks to my literary agent, Sandra Bond, who looks out for my best interests in my writing career.

And last but not least, thanks to my family for their support and enthusiasm.

ONE: SNOW ACCIDENT

CLAIRE HANOVER'S KNEES SLAMMED up toward her chest. She shoved them down and around the mogul and braced for the next impact. *Oof!* Then the next and the next. All she could hear were her own labored breaths and her skis swishing through three inches of Colorado champagne powder sprinkled over the bumps of packed snow.

Her body lurched, thrown back on her skis. Punching out with her fist, she drove her downhill knee forward to regain her balance. It screamed in protest. She stabbed her ski pole into another mogul and swung around it. *Three more turns*, she promised her forty-six-year-old knees. *Then we'll rest.*

After rounding three more body-sized bumps, she hockey-stopped in a soft patch of loose snow. Leaning forward on her poles, she eased the pressure on her knees. They stopped cursing her for pushing them so hard during her first day on skis in months. The pain slowly receded. She sucked in gasps of clean, cold air, unzipped her jacket a few inches to cool off, and glanced uphill.

The T-bar was no longer in view, inching its way above the tree line on Peak Eight of the Breckenridge ski resort. The smooth upper slope of Ptarmigan, the easiest black diamond run north of the T-bar, sparkled in the brilliant sunshine of a cloudless March sky. Claire had carved pretty S-turns up there, but when the slope plunged into the trees, growing steeper, the resulting moguls thrown up by countless skiers had forced her to sacrifice her grace. Now she was in survival mode.

She looked downhill. Three skiers stood off to the left below the mogul field, waiting with faces upturned toward her. Her husband, Roger, would be secretly grateful for the opportunity to rest, but Judy, her twenty-one-year-old daughter, and Judy's companion, Stephanie, would be anxious to move on.

Claire took a deep breath and pushed off.

She fought through the remaining moguls, conscious of the others watching her as her knees resumed their cries of agony. *Why did I let Roger and Judy talk me into this run? It'll be the death of me.* Finally, she carved one last long turn and slid to a stop between the culprits.

Roger grinned at her from beneath his tinted goggles. His graying hair stuck out in all directions around his bald spot. He refused to wear a ski hat or helmet, so Claire constantly had to slather sunscreen on his head.

He raked his hand through his tousled hair. "Great run, huh?"

"And we've got it almost to ourselves. That's the advantage of skiing on a weekday." Judy nodded at a lone snowboarder speeding through the mogul field.

Barely under control, the boarder launched off one bump, slammed into another, rolled and righted himself before launching into the air again. His goofy hat streamed multi-colored fleece dreadlocks behind him as he bounced down the slope toward them, picking up speed.

Claire tried to gauge where the young man's erratic trajectory would take him. "Think we should move?"

"It's his responsibility to steer clear of us," Roger said.

Claire shuffled backward toward the trees on her skis. "But is he capable of steering?"

Before Roger could answer, the boarder raced past. Leaning hard on one edge of his psychedelic orange-swirled board, he sprayed them with snow.

"Hey!" Judy cupped her hands around her mouth and yelled at the boarder's receding back. "You cut that too close!"

Stephanie whirled to watch the boarder's progress, whipping long black hair across her face. She swiped her locks away and tsked at Judy. "He needs to be taught some manners."

"How right you are," Judy said.

Surprisingly compatible, Stephanie and Judy hadn't known each other before last night. The connection was Nickolas Contino, Stephanie's brother and Judy's boyfriend, who currently was skiing Copper Mountain's back bowls with his father. Unbeknownst to Claire, when she arranged to fly Judy home from her spring semester in France for this ski trip, Nick made plans for his family to vacation in Breckenridge at the same time. Having just met the young man, Claire was reserving judgment.

In fact, she still felt miffed Judy had gone out with Nick only a few hours after the family arrived for their two-week vacation.

Claire and Roger had collected Judy at the Denver airport Saturday, taken her home to Colorado Springs to do laundry and repack, then driven to Breckenridge on Sunday. Claire would have liked one unhurried night with just family before Judy started socializing. Here it was Monday, their first day on the slope, and Judy already had someone tagging along.

Judy tossed her mane of long chestnut-brown hair, glanced at her mother, and pursed her full, plum-colored lips. She quickly plastered an "I'm having a good time" smile on her face, but as if it had a mind of its own, one foot stamped its ski in the snow.

Some would take the gesture to mean Judy needed to warm her feet, but Claire knew the action signaled impatience. Impatience with her slow, uncool mother, who cramped her style. Even though she tried to hide it, Judy pawed at the snow like a thoroughbred racehorse anxious to be given her head.

Claire sighed. She had hoped to spend the day skiing as a foursome, snatching some long-missed conversation time with her daughter on the lift rides. Now, only an hour after they had started skiing, Judy had had enough.

Claire released the reins. "Judy, you and Stephanie go on ahead. You don't need to keep waiting for me. Your dad and I will meet you in the Vista Haus at noon for lunch."

Judy flashed a grin. "Thanks, Mom."

She and Stephanie pushed off and skied toward the upper part of the Claimjumper run. Their willowy bodies leaned gracefully into their fast, carved turns. Stephanie had the better skiing form, but Judy managed to keep up.

Ah, to be young, fit, and fearless.

Roger laid his hand on Claire's arm. "I know you wanted to spend the day with her, but you did the right thing."

"Yeah, but that doesn't mean I have to like it. First Michael couldn't leave his project in Boston to join us. Now Judy can't wait to get away from us."

Claire knew she should feel proud that management at Electronic Data Systems thought her son's engineering skills were so important they couldn't release him, but she missed him. And now Judy stood poised on the brink of leaving the nest, wings fiercely flapping to catch the winds of freedom. Soon, no one would need the mothering skills Claire had honed over two dozen years.

Roger bent and gave Claire an awkward kiss, their goggles rubbing against each other. His brown eyes twinkled behind the plastic lenses. "You've still got me."

She smiled at him and patted his cheek. "Yes, I do, and I'm not letting you go. You ready to hit the slope again, Handsome?"

"After you, Beautiful."

To the rest of the world, Claire was sure their words rang false, with their middle-aged paunches and graying hair—Claire's dyed blond. But Claire still saw traces of the handsome athletic MBA candidate she'd married twenty-six years ago during the summer before her senior year of college. She hoped Roger's gaze was similarly rose-colored.

She pushed off and followed Judy's and Stephanie's tracks down the hill. Roger trailed behind, letting her set a leisurely pace. They wound through the widely spaced fir and spruce trees above the snowcat track connecting the top of the Independence chairlift with the bottom of the T-bar.

A scream pierced the thin mountain air.

A tight fist of fear squeezed Claire's heart. *Oh, God.* "That sounds like Judy!"

Claire hunkered down and picked up speed, scanning the slope before her with anxious eyes. Roger's skis schussed right behind her as he raced after her.

She spotted Judy in the woods off to the right, bent over a form in the snow. Her skis lay abandoned on the slope nearby, but she didn't look hurt. Relief washed over Claire, loosening clenched muscles. *Thank God, but where's Stephanie?*

Claire tore her gaze from her daughter. The form by Judy took shape. A body lay on its side, with its back facing Claire and wearing Stephanie's ski jacket.

Claire skied over to Judy's skis and clicked out of her own. She slogged through the soft snow on the trailside to Judy. "What happened?"

Tears streamed down Judy's cheeks. "Ste—, Steph—" She pointed.

Claire stepped closer and peered over Stephanie's back.

Stephanie's face came into view, scratched, swollen, with blood streaming out of her misshapen nose. A bright red pool stained the snow by the young woman's head, but its source wasn't just her broken nose. Blood oozed out of her ear, a sure sign of a traumatic head injury.

Horror-stricken, Claire fell to her knees, clutching her chest. Her heart pounded. "Oh, God."

"Holy shit!" Roger stood over her. He gaped at Stephanie, then looked around.

"She must have hit this." He pointed to the tree straddled by Stephanie's skis. Bits of bark littered the snow around the base of the tree.

Claire tried to clear her mind and remember the first-aid mantra she had learned years ago when she had been Judy's Girl Scout leader. *Check, Call, Care.* She licked her dry lips and reached out to feel Stephanie's neck. A faint pulse fluttered under her fingertips. She bent over the young woman's face. A small breath whiffed out of her lips and blew against Claire's cheek, followed by an almost imperceptible rise of Stephanie's chest.

"How'd she hit the tree?" Claire asked Judy.

Judy gulped and took a shuddering breath. "I don't know. I didn't see."

Roger stumbled over to Judy and gathered her in his arms, pulling her head away from the shocking scene. She squeezed her eyes shut and clutched her father.

"Roger, call nine-one-one," Claire said. "Tell them we have an unconscious victim with shallow breathing and a head trauma."

While he dug out his cell phone, Claire's mind raced. *Stephanie doesn't need CPR yet, but we should try to stop the bleeding without moving her.* Claire shivered, but not from the cold. While holding Stephanie's head still with one hand, Claire gingerly pinched the bleeding nose with her other hand and checked that air was still flowing through Stephanie's mouth.

Roger reached the emergency dispatcher and started relaying information.

Claire glanced at Judy. "Why didn't you see what happened?"

Judy shook her head and sniffed. "Sh . . . she got ahead of me. Then that snowboarder came out of the woods up there." She pointed uphill, at a curve, and swallowed hard.

"What happened next?"

"He sped past me and around the curve. A few seconds later, I heard a thump and saw Stephanie-eee." She wailed and buried her head against Roger's chest again.

"You think he hit her?" Claire asked.

Judy nodded.

Roger clutched her while he gave directions over the phone.

Claire un-pinched Stephanie's nose and checked it. The bleeding seemed to have stopped, and the flow out of her ear had slowed. Stephanie was still breathing, though the breaths were shallow.

Claire's hands hovered over the frighteningly still young woman, yearning to comfort, to make the hurt go away, to mother. But how? Stephanie shouldn't be moved. If she hit the tree hard enough to break her nose, she could have a neck injury as well as the head trauma.

Claire couldn't think of anything else to do that would not make Stephanie's injuries worse, but she ached to do something, anything, useful. She focused on their skis lying above them. At least she could help the ski patrol find them.

"Watch her breathing, Roger, and let me know if it stops."

Pushing off her sore knees, Claire rose and tromped through the snow to their skis. She hoisted hers and walked them out to the center of the slope, where she slammed them into the snow, making the sign of an X, the universal call for help at ski areas. She searched uphill for other skiers but saw none. Tracks in the snow caught her eye. Only a few showed in the fresh layer that had fallen overnight.

She traced Judy's, hers, and Roger's tracks up from where they had stopped and clicked out of their skis. Then she saw the single track of a snowboard making wide turns. She followed the track, looking for the impact point with Stephanie's ski tracks.

Claire found where Stephanie's tracks changed from a carved turn to an out-of-control skid veering into the woods. The snowboarder's track intersected with Stephanie's near there, but one last set of ski tracks appeared in the snow, too.

Where Stephanie's tracks veered into the woods, the extra set carved toward hers, approached within inches, then veered off in the opposite direction. *Could the skier have hit her instead?* Claire searched uphill, following the extra tracks until they disappeared into the woods off to the right side of the slope. A broken branch swung in the light breeze.

I need to see the tracks up close. If she could tell which track went over the top of which, maybe she could figure out who reached the spot at the same time as Stephanie.

Claire started uphill, but before she could take more than a few steps, three ski patrollers came into view. They wore red jackets emblazoned with white crosses, and one towed an evacuation toboggan. They rushed toward Claire's X'ed skis. She waved her arms and pointed to Stephanie.

The patrollers skidded to a stop, their toboggan obliterating all the tracks around the impact point, and ran over to examine the young woman. Claire could tell from the tenseness in their voices when they saw the head injury that Stephanie's chances were slim. They worked efficiently nonetheless, immobilizing her head, lifting her onto the sled and zipping her into the yellow, vinyl-coated bag that kept hurt skiers warm for the ride down the hill and their injuries masked from public view.

Once they had strapped in Stephanie and her ski equipment, two of the patrollers took off with her. One crouched next to her on the toboggan and pumped an air bag into the mask covering her lower face. *So, Stephanie has stopped breathing.* Claire's throat constricted with unshed tears. She murmured a silent prayer.

The third patroller, a lean, sandy-haired man in his thirties, approached them. He pulled out a small notebook and a pen. "I'm Hal Matthews, senior ski patroller. I need to ask you some questions about the accident. Did anyone see what happened?"

"Not exactly," Roger said before telling him about the snowboarder and describing his board and attire. Judy choked out her part of the story in response to the patroller's gentle questions.

Their voices faded in Claire's mind as she studied the spot where the tracks of the impact had been. She tried to make sense of what she had seen. If a skier took off from the woods without checking uphill first, then the skier could have run into Stephanie instead of the snowboarder. But if so, why didn't the person stop? He or she had to have seen Stephanie hit the tree. Why didn't the snowboarder stop? And if the snowboarder hit Stephanie, why again did neither one stop?

"Mrs. Hanover?"

The patroller's question broke into Claire's train of thought. Realizing Roger must have given the young man their names, she answered, "Yes?"

"Do you have anything to add?"

"As a matter of fact I do, though the evidence is gone."

He crooked an eyebrow, and Roger and Judy stared at her.

Claire launched into an explanation of the tracks she had seen, ending with, "Unfortunately, none of us saw this skier, though that young snowboarder may have. Either one could have hit Stephanie, and the other one probably saw what happened."

"Then we have all the more reason to find the snowboarder." Matthews called in the snowboarder's description to ski patrol headquarters and returned his radio to his belt. "I'll also get this description to the Summit County Sheriff's Office and the Breckenridge Police Department. Now, how are you related to Stephanie Contino?"

"Oh, we aren't," Claire said. *Not yet.* "Her brother and my daughter started dating at the University of Colorado last fall before she went abroad for an art study program in January. Both families are in town this week to ski."

"Do you have contact information for Miss Contino's family?"

After Judy gave him the phone number, she asked, "What about Stephanie? Will she live? Where will they take her?"

Matthews tugged his collar. "She'll be taken by ambulance to the Summit County Medical Center in Frisco. Depending on her condition, they'll decide where she goes next."

While he tried to make his voice carry hope and sympathy, the despair he couldn't mask in his glance to Claire told her what she already knew. Stephanie's next likely stop would be the morgue or a funeral home.

He held out a card to Roger. "Call me if you think of anything else. I'll escort you down the hill, if you're ready." He walked over to the skis left by the patroller who had crouched over Stephanie's body and picked them up.

Roger helped Judy up, and the four of them trudged to their skis. Silently, they clicked into their bindings and headed slowly down Claimjumper.

As Claire followed Judy, she noticed her daughter's awkward form. *The poor girl can barely focus on her skiing.* Then Claire caught her ski edge and fought to regain her balance. *Neither can I.*

She blinked back tears as she envisioned the reaction of Stephanie's parents and her brother to the news. *How are we going to get through the next few days?*

One thought came through clear. *Our nice family vacation has sure gone to hell in a handbasket.*

TWO:
WAITING FOR THE CONTINOS

UNDER THE STERILE GLARE of a fluorescent light, Claire sat twisting her hands in the waiting room at the Summit County Medical Center. Her gut churned as she vacillated between despair and hope for Stephanie's life. The staff had been mute about the young woman's condition, since the Hanovers weren't family.

She rehearsed and discarded inane-sounding expressions of condolence to Stephanie's parents and brother. Nothing sounded right. And guilt kept nagging. Could she have done anything before or after the accident to prevent Stephanie's death?

Right after Hal Matthews left them at the base lodge to call Stephanie's family, Claire, Roger, and Judy had driven to the medical center. Since then, time had slowly ticked by on the wall clock as they waited for the Continos. Roger sat at the other end of the sofa with his arm around Judy. She leaned against his shoulder and quietly sniffled.

Feeling prickly heat soon after coming inside, Claire had taken off her ski jacket and sweater. She couldn't remove the heavy, waterproof ski pants, though, because all she wore underneath was long underwear. She tugged at the collar of her turtleneck and fanned her face.

Maybe Claire's warmth was more than being overheated. She remembered reading that stress could bring on perimenopausal hot flashes. She studied Judy and Roger, who seemed comfortable. *Yep, hot flash.*

Roger caught Claire's eye. "Maybe we should leave a message for the Continos and go home to wait."

Claire shook her head. "I can't leave Stephanie here alone." Even if nothing more could be done to save her, Stephanie deserved to have people who knew her, at least a little, watch over her until her family arrived.

"I don't want to leave either," Judy said.

"Besides, if I were Stephanie's mother, I'd want to know every detail of what happened right away, particularly what Stephanie was doing and how she felt before she…" Claire glanced at Judy. "Before the accident. We owe it to them to answer whatever questions they have as best as we can."

"But we didn't see the accident." Judy's eyes were puffy and her face was tear-blotched.

Claire took Judy's hand. "Honey, you'll have to be strong, especially for Nick. This will be quite a shock for him."

Judy squeezed her mother's hand. "You don't think Stephanie's alive, do you?"

"What do you think?"

"She looked bad, really bad." Judy sucked in a deep, shuddering breath. "But she had her whole life ahead of her. It's not fair for her to die so young, from such a stupid accident!"

"Life's not fair. Nor is death." Claire squeezed her eyes to stop the tears. She agreed with Judy and wished her daughter hadn't had to learn the harsh lesson so young.

The sound of a door opening and a cold gust made Claire look up.

With a solemn expression, Hal Matthews held open the outside door. The couple who followed him in had to be Stephanie's parents. Claire remembered Judy telling her the names of Nick's parents the night before.

Anthony, Stephanie's father, entered first, his olive-skinned face grim under a regal mane of dark hair sprinkled with gray, the perfect picture of an Italian-American gentleman. He wore black ski pants and jacket, as if he had just come off the slopes. He turned to take the hand of his wife, Angela.

Angela's shiny black hair was perfectly coifed, and her petite figure was clothed in a maroon-and-black embroidered pant set that must have cost a fortune. Obviously, she hadn't gone skiing that day. Her face held a raw edge of despair.

Claire's chest contracted. No mother should have to go through what Angela was about to face. Outliving one's child is a mother's worst nightmare.

Last came Judy's Nickolas, or Nick as she called him. Tall, thin, and black-haired like his parents, his sharp features looked as if they had been chiseled out of stone. Like his father, he was dressed for skiing. Worry furrowed his young brow as he scanned the waiting room. When his gaze fell on Judy, he stepped toward her.

Judy ran into his arms, burying her face against his chest. "Oh, Nick, it was awful. Oh, God."

Claire stood and approached the Continos, her feet feeling as if they were made of lead.

Roger followed and put a steadying hand behind her back. "Mr. and Mrs. Contino, I'm Roger Hanover and this is my wife, Claire."

The fear in Angela's eyes was a deep, sucking void.

Claire clasped the woman's icy hands. "We're so sorry this happened. If you need anything, anything at all, we're here." *God, that was lame. After all that thinking, that's the best I could come up with?*

With tears pooling in her eyes, Angela nodded mutely.

Anthony laid a comforting arm around his wife's shoulders. "Thank you."

While they talked, Hal Matthews had checked in at the desk. An attendant buzzed open the door from the waiting room to a hallway leading to treatment rooms. Matthews stood next to her at the open doorway. "Mr. and Mrs. Contino?"

As Anthony stepped through with Angela, he called Nick's name. Nick mouthed "later" to Judy and followed his parents.

The Hanovers returned to their seats. Judy slipped her hand into Claire's again. Dully, Claire stared into space until she realized her hand had gone numb, squeezed so hard in her daughter's. She gently extracted her hand and swallowed. Her throat was dry. "Roger, could you get us some water, please?"

As he stood and moved to the water cooler, Judy let out a long sigh, her gaze glued to the waiting room door.

"I know this is hard, honey." Claire ran her hand along Judy's hair. "Anything I can do for you?"

Judy had found comfort in the caress as a child but had shied away from her mother's touch as a teenager. This time, she remained motionless, except for a small shake of her head in answer to her mother's question.

Roger returned with two paper cups filled with water.

A muffled noise filtered down the hallway and out the reception window into the waiting room—a woman's scream, followed by hysterical sobbing.

Roger's hands shook, and he spilled some water.

Claire took her cup and glanced at the only other occupant of the waiting room, a young mother with a lethargic toddler, who stared at the empty reception window. Slowly, her head turned toward Claire and their gazes locked, she clutching her sick child to her chest and Claire's hand still on Judy's hair.

In her maternal bones, Claire knew the woman thought the same thing as she. *Dear God, please never let that be me.*

The receptionist returned and called a name.

Like an automaton, the young mother stood, breaking the spell of that mutual look of horror. She walked with her toddler slung across her hip through the door into the hallway.

Needing the contact, Claire stroked Judy's hair again.

Judy hunched her shoulders and slid her head away from Claire's hand. "Stop petting me like a dog, Mom."

"Sorry. Old habits die hard." Claire forced herself to take a swallow of water. Realizing Judy hadn't taken her cup from Roger yet, Claire placed it on the end table beside them.

Without a word, Roger turned to pour another for himself. The three sat quietly for a few more minutes, lost in their own morbid thoughts.

The doorway to the examining rooms opened. Nick Contino stepped through, his eyes red-rimmed.

As if drawn to him by a powerful magnetic force, Judy leapt to her feet and ran to him. They hugged for a long time, then Judy pulled away to say, "I'm so sorry." She led him by the hand to Claire and Roger and sat with him on the sofa facing theirs, their arms intertwined and hands locked in a tight hold.

A surge of jealousy engulfed Claire. Judy had shrugged off her mother's attempts at comfort, and now she clung to her boyfriend like ivy sucking life from a tree. *Don't be stupid, Claire. Be happy she can find comfort with him.*

Judy glanced nervously at her parents then licked her lips as her gaze returned to Nick. "Is Stephanie . . . ?"

"She's gone," he said in a hoarse whisper.

A whimper escaped Judy's lips before she clamped them shut and gazed at their clasped hands.

"Nick, we all feel awful," Claire said. "I wish we could have done something, anything, to prevent the accident or to help her afterward."

Nick shook his head. "They said she was lost as soon as she hit the tree. The blow to her head was too severe." He swallowed hard. "She probably never felt it. You couldn't have done anything."

Claire felt some relief. At least Stephanie hadn't suffered. Her family, however, would suffer for years to come. "Did Mr. Matthews tell you what happened?"

"Yes, but I wanted to hear the story directly from you." Nick peered at Judy. "If you're up to it."

Judy sucked in a deep breath and sat tall. "I'm up to it."

Claire felt a surge of pride and a twinge of nostalgia. *When and how did Judy grow so strong?*

Judy told Nick about the snowboarder and about finding Stephanie lying in the snow. She swiped at a tear running down her cheek. "I feel so guilty, Nick. I should have kept up with her, so I could warn her about the snowboarder."

Nick hugged her again, but seemed unable to speak, to assure her that she deserved no part of the blame in Stephanie's death.

Claire felt she had to say something. "None of this was your fault, Judy."

Judy stared at her. "You're just saying that."

Claire realized Judy needed to hear it wasn't her fault directly from the Continos, but she tried to offer what assurances she could. "There's still a possibility that the snowboarder didn't do it."

"Mr. Matthews sure made it sound like the snowboarder did it," Nick said. "He said the resort posted a description of the slimeball, asking anyone who knows him to contact them. They gave a description to all the patrollers, too." His jaw worked. "The guy better hope they find him before I do."

Judy tugged at her hand that was clenched tight in his fist. "You're hurting me."

Nick jerked his hand away. "Damn. I'm sorry."

"I understand," Judy said, rubbing her knuckles. "How did they find you? Weren't you and your dad snowcat skiing in the back bowls at Copper Mountain?"

Nick shot her a glance then quickly said, "Mr. Matthews called the house. Mom gave him Dad's cell phone number, and he called that. Good thing we got good reception at Copper. By the time we drove here, Mr. Matthews had picked up Mom and brought her here. We met them in the parking lot."

Claire wondered why Nick seemed rattled by the question. She scanned his clothes. No wet spots, even on the bottom hem of his ski pants. She hadn't seen any wetness on his father's ski clothes either. Their outfits must have been made of awfully quick-drying cloth, or the two men were excellent skiers who never fell. She realized Nick was watching her and met his gaze.

"Mom and Dad will probably want to talk to you, too," he said.

Claire nodded. "That's why we stayed."

Nick pursed his lips. "I don't think Mom can handle it now. Could you come by our house tomorrow?"

"Sure," Roger replied. "What else can we do?"

Nick turned his gaze on Judy and his expression softened. "Take care of my girl here."

Noting Judy's answering look of adoration, Claire felt a sudden shock of realization. These two had fallen hard for each other. She studied the handsome, mysterious young man in a new light and vowed to find out more about him.

Nick extracted himself from Judy's clutches and stood. "I should go back to my folks now. The doctor gave us the number of the only funeral home in town."

His eyes glistened, and he took a moment to compose himself. "They're coming to get Stephanie soon." He turned away and, with clenched fists, walked through the reception door.

Judy held her hands over her mouth as tears slid down her cheeks.

Claire handed her a tissue. Judy would take that from her, at least.

While Judy dabbed her tears, a man wearing jeans, a brown work shirt, and a black fleece vest with a sheriff's star logo sewn onto it walked into the waiting room. He appeared to be in his mid-thirties, tall, lean and well-muscled with short-cropped black hair. His cold, gray-blue eyes studied Claire's family before he walked over to them.

"I'm Owen Silverstone, detective with the Summit County Sheriff's Office. Are you the Hanovers?"

"Yes we are," Roger said.

The man's high, prominent cheekbones bespoke his Native American heritage. "I need to ask you some questions."

Startled, Claire asked, "Why?"

"We're required to investigate all deaths at the ski resort, but first I have to talk to Hal Matthews. Do you mind waiting here?"

Roger spread his hands wide. "That's what we've been doing already."

Claire's gut rumbled. The wall clock showed it was already after one, and they hadn't eaten lunch. Not that she could stomach anything yet.

Detective Silverstone thanked them, then went through the reception door, leaving the Hanovers alone again.

After three more patients had entered the waiting room, the detective returned. "The Continos have left, and Hal's available to join us. I found an empty office in the doctors' center next door so we can talk in private."

He held the outside door open and ushered them across the parking lot, then into the adjoining building and an office inside. Hal Matthews was already there, perched on the side of the desk.

Three chairs crowded the space in front, and he indicated the Hanovers should sit in them.

Detective Silverstone sat in the chair behind the desk and took out a notebook. "Hal already filled me in on what you told him about the snowboarder. We have an ongoing problem with recklessness on the slopes, and we're working hard to curb it. Hopefully, if enough of these kids get charged with assault or manslaughter, they'll get it through their thick heads that they need to slow down."

Confused, Claire looked at the senior ski patroller and back at the detective. "But didn't Mr. Matthews tell you about the tracks I saw?"

Silverstone checked his notes. "He said you thought you saw an extra pair of ski tracks in addition to Miss Contino's and the snowboarder's."

"Yes," Claire said, "And I believe—"

"I'm surprised you only saw one extra set, or that you could distinguish the tracks. Lower Ptarmigan's usually crisscrossed with tracks by that time in the morning, not to mention ones from the day before. It's not a slope that gets groomed every night, is it, Hal?"

Matthews shook his head.

Feeling a twinge of irritation, Claire gripped the arms of her chair. "But three inches of snow fell last night, so that covered yesterday's tracks. And the T-bar didn't open until a few minutes before we got on."

"That so, Hal?"

"I talked to the lift operators," Matthews said, "to see if they remembered the snowboarder. They remembered the goofy hat, but that's all. And they said they started up the T-bar at ten fifteen."

"So, we were some of the first skiers to make tracks in the fresh powder." Claire edged forward in her chair, anxious to make her point. "Not only were the tracks clear, but both the skier's tracks and the snowboarder's went close to Stephanie's where hers veered off into the woods."

Silverstone quirked an eyebrow at Matthews. "Did you see that?"

"No. Mrs. Hanover claimed the sled went over them, so they were gone when she told me about them."

Claimed? Realizing the senior ski patroller didn't believe her, Claire kept pushing. "The ski tracks came straight out of the woods above the collision point. No turns. If the skier was the one who hit her, either he never saw Stephanie or he deliberately hit her."

Judy stared at her mother. "You think someone killed her on purpose?"

"Whoa." Matthews put out his hands. "You're getting carried away here."

Claire focused on the detective. "No, I'm just covering all the possibilities."

Silverstone stroked his chin. "We always look for the simplest explanation first. Accidental collisions happen all the time on the mountain, though they rarely result in death."

He checked his notes. "You said the snowboarder passed the four of you, then he passed Miss Hanover again, presumably after stopping somewhere, before he reached Miss Contino?"

"Either he hit Stephanie and the skier must have seen it," Claire said, "or the skier hit her and the snowboarder saw it. What's still puzzling me is why neither one stopped to help her."

"Not everyone's as responsible as you," Matthews said. "It's amazing what assholes some of our patrons can be."

"Well, we know nothing about this skier," Silverstone said, "or if he or she even exists. Our best course of action is still to find the snowboarder." He flipped his notebook closed and glanced at Matthews.

"I called in while you were fetching the Hanovers," Matthews said. "The patrollers haven't spotted him yet. One more thing. The ski resort prefers to be the primary contact with the press on this."

Silverstone addressed the Hanovers next. "Until we determine if criminal conduct was involved, none of you should talk to the press. It could harm our case if we need to bring charges. And, as you can imagine, a death on the slopes can be very damaging to the local economy if it's blown out of proportion."

Anger boiled in Claire's gut. *They're more concerned about bad publicity than the truth.*

Roger covered her clenched hand with his. "We understand."

Matthews stood. "The lifts will start shutting down in less than an hour. Would any of you be willing to ski Peaks Seven and Eight again tomorrow and help us look for that snowboarder?"

Claire looked at Roger and he nodded.

Judy shifted in her chair. "I think I should be with Nick . . . if he wants me."

Claire turned to Matthews. "We need to visit the Continos in the morning, but Roger and I should be able to ski after that."

"Both the ski patrol and the sheriff's office would really appreciate it." Silverstone plucked a card out of his wallet and handed it to Roger. "I understand you've already got Mr. Matthews's card. Carry both with you tomorrow along with your cell phone. Call either one of us if you spot the boarder."

He peered at Claire and Roger in turn, as if to assure he had their full attention. "Under no circumstances should you approach him yourself."

THREE: SUSPICIONS

WHILE ROGER DROVE TO the Contino home the next morning, Claire warmed her backside on the BMW's heated seat, wishing the heat could penetrate the cold knot of grief and dread churning her insides. She scanned the hastily written directions in her hand. "The turn for the Highlands is just north of town, right?"

"Mom," Judy replied, "I told you I could give Dad directions. I was there with Nick two nights ago, remember?"

Claire faced Judy in the back seat. "I know, honey, but it was nighttime, and you were only there once. That's why I called the Continos this morning. I also wanted to make sure they were ready for us."

Judy rolled her eyes. "Turn right at the light, Dad." She avoided her mother's gaze and stared out the window.

Claire wished she'd had time to put together a sympathy basket. She had brought supplies to Breckenridge so she could construct and donate a gift basket to the upcoming Summit Foundation auction, but she didn't have suitable items for the Continos.

Nothing would ease the raw pain of losing Stephanie, but Claire wanted to at least let her family know that the Hanovers cared.

As Roger drove the winding curves of Highland Drive, he let out a low whistle. "This is some neighborhood. I don't see a single home that looks like it would sell for less than two million."

Lining the road, cemented river stone and peeled-log mansions sat back on large treed lots. Huge, dark windows faced the ski-area mountains and seemed to stare at the car like sunken eye sockets in hollow skulls.

Claire shivered. "Most of them look empty. They must be second homes. Did the Continos rent like us, or do they own a vacation home here?"

"They own it," Judy answered. "They usually come up from Denver once a month or so."

"They must be doing well." Roger's tone was wistful.

Claire glanced at him. After Enrique, a massage therapist, was shot and killed in Claire's bedroom two months earlier and the Colorado Springs police accused Roger of the crime, Roger had lost his corporate job as a chief financial officer during the resulting lurid publicity. He had been exonerated for the crime, but he hadn't gotten his position back. Or found another one yet.

She smoothed her hand across his shoulders. "We're doing well, too, Roger. Well enough for me." Thank goodness they were diligent savers and had a considerable cushion.

He flashed her a half smile, as if he half-believed her.

Claire pointed at the sign for the Continos' street. "There's the turn."

"The house is the third one on the right," Judy added.

Roger pulled into the long driveway and parked behind a large black SUV. "A Range Rover. I should've known."

He can't be that envious. "I'm sure your X-Five is just as classy as his Range Rover."

"That Range Rover costs twenty to twenty-five K more than my car." At Claire's sharp glance, Roger patted her hand. "Wishful thinking. That's all." He stepped out, his shoes crunching on the frozen snow.

While Claire climbed out, she pondered why men always had to measure themselves against other males. Even when they were doing well, like Roger, they always managed to find someone who made more money, was a better athlete, had a larger banana. She sighed. *That's why we women have to keep telling them their bananas are plenty large enough for us.*

When they walked onto the porch, Judy slipped her hand into her father's, reminding Claire why they had come. Claire took a deep, steadying breath as Roger rang the bell. The cold mountain air chilled her lungs.

Nick opened the door, and Judy fell into his arms. He hugged her then shifted her to his side. He held her protectively against himself, as if he already felt responsible for her.

The intimate gesture brought out Claire's protective maternal instincts. She wasn't ready to turn over her daughter to this young man. Not yet. Not until she was sure he valued Judy as much as Claire did.

Nick stepped back to make room for Claire and Roger. "Come inside, please. Thanks for coming." Dark shadows edged his eyes, accentuating his heavy brows, almost black eyes, and sharp nose.

His sleek, predatory features reminded Claire of a hawk, but a stressed-out, exhausted hawk.

Roger shook the young man's hand. "I wish we were getting to know your parents under better circumstances, Nick."

"So . . ." Nick's voice caught in his throat, and he cleared it. "So do we. Mom and Dad are in the living room. I'll take your coats." After piling their coats on a nearby bench, he led the Hanovers down the hall.

Claire clutched Roger's arm, dreading the tears and anguish to come.

When they entered the living room, Anthony Contino stood and offered his hand to Roger. He, too, had dark circles under his eyes. "Thank you for coming, Mr. Hanover."

"Please, call me Roger. And call my wife Claire."

Claire shook Anthony's hand. She looked at Angela, sitting on the green leather sofa. The woman was misery incarnate. Her formerly styled hair was pulled back into a severe ponytail. Obviously, she had tried applying some lipstick and blush, but most of it had rubbed off on the pile of wadded tissues before her. Tears still brimmed in her eyes, and her chin shook as she bit her lip.

Claire did what came naturally. She sat next to Angela and put her arms around the woman. She whispered, "I'm so sorry."

That set them both to weeping again. Claire held Angela for a while, until they needed to snatch tissues from the box on the coffee table to wipe their faces.

The men had stood awkwardly with hands in their pockets and gazes averted from the sad scene. Judy quietly joined the mothers at the tissue box, pulling one out to wipe her eyes.

Angela picked up a cup of coffee and took a sip. Once she could speak, she said, "Please, tell me what happened. Everything."

The others sat on the color-coordinated leather easy chairs and loveseat clustered around the stone-inlaid coffee table. Judy, Roger, and Claire took turns describing the events of the previous day.

When Claire began talking about the tracks she saw, Judy interrupted, "Mom, I think Mrs. Contino has suffered enough."

The tissue pile had grown to twice its original size. Angela twisted another one in her hands. "No, please, I must know."

Claire shot a *hush* glance at Judy and rubbed Angela's shoulder. "I understand. I would want to hear everything, too." She diagramed the ski tracks and snowboard track with her finger on the coffee table while she described them to the Continos.

Nick released Judy's hand and sat forward. He ran his finger along the imaginary path of the unknown skier's track. After a sharp glance at his father, he asked, "So you think the skier might have come straight out of the woods, right at Stephanie?"

Claire nodded. "She would've had no time to react."

Anthony drew in a sharp intake of breath. He and Nick locked gazes.

Claire saw a clear message of fear pass between them. *What the hell?*

A frown of confusion passed over Angela's face. "Do you think this skier ran into her on purpose?"

"The ski patrolman said it was an accident, Mom." Nick glanced at his father.

"Yes, an accident. It must have been," Anthony said quickly. "Anything else would be unthinkable, impossible." He glared at Nick as if warning him not to say more.

"We just don't know." Claire realized from Nick and Anthony's scowls that they wanted Angela to be assured that Stephanie's death was an accident. She took Angela's hand. "He probably took off from the woods without checking uphill first, so he never saw Stephanie."

"Why do you say 'he'?" Anthony asked sharply. He stared at Claire.

She shrugged. "I'm assuming the person had to be bigger than Stephanie to knock her so violently off track. The snowboarder was. If the snowboarder did it, the skier could have been a woman or a small man, I guess." *Was that why the skier didn't stop? Could he or she have been afraid of the snowboarder and what he might do to him or her?*

Nick bit his lip and watched his father, his finger tapping a solemn beat on the coffee table.

Anthony stood, smoothing his palms down his thighs, as if wiping off nervous sweat. If anything, his twisted face looked even more anguished than before. "We've been remiss. We haven't offered you anything to drink. We have coffee, and I can make tea or hot chocolate."

"Don't go to any trouble on our account." Roger stood. "You have enough to deal with. We just came to answer your questions and convey our condolences."

Claire glanced at Angela, who seemed frail and worn out. "I'm sorry if I went on too long."

"No, no," the woman replied. "I needed to know."

"Can we tell you anything else?"

Angela shook her head. "All we can do is wait for the ski patrol or the sheriff to find who did this to Stephanie."

Claire rose and joined Roger, causing the others to stand too. "Roger and I will be on the slope today, too, looking for the snowboarder."

"I wish I could look, too." Nick's fingers clenched and unclenched at his sides as if he itched to put those hands around the neck of the person who killed Stephanie, accident or no.

Judy looped her arm through Nick's and looked at Angela. "I'd like to stay here today, if you'll have me, to help with the . . . arrangements."

Proud of Judy's initiative and willingness to help, Claire gave her daughter a warm smile. A worrying thought struck her. Judy was acting like a daughter-in-law, volunteering to take on such a large role in Stephanie's funeral arrangements. Was she that serious with Nick? *Cut it out, Claire. Be glad she's assisting Angela in some way. God knows the woman needs it.*

"Thank you, Judy. I'd appreciate that. It's all rather overwhelming." After giving Judy a sad smile, Angela turned to Roger and Claire. "We want to have the service here, rather than in Denver. Stephanie loved the mountains, and—" Her voice caught, and her hand went to her mouth.

Nick finished for her. "We plan to spread her ashes somewhere in the mountains."

Claire gave Angela a hug, quick enough to prevent another onslaught of tears. "We'd like to come to the memorial service."

Angela nodded.

Anthony escorted Claire and Roger to the door and gave Roger a stiff handshake. While they walked to their car, Claire hunched her jacket around her chilled neck and reviewed the conversation in her mind. Something troubled her. Nick and Anthony's strange reactions to the possibility that the skier had deliberately hit Stephanie.

What are they afraid of?

⤜⤝

Hours later, exhausted after hunting for the snowboarder on the ski slopes, Claire lay on one side of the L-shaped sofa in the living room of their rented townhouse. She groaned and stretched her sore muscles. Roger lay on the other side, nursing a beer. They had stripped off their outer ski clothing and sweaters, so they lounged in turtlenecks, long underwear bottoms, and slouched ski socks.

As the waning afternoon sun threw long shadows across the floor, Roger asked, "Who's getting up for the ibuprofen?"

"I guess I will." With a grunt, Claire pushed herself to her feet, staggered a bit until her stiff legs remembered how to walk, then padded upstairs to the bedroom. She returned with the bottle and passed it to Roger before plopping down on the sofa again. After swallowing two pills with some water, she said, "I wish we'd spotted that snowboarder."

"He's probably lying low or boarding at another Summit County resort," Roger said. "Especially if he or one of his buddies saw the signs the ski patrol posted."

"Either that or he could've been here for the day from somewhere on the Front Range, Denver, Boulder, or Colorado Springs—like us."

"On a Monday? I don't think so. A weekend day, maybe. I bet he's a local or he's here for a week or two, like us."

"So there's a chance we'll still find him."

Roger took another sip of beer. "He moved like someone hooked on snowboarding. I doubt he'll give up more than a day or two of it, especially if he's here on vacation. He'll probably ditch the goofy hat, though."

"But not his board, unless it was a rental. I remember that swirly orange pattern." Claire rested her head against the sofa back. "I hope we find him. I want to do *something* for the Continos. I feel so helpless."

The front door opened and Judy walked in. Her gaze swept over her parents sprawled on the sofa, and she cracked a wry grin. "Don't you two look attractive."

Claire sat up and peered beyond Judy. "Is Nick coming in? I'll change into sweats if he is."

"No, he just dropped me off. They still need to contact some more relatives." Judy shucked off her coat, slid onto a barstool next to the kitchen counter, and leaned her chin on her hand.

Claire studied her daughter's face. Judy looked tired, sad, and blotchy, as if she had done some crying.

"Poor Mrs. Contino," Judy said. "Nick and Mr. Contino decided to call the relatives so she wouldn't have to. But then, she and I met with the funeral director and she had to make all those decisions about the service. She kept asking me what I thought, and I had no idea how to answer her."

"I'm sure your presence was a comfort to her."

Judy took a moment to think. "I'm not so sure. Sometimes I'd catch her looking at me with a wistful expression on her face. I think it's weird for her that I'm alive and Stephanie's not. It was a little too overwhelming, so finally I had to get out of there, at least for a minute. I went to find Nick. He was with his dad in the study. That whole scene was a little odd."

"Odd? How?"

"The door was open, so I walked in. Mr. Contino was pacing the room and crying. He kept saying over and over, 'It's all my fault.'"

Every time Judy or Michael had gotten hurt, Claire had felt that parental guilt—*if only I had been there, protected them more, made them take fewer chances.* "He probably feels he and Nick shouldn't have gone to Copper, that if he'd been with Stephanie, he might have been able to protect her."

"But how?"

"I know it doesn't make sense, honey, but that's the way parents are. He could also be feeling survivor's guilt. Did you leave them alone?"

"I tried to sneak out, but Nick saw me. He jumped up and followed me into the hall, said their conversation was private. When I said I realized that and had decided to leave, he grabbed my arm and asked me how much I had seen and heard. He seemed really worried about me seeing his dad like that. It was probably the most upset I've ever seen him."

A chill raced down Claire's spine. *If that young man's abusing my daughter, he'll have to deal with Mama Bear.* "Has Nick ever hurt you, Judy?"

"Of course not, Mom." Judy's nose wrinkled in disgust. "Jeeze, don't blow this up into some huge issue. He didn't grab me in that way. You know I'd never date a guy who hurt me."

Claire relaxed. Yes, she had raised Judy to be strong and independent. Maybe too independent. "He was probably just concerned that his dad would be embarrassed that you'd seen him crying. What happened next?"

"I told him I hadn't heard much, and I apologized for walking in on them. I said I would knock next time. Then Nick said not to worry, that he and his dad were just really stressed out. I decided we all needed a break, so I offered to make lunch for everyone."

"Oh." Claire checked her watch. Almost five. "I should bring over a dinner for them."

"You don't need to. Nick's going to pick up a pizza on the way home, but I doubt they'll eat much of it. They just picked at the sandwiches I fixed them."

"I haven't even thought about our dinner," Claire said. "Food doesn't seem so important at a time like this."

"Maybe I should order some Chinese takeout," Roger said.

"Not for me," Judy said. "Some friends from CU-Boulder rented a condo here for the week. Nick and I called to tell them about Stephanie. They asked us to join them for dinner tonight. He can't, but I thought I would."

"But we've barely spent any time with you since you returned from France. Not that it's anyone's fault," Claire hastily added, "with Stephanie's accident, but I thought we could spend a quiet evening together and comfort each other."

Judy made a face. "I don't think spending the evening with two old people in their long underwear is what I need right now."

Claire bristled. "That's not fair, Judy. We've been out skiing all afternoon looking for that damn snowboarder, and we're pooped."

"C'mon, I was trying to make a joke. I'm not blaming you for how you look. Or feel." Judy got up and paced the floor. "It's just . . . after spending the whole day with the Continos, I can't stand being serious and sad anymore today. I want someone to cheer *me* up."

Claire's heart went out to Judy. "We'll cheer—"

"She's right." Roger laid his hand on Claire's arm. "Let her go. She needs her friends. And we could use some one-on-one time ourselves. Maybe instead of Chinese takeout, we should go to that fondue place you like. What was the name?"

"Swiss Haven."

"That's it. Just the two of us." Roger winked. "Judy, toss me the phonebook, and I'll make a reservation."

"Make it for the late eight o'clock seating," Claire said. "We still need to shower."

After handing her father the phone and phonebook, Judy sat next to Claire. "I promise, Mom, I'll spend tomorrow night with you."

Claire sighed. "All right. I'll hold you to that. Where are you meeting your friends?"

"Their condo. Could you guys drop me off on your way to the restaurant? We'll probably go out somewhere, but I don't know where yet."

"At least you know where to find Dad and me if you need us."

By nine-thirty that night, Claire was feeling none of her skiing aches and pains. Instead, her head buzzed pleasantly from half a bottle of plumy cabernet sauvignon. Her stomach comfortably bulged from a Gruyère cheese fondue, followed by a broth fondue *chinoise* into which she and Roger had dipped slivers of chicken and beef.

Their table in the back room of the Swiss Haven had given her and Roger some privacy while they talked out their feelings of horror over Stephanie's death. When she expressed her concern about the effect on Judy, he reminded her how strong and independent Judy had grown. He was more concerned about how Nick would deal with his sister's death.

Their table also had provided a vantage point for watching waiters waltz between tables filled with customers. They expertly balanced platters laden with grills, fondue pots, bread baskets, and plates of raw meats and seafood. The low murmur of voices, the sizzle of grilling meats, and the occasional pops of wine corks provided a relaxing filler for the gaps in their own conversation.

Claire hadn't realized how much stress she had been feeling until it had slunk away to lurk in a dark corner. She picked up her almost empty wineglass, took a sip, and looked at Roger. His frisky answering smile told her what plans he had for the rest of the evening. *And I'm more than willing to go along with his plans.*

This family ski trip had another purpose besides a reunion with Judy. The getaway was part of the healing process to repair their marriage after the Colorado Springs murder. Claire had finally convinced Roger she hadn't slept with the handsome young massage therapist. But restoring their loving partnership was a more daunting task. A task she was determined to succeed at, by God.

Roger covered her hand with his and gave it a gentle squeeze. "Isn't this better than eating Chinese takeout with a twenty-one-year-old daughter who needs cheering up?"

Claire smiled. "You said it. Though, she did pique my curiosity when she mentioned Nick's odd behavior."

"What was odd about it?"

"That he was so secretive about his father's grief."

Roger rubbed his chin. "Could be their culture. Maybe they're very private and keep things inside the family."

"Maybe, but I get the feeling that Judy's pretty close to being family herself."

Arching a brow, Roger said, "Really?"

"Really. I'm seeing signs that she and Nick are getting serious. This family could be our in-laws someday. We need to get to know them better." Claire ran a finger over her wineglass. "Something else was odd. Did you notice how strange Nick and Anthony acted when I told them about the ski tracks?"

Before Roger could reply, their waitress brought a steaming pot of dark chocolate fondue and a tray of pound cake and fruit. Roger speared a cube of pound cake, dipped it in the chocolate, and popped it in his mouth. After swallowing, he said, "I'll fight you for the rest of this."

"Oh, no you don't." Claire speared a strawberry, dragged it through the dark sauce, and took a bite. "This is heavenly."

With a grin, Roger quickly stabbed a banana slice, and the battle was on. They both fell into serious eating, lapping up as much chocolate as they could, until the pot was polished clean.

Roger leaned back, folded his hands over his belly, and asked, "What were you saying before? Something about the Continos acting strange?"

Claire gave up on trying to scrape a fragment of dried chocolate off the rim of the pot and put down her fondue fork. "When I raised the possibility the skier could have deliberately hit her, I swear I saw fear in Nick's and Anthony's faces. Then they got nervous."

"What would they have to fear?"

"I don't know. And another thing. Supposedly they were at Copper Mountain skiing in the deep powder of the back bowls when Stephanie was killed, but their ski clothes were dry when they got to the medical center."

"Copper is a twenty-minute drive away. Their clothes could have dried in that time."

"Ours take hours to dry if we've been in deep snow. And Nick acted nervous when Judy asked how the Breckenridge ski patrol contacted them there."

Roger peered at her. "You're not trying to turn into a PI on this thing, are you?"

After risking her life to find Enrique's killer, Claire had developed a reputation as a sleuth. One she didn't want. *I'm a gift basket designer, a mother, and a wife, and that's all.*

She rubbed her knee against Roger's. "No, this vacation is for other things. I'm only trying to make sense of what I saw."

Roger leaned in close, nipped her earlobe, and whispered, "Speaking of other things, let's forgo the after-dinner coffee and head straight home."

"Sounds like a plan." Claire polished off her wine.

Roger raised his hand to signal the waitress, but a disturbance at the front door diverted his attention.

Judy stood in the middle of the restaurant, scanning the tables. When she saw Claire and Roger, she rushed toward them. "Mom. Dad. You've got to come quick."

Claire straightened. "Why? What happened?"

Judy leaned her hands on the table, brought her head close to theirs, and spoke in a whisper. "When we were at Downstairs at Eric's, I saw a hat on a wall peg by the video games that looked like the one the snowboarder wore. I tried to keep an eye on the hat to see who it belonged to, but it disappeared while I was giving the waiter my order."

"Tough luck," Roger said.

"No, listen. When I saw the hat was gone, I asked people playing the games if they saw who took it, pretending I wanted to buy one like it. Finally, one guy said it belonged to somebody called Nail-It."

"Sounds like the nickname of a snowboarder." A shiver of excitement stirred in Claire's belly.

Judy nodded, her eyes wide. "I thought so, too. I asked the guy if he knew where Nail-It went, and he said Nail-It usually hangs at Sherpa & Yeti's."

"What's that?" Roger asked.

"An underground grunge bar on the other side of Main Street. I decided to follow him there, but my friends refused to go with me. They said they'd just ordered and wanted to eat."

"A grunge bar?" Claire asked. "I'm not sure you should be exposed to that environment."

"Mom! Grunge is a way of dressing. It doesn't mean the place is dirty."

"No, what I mean is, I don't think you should be going to any bar."

Judy placed her hand on her hip and looked askance at Claire. "I've been twenty-one for three months now. I've been in lots of bars in France. I know my way around them."

Oh, God, my daughter is drinking and hanging out in bars now. Claire stared at Judy while visions of drunken debauchery starring her daughter crowded into her mind. She rubbed her forehead. *No, don't be ridiculous. Judy's responsible. She wouldn't go overboard. Would she?*

"We should call Detective Silverstone instead of confronting this snowboarder ourselves." Roger opened his cell phone and pulled the detective's card out of his wallet.

"Nail-It might be long gone before the cops get there." Judy grabbed Claire's hand. "C'mon. We've got to hurry. Here's our chance to find the guy who killed Stephanie."

Claire glanced at Roger. "She's right on both counts. We can't wait for the police and she shouldn't go alone."

"Foiled again." Shooting a look of regret at Claire, Roger stood. "I'll go with her while you pay the bill."

"But I can't. I left my purse at home."

"All right, you go, but if you find the guy, don't approach him. I'll call Silverstone, pay the bill, and catch up." He punched the detective's phone number into the cell phone.

Claire grabbed her coat and zipped it shut as she followed Judy out of the Swiss Haven into the dark night. Streetlights cast puddles of light on the ground, while a swath of bright stars shone overhead. Claire trotted to keep up with her daughter's fast pace and maintain her footing across the frozen slush piles lining the sidewalk.

As they headed across Main Street, breathing clouds of vapor in the frigid air, Judy asked, "What did Dad mean by 'foiled again'?"

Claire pulled her collar tighter around her neck. *I'm not about to discuss my sex life, or lack thereof, with my daughter.* "Never mind."

They passed in front of a cream-colored building with maroon and teal trim, one of many Victorian-style buildings in the historic downtown district. Judy stopped by a sign advertising the businesses within—an insurance office, a souvenir shop, and a black square with "Sherpa & Yeti's" scrawled in red, as if it had been painted in blood.

Claire stared at the flyer advertising that month's entertainment —Jungle Brothers, Bongo Love, De La Soul—listed as hip-hop, funk, and African dance bands. She wasn't even sure what those music styles sound like.

"It's down here." Judy beckoned to her from halfway down a narrow flight of concrete stairs leading to the basement. A rhythmic thumping pulsed from the open doorway, and the distinctive purplish glow of a blacklight painted the bottom of the dark stairwell.

As Claire hesitated, a trio of young men in baggy jeans brushed past her and clattered down the steps. Though the temperature was below freezing, only one wore a jacket—a hooded sweatshirt with a grenade logo stenciled on the back.

A grenade?

"Mom?"

Feeling as if she was descending into Dante's Inferno, Claire walked slowly down the stairs.

What are we getting into?

FOUR: THE SNOWBOARDER

When Claire reached the bottom of the stairs, she grabbed Judy's arm and whispered, "Did you see that sweatshirt with the grenade logo?"

Judy tsked. "You're such a dinosaur, Mom. That was a hoodie, and Grenade is a brand of snowboard wear." She dragged Claire into the small, dark alcove inside the door.

A young man with a scraggly beard sat perched on a stool behind a cash register. "Three dollar cover."

While Claire blinked to adjust her vision to the dark interior, Judy dug some bills out of her pocket and paid him. A larger and more muscular young man lounged on a stool beside a small coat-check counter. Presumably the bouncer, he looked Claire up and down then gave her a mocking half smile, as if to say, "You don't belong here, do you?"

She and Judy took off their coats and handed them to the young woman behind the counter. They headed down another dark flight of stairs lined with a flexible red tube light. The noise picked up as they rounded the corner into a room no larger than their basement rec room in Colorado Springs. Packed with young people, the room held a pool table and a bar along the far wall. Art Deco posters lined the black and red walls.

Underlying the chatter of voices and strains of a wailing guitar, the deep thump of a persistent bass echoed in Claire's stomach. Her full tummy churned from the stench of cigarette smoke, beer, and hormone-drenched young bodies. Claire realized she had at least twenty years on everyone else in the room.

Skirting the outstretched cue of a man aiming a shot, she followed Judy around the pool table into the larger back room, the source of the heavy thumping.

A pimply faced disc jockey with large earphones looped around his neck bopped on a tiny stage behind a stand of stereo equipment. Flanking the stage, huge speakers pulsed a primitive dance beat. The disc jockey loaded a vinyl record on one of the two turntables in front of him.

Claire wondered why he wasn't playing CDs. When he rubbed the record under the needle, producing a scratchy repetition of a section of music, she realized why.

People stood talking in clumps in front of the stage, but no one danced. The ratio appeared to be about two men to every woman, and most of the clumps were single-sexed. Everyone held drinks. Claire presumed that later in the evening, the liberal lubrication of alcohol would facilitate more mixing.

While she and Judy pushed through the crowd, a rotating mirror ball bathed faces with multiple colors. Posters of bands Claire had never heard of lined the black walls, along which young people lounged on tall stools, smoked, and drank beer. That seemed to be the only beverage everyone was drinking, though the mirrored bar stocked bottles of liquor.

When they reached the bar, Judy put her head next to Claire's so she could be heard. "Beer, Mom?"

"Why not?" Maybe a beer would settle her stomach and help her to not feel so out-of-place. She had already received a few stares. Remembering why she was there, Claire searched the room. Though many of the young men wore baseball caps, some backward, or knit beanies, none sported a hat of multi-colored fleece dreadlocks. Claire doubted Nail-It would wear such a hat in the warm room.

As Judy handed over a glass of beer, Claire said, "I bet we won't see that hat in here. He would probably leave it at the coat check. We'll have to ask around."

Claire leaned over the bar as the bartender brought Judy's change and shouted, "You know a guy named Nail-It?"

"Nope." He moved on to fill another order.

Claire turned to the young man on her right. "How about you? You know a snowboarder named Nail-It?"

The guy gave her a suspicious glance, shook his head, and turned his back to her.

"You're embarrassing me, Mom." Judy clutched her beer as they stepped away from the bar. "You can't ask everyone here if they know him."

"Why not? How else are we supposed to find him?"

"Go up the stairs and ask the coat-check girl if a guy has already checked the hat. If he hasn't, wait and watch for him."

"Good idea. You do that. But remember what your dad said. Don't talk to the snowboarder. In the meantime, I'll keep asking around." Claire took a sip of beer for courage.

Judy shot her mother a dubious look then walked into the billiard room.

Claire approached a quartet of young women clustered at the other end of the bar and spoke with a raised voice so it would carry over the music. "Excuse me. I'm looking for someone. Do any of you know a snowboarder named Nail-It?"

"Nail-It Naylor?" the brunette on the end asked. "Why're you looking for him? If he owes you money, join the crowd."

The others laughed.

"No, he doesn't owe me anything," Claire said. "He witnessed an accident on the slope yesterday. It involved a friend of mine, and I just want to ask him what he saw."

The tall blonde tossed back her long hair. "You mean the woman who bashed a tree?" Her expression softened. "You knew her? I'm sorry."

Refusing to succumb to grief, Claire reminded herself why she was here. "Thanks. Could you describe this Naylor guy to me? All I saw of him was his outerwear and that multi-colored hat."

The blonde laughed. "Boyd likes to have all eyes on him, especially when he's flipping tricks or grinding rails."

What the heck is she talking about? "Is Boyd his first name?"

"Yeah, he hates it, which is why he goes by Nail-It. Matches his last name, and he does nail his jumps."

"He shreds with the best," one of the other young women added.

Shreds? "What does he look like?"

The blonde cocked her head and stared into space as if trying to picture him. "Fuzzy blond hair down to his shoulders, blue eyes, a few inches taller than me."

A young man wearing a backward baseball cap stumbled into the group. His open coat slouched off his shoulders, and his red-rimmed eyes wandered unfocused over the faces of the young women. "Any of you ladies care to dansh?"

He swayed before them, obviously well on his way into a good bender. His beer sloshed on the gray carpet underfoot. The blonde and her friends turned their backs as a group.

Not as fast, Claire was left alone with him. *Darn!*

A look of disappointment crossed the drunk's face, then he focused on Claire. "How 'bout you? Let's boogie." He shuffled his feet, causing more liquid to slosh from his glass.

She tried to keep the distaste out of her expression. "No, thanks."

He grabbed her arm and tugged her toward the stage. "C'mon."

Claire planted her feet and pulled his hand off. "I said, no thanks."

He lurched close, his stale beer breath overpowering. "Jus' one." He held up a finger, which swayed between their faces.

Roger appeared next to Claire and took her arm. "The lady said no."

The drunk eyed him, taking in Roger's advantage in height and weight and the angry set to his jaw, then put out his hand, palm out. "No offensh, man. Didn't know she was your lady." He spun, put out a foot to catch his balance, and stumbled off.

Roger dropped his grip on Claire. "I leave you alone for a few minutes, and you're already attracting young drunks."

Ready with a retort, Claire noticed the grin on his face, and swallowed her angry words. She lifted her beer glass as if toasting him and took a sip. "Always ready to dance with a handsome fellow like yourself."

Roger glanced at the stage. "Not sure I'd know what to do to this music." He scanned the non-dancing crowd. "No one else seems to either."

"Did you see Judy when you came in?"

"She was talking to the coat-check girl and told me where to find you."

He steered Claire toward the back of the room, away from the stage, though the noise level didn't dissipate much. "I called the sheriff's office. The dispatcher said she'd locate Detective Silverstone and send him over here, but she had no idea how long that would take. She seemed to know the place, as if they've had trouble here in the past. So, did you find this snowboarder?"

"No, but I have a name, Boyd Naylor, and a description from the young women over there." She tilted her head toward the quartet at the bar.

Judy walked up beside Roger, her beer glass already half empty. "Oh, good. You found Mom. Nail-It seems to be here. The girl behind the coat-check counter found a hat that looks like his."

A young man in baggy black jeans and a T-shirt with a marijuana leaf on it stepped out of the men's restroom and walked toward the billiard room. His fuzzy blond mop looked like a whole family of gerbils could nest in it.

Claire walked over to the tall blonde who had given her Naylor's first name and tapped her on the shoulder. "Is that Boyd?" She pointed at the receding back of the young man.

"That's him," the blonde replied.

Claire grabbed Roger's arm. "Let's go."

They walked into the billiard room and found Naylor leaning on the small bar there, ordering a beer.

When the bartender brought the glass, Roger slapped a twenty on the counter. "It's on me."

Naylor whirled around and stared at Roger. "Who're you and why're you buying me a beer?"

Roger stuck out his hand. "Roger Hanover. This is my wife, Claire, and my daughter, Judy."

Claire and Judy nodded at the puzzled snowboarder.

"Are you Nail-It Naylor?" Judy asked.

He drew back but had the presence of mind to take a swig of his free beer. "How do you know who I am?"

Judy smiled. "No need to worry. We just have a few questions. First, you wear a hat with multi-colored fleece dreadlocks, don't you?"

His brows furrowed. "Yea—ah."

"And your snowboard is orange with swirls on it," Claire said.

"Where's this going?" Naylor peered at each of their faces as he drank some more beer.

Roger pocketed the change the bartender returned to him and faced Naylor. "We're friends of the young woman who was killed on Peak Eight yesterday."

"Shit!" Naylor slammed the glass on the bar, sloshing the beer, and turned to flee.

Roger laid a restraining hand on his arm. "We want to hear your side of the story."

"No way. That dude'll get me for sure." Naylor's eyes widened with fear. "I didn't see nothing."

"That dude?" Claire advanced on Naylor. "What dude?"

Naylor shook his head.

Claire's mind raced. Obviously, the young man was afraid of someone. Was he already in trouble with the ski patrol, Breckenridge police, or the Summit County sheriff? Or maybe the dude was the skier—the one whose tracks she had seen. If Naylor saw the skier hit Stephanie, the skier could have threatened him with harm if he divulged anything.

How could she get him to open up? Claire got an idea. She caught her daughter's eye, pointed her chin at Naylor, and gave Judy a nudge.

"Look, we're not the authorities," Claire said. "We knew the young woman who died. We need some closure, to understand what happened to her. So do her parents and brother."

Judy removed her father's hand from Naylor's arm and slipped her arm through the snowboarder's. "She was my friend. It's very important to me. I'd really appreciate it."

Though Naylor still looked edgy, his desire to flee seemed to wilt under her sweet gaze.

"If you want," Claire added, "whatever you tell us won't go beyond us and Stephanie's family."

Sorrow joined the fear in his eyes. "Oh, man. I didn't want to know her name."

"Please help us." Judy stopped just shy of batting her eyelashes at him.

When did she become such an expert flirt, Claire wondered. And how much practice did it take?

Naylor licked his lips. "You won't go to the cops?"

Claire damn well would, but she could convince him of the necessity of that later. Right now, she had to get him to trust them and tell them what he knew. She was terrible at lying, but a delaying tactic was different, right?

"We won't tell a soul unless you approve it first." Claire glanced at Judy and Roger. "Okay?"

Roger shot her a dubious look but appeared to be willing to follow her lead. "Okay."

Judy nodded.

"Let's go somewhere quiet, so we can hear each other talk." Claire scanned Naylor's thin frame. "How about the outdoor crepe stand across the street. You hungry? We're buying. It'll only take a few minutes."

Naylor downed the rest of his beer and wiped his hand across his lips. "Okay."

He led them up the stairs and retrieved his snow jacket and goofy hat from the coat check. Claire, Roger, and Judy got their coats, too, and Roger tipped the young woman.

Once outside, Claire led the way across the street and talked Naylor into ordering two dessert crepes, chocolate and strawberry. She also ordered a round of hot chocolate, so he wouldn't feel self-conscious about eating alone. Once they were seated at an outdoor table beneath an overhead gas heater, Naylor dug into the crepes, wolfing down big bites like a stray dog on the run.

The sight reminded Claire of her son in the midst of a growth spurt. *Poor guy probably skipped dinner.*

Roger leaned forward. "Judy saw you zoom past her seconds before Stephanie was hit. You were going awfully fast." The accusatory words came out in a cloud of frosted breath.

After taking a swig of hot chocolate as if to bolster his courage, Naylor said, "It's like this. I may look like I'm booking too fast down the slope, but I know what I'm doing. I've been riding board for eight years, since I got hooked on it in junior high. I can catch major hang time and still land on a dime. Just ask around."

"A young woman in the bar said you shred with the best," Claire said. *Whatever that means.*

Judy lifted a surprised brow at her mother.

Naylor sat back, folding his arms across his chest. "There. You see?"

A frown creased Roger's face. "That's precisely the problem. We don't see. We don't know who hit Stephanie or how."

Firmly, Claire pushed him away. She decided to establish some rapport. "Ski patrol's looking for you because they think you hit her. I think someone else did, for reasons I'll tell you later, but I need to hear your story first."

Naylor swallowed a huge bite. He leaned his elbows on the table and peered nervously up and down Main Street. No cars moved along the street. The only other people in sight were the two workers manning the crepe stand, chatting quietly between themselves. He opened his mouth to speak then closed it again.

Judy ran her hand along Naylor's forearm in a gentle caress. "Please tell us what happened."

Good girl.

Looking extremely disappointed after Judy removed her hand, Naylor cleared his throat and started in. "I remember passing the four of you below the bump field on Ptarmigan." He looked Claire and Roger up and down. "You must know your stuff to have made it down that."

Roger cracked a wry smile. "We try."

"Anyway, after I passed you, I stopped in the woods to take a piss. Then she and her friend came by." He jabbed a thumb in Judy's direction then scratched his head, jostling the hat perched on his unruly hair. "I kinda thought that since they'd peeled off from you two, I might catch them in the lift line. Strike up a conversation, you know." He grinned sheepishly.

Judy pursed her lips, but thankfully knew to stay quiet and sip her cocoa.

"And then?" Claire prompted.

"I passed her." Naylor indicated Judy. "And slowed down, looking for the other one. Right when I spotted her, this dude dressed all in black came shooting out of the woods right at her. He smacked into her like that." He clapped his hands together, startling Claire.

Judy gasped.

"She didn't fall right away, but she lost her balance. I could see her fighting for it. But she never got it back. Then she smashed into the tree." He stopped, his eyes glazed over as he relived the crash. "Shit," he whispered and cast his gaze toward the ground.

Claire gave him a moment then asked, "Do you think it was an accident? That he didn't look uphill before he came out?"

"Hell no." Naylor ground his teeth and raised his head. Unshed tears glistened in his eyes. "He was looking uphill all right. Right at her. He waited until she got close, then he pushed off and rammed her."

"Oh, God." A tear dribbled down Judy's cheek. She pulled a tissue out of her pocket.

Gently, Claire asked, "Why didn't you stop to help her?"

Naylor jerked and stared at her. "I saw her head smack into the tree and the blood on the ground. I couldn't help anyone hurt that bad, and I didn't have my cell phone on me. I figured the best thing to do was to get the ski patrol. So I booked."

"What about the skier? Why didn't he stop?"

"'Cause he was chasing me, man."

"What the hell?" Roger's eyes went wide.

"I passed him on my way down," Naylor said. "He was standing on the other side of the slope, farther down, staring at her, cool as a frozen cucumber, like he was waiting to see if she moved or something. I couldn't believe it. Then he took off after me, and all I could think was that I'd be next. My heart was pounding, man. The dude was good, knew his stuff. And he was fast, as fast as me. I couldn't shake him."

Claire gripped her cup. "What did you do?"

"I figured my only chance was to head into Toilet Bowl." At their quizzical glances, he said, "That's what we boarders call the treed area between Northstar and Claimjumper. It's full of big bumps, tree wells, icy spots, all kinds of nasty, fun shit. It's where we hang out, shoot the breeze, smoke some weed. Just to party a little, know what I mean?" He looked at Judy.

She nodded, silently shredding the tissue in her hands.

Claire stared at her daughter.

Judy shrugged, as if to say she was only playing along with Naylor.

"I know that place backward and upside down," Naylor said. "I know every bump and tree, so I figured I could lose him there. And I did. After I couldn't see him anymore, I spotted a couple of riders hanging off to the side, finishing a joint. I asked 'em to ride down for me and get ski patrol to help your friend 'cause I had a maniac on my ass. What was her name again?"

"Stephanie," Judy whispered.

Naylor glanced at her and his expression softened. "Stephanie. Yeah. Well, after that, I peeled out of Toilet Bowl as fast as I could, hit the base, stepped out of my board, and ran for the first bus heading off the mountain."

Roger looked skeptical. "Why didn't you contact the ski patrol and tell them about the skier chasing you?"

"You think they'd believe me? You don't believe me yourself, man. I can tell from your eyes. I've had some run-ins with the patrol in the past. They'd assume I did it, pull my season pass, and who knows what else."

A manslaughter charge is what else. Claire was amazed that what the young man seemed to be most concerned about was his ski pass.

"Well, I'm willing to believe you," Claire said, "because your story meshes with what I saw. I spotted the skier's tracks coming out of the woods and meeting up with Stephanie's right before hers veered off. You said the skier was dressed all in black. Can you be more specific?"

"Black skis, those skinny graphite black poles, black gloves, and Spyder pants and jacket."

"Spider?"

"It's not what you're thinking, Mom," Judy said. "It's S-P-Y-D-E-R, a brand of ski clothing, with a big logo of a spider on the pieces."

"What about his head?" Claire asked Naylor. "Could you see his face or hair?"

"He wore sunglasses, but no hat. His hair was kinda gray, or a mix of black and gray. I was surprised an old dude could ski that fast."

"Was he heavy?" Roger patted his own paunch.

"Nope. Thin."

Judy leaned forward. "I think I saw the man. He rode up the T-bar a few positions behind Stephanie and me. I remember him because he shoved past a couple of guys adjusting their gear at the top of Ptarmigan like he was in a big hurry. I thought he was rude."

"Can you add anything to the description Boyd gave us?" Claire asked.

Naylor winced.

Claire caught the movement. "Sorry. Nail-It."

"The man was on the other side of the slope from us," Judy said, "so I didn't get a look at his face. I asked Stephanie if she'd seen how rude he was." Judy's voice caught, and she grabbed her cocoa cup to take a sip.

Claire rubbed Judy's shoulder. "Did she see him?"

Judy shook her head. "She was fixing her gloves and didn't see him at all."

Tapping his plastic fork on his empty paper plate, Naylor seemed to formulate some decision. "I drew a picture of him."

"The skier?" Roger asked.

"Yeah, I'm majoring in art."

"Me, too," Judy said.

"Cool." Naylor looked at Judy, as if assessing her with a fresh eye, but when she showed no return interest, he sucked on his fork and focused on Claire. "I couldn't get to sleep last night. I kept seeing the dude in my head. So I decided if I drew him, maybe he'd leave my dreams and live on paper, you know?"

Claire didn't know, but she nodded.

"Anyway, it worked."

"We'll need to get that drawing." Claire reviewed what they knew. An older man, dressed in black Spyder ski clothes, who was an excellent skier, had deliberately killed Stephanie. "I want to take the information you gave us to Detective Silverstone at the Summit County Sheriff's Office."

Naylor shook his head and sat back, his palms pushing against the table, as if ready to bolt. "You promised you wouldn't go to the cops."

Claire spoke quietly, but firmly, "No, I said we wouldn't tell a soul unless you approve it first. I'm asking for your approval. You're in danger, Boyd. Look how easily we found you. Not only will the police have no trouble tracking you down, but this skier-in-black could do the same and come after you."

"I can take care of myself," Naylor said.

"Not if he has a gun," Claire replied. "Detective Silverstone needs to hear how the skier chased you, so he knows how dangerous this man is. This isn't only about your safety. What if the skier gets his kicks from crashing into people on the slope? What if he kills someone else? Do you want that on your conscience?"

Naylor tucked his hands under his armpits, hugging himself. His gaze shifted up and down the street, searching once more. "What if the cops can't find him, and he gets to me in the meantime?"

"How about this? I'll tell Detective Silverstone your concerns and see if he can offer protection."

"I don't want cops hanging around my place."

"So you live here?" Roger asked.

"For the season, at least."

"Let me see what the detective has to say," Claire said, "then I'll call you and let you know. Maybe they can protect you without being so obvious. Can I have your phone number?" She dug a pen and an old grocery receipt out of her purse and passed them to Naylor.

He hesitated then scribbled his cell phone number. "You won't give him my name until I say so, right?"

Claire looked directly into his eyes. "Right." What she didn't add was that she would keep hounding him to give himself up for questioning until he did.

He returned the stare and worried his lip. "Okay." He stood and hunched his shoulders against the cold. "I'm going back to Yeti's now. Some people are expecting me."

"Thanks for talking to us, Boyd—Nail-It." Claire extended her hand.

Naylor shook it. "Thanks for the crepes." He walked to the street, glanced both ways, and stepped out. His head was bowed, as if pondering their conversation.

Tires screeched. Aimed straight at Naylor, a black SUV roared along the asphalt.

FIVE: THE BLACK SUV

CLAIRE LEAPT UP, TOPPLING her chair. She screamed, "Look out!"

Judy jumped up next to her. "Nail-It!"

Roger's chair fell over with a loud clang as he shoved himself to his feet.

Boyd jerked his head up but had no time to react before the black SUV rammed him. Arms flailing, his body was catapulted over the hood.

Claire tensed, almost as if she had been hit, too. She gaped in horror at the scene unfolding in slow motion before her.

Beside her, Judy gasped. Her hand flew to her mouth.

The SUV jolted to a stop.

Boyd slid off the side of the hood and slammed to the ground.

The vehicle started moving again. Its rear tire ran over Boyd's groin with a sickening crunch. Once free of Boyd's body, the rear tires spun on the slick street, spewing crystals of brown ice on his still form. All four tires caught, and the SUV shot down the street, with the dark silhouette of the driver inside sitting stone-still.

Roger ran after the vehicle and peered at the back bumper.

"Ohmigod," Judy shouted, "that car smashed into Boyd and never stopped."

Claire grabbed Judy's shoulders. "Yes, and we've got to help him."

Judy gazed at her, glassy-eyed, then blinked and nodded.

Claire ran to Boyd, dragging Judy behind, and knelt on the asphalt next to the young man, who lay sprawled on his back in a widening pool of blood. "Boyd, can you hear me?"

He groaned softly but his eyes didn't open.

Roger met them there, already pulling out his cell phone. "Christ, that driver hit him deliberately." He stared at the young man's mangled body.

Feeling slow and stupid as if she had just woken from a nightmare, Claire asked, "Did you see the license plate?"

"Some of it. I'm calling nine-one-one." He punched in the numbers.

Claire called Boyd's name again. He remained silent and unmoving. *At least he's breathing.* She took a deep breath herself to still the wash of panic flooding her heart. Here it was only the day after Stephanie's accident, and Claire needed to rely on her rusty first-aid training again.

Check the scene first. She scanned the road. No cars approached, but Boyd and the rest of them were vulnerable out in the middle of the street. The two crepe-stand workers, a young man and young woman, had run over to the side of the street. They stood craning their necks and wringing their hands in their aprons.

Claire pointed to the young man and yelled, "Hey you. Stop any cars that come. Got it?"

He nodded, as if grateful for something to do, and ran into the street, south of where Boyd lay. Roger moved to the north, ready to stop traffic coming in the other direction.

Check the victim. Blood stained the top of Boyd's jeans, which were scored with black tire tracks. Likely his pelvis was crushed. *Oh, God, the pain.* She hoped he would remain unconscious.

Gently, Claire pulled away one side of his open jacket to examine his torso, which had borne the brunt of the initial impact. Blood soaked his T-shirt. *Not good.*

She ran her trembling gloved hands along his scalp and behind his neck, being careful not to move his head. Her gloves came away blood free. At least he didn't have an open head wound.

"Here." Judy held out his hat. She must have recovered it from the street.

"Good thinking, honey." Claire grabbed the hat and perched it gently on top of his head to keep him warm.

Step three. Call. She heard Roger giving directions on the phone. *Good.* "Tell them he's breathing, but unconscious and bleeding from multiple injuries."

Roger relayed the information.

Step four. Care. What the hell can I do? His life is pouring out of him onto the ground. Claire rubbed her forehead with a shaky hand and took a deep breath. *Focus. You can do something. Must try to stop the bleeding.* Claire's gaze lit on the young woman at the side of the road, still wringing her apron. "Get some towels, cloths, whatever you have that I can use to stop the bleeding."

As the young woman ran to the crepe stand, Claire said to Judy, "Go with her. Bring back whatever you find."

Claire shucked her jacket and laid it on Boyd's chest. She had to keep him as warm as possible, or he would go into shock. She looked up at Roger. "Give me your coat."

He took it off and handed it to her, then returned the phone to his ear.

She placed Roger's coat on Boyd's legs. Gingerly, to avoid jostling his pelvis, she slid one side of the coat under his lower legs to protect them from the cold ground. Boyd's own coat would provide a layer of protection for his back.

Judy and the crepe worker returned with arms full of towels and paper napkins. Judy dropped to her knees next to her mother.

Claire lifted her coat and Boyd's T-shirt. A jagged red cut slashed across half his stomach.

Oh, God. Claire's stomach lurched. She swallowed the bile rising in her throat and willed it back down to where it belonged.

Judy sucked in a breath and turned away.

The crepe worker dumped her armload of towels and stepped back, eyes wide with horror.

Claire knew the young woman would bolt if she let her. She stared down the crepe worker and forced her voice to be stern. "Don't leave. I need your apron."

Slowly, the young woman moved her hands behind her back to untie the strings.

Claire pulled a towel from Judy's pile, folded it, and pressed it on the wound. She peered at Judy. "Another one."

Keeping her gaze averted from Boyd, Judy folded a towel and handed it to Claire.

Good girl, you're hanging in there. Claire slipped the second towel over the first, now blood-soaked, towel and pressed her gloved hand down again. "Now the apron."

Judy reached up for the apron held out by the crepe worker and tried to hand it to Claire.

Claire shook her head. "No, you have to slide it under his back, without moving him at all, so we can tie it around his stomach and keep pressure on this wound."

When Judy hesitated, Claire said firmly, "Now."

With trembling hands, Judy slid one side of the apron under the hollow of Boyd's lower back and gently pulled from the other side to bring it up and around.

"Now tie it tight. I'll slide my hand out of the way."

Judy did as she was told.

"Good job, honey." Claire turned her attention to Boyd's pelvis. It didn't seem to be bleeding as badly as the cut on his stomach, and pressing on the broken bones might make things worse.

The siren of an approaching ambulance interrupted her thoughts. *Thank God. No more decisions.*

Two emergency medical technicians ran over with a stretcher. As they hooked up a heart-rate monitor, IV, and oxygen to Boyd, Claire briefed them on what she had done.

She stood to get out of the way and swayed. Stars revolved around her head as her knees buckled.

Roger caught her, and he and Judy sat her on the curb. He pushed Claire's head between her knees.

One of the EMTs shouted, "You going to be all right, ma'am?"

Claire took a deep breath. The world stopped spinning. "I think so."

"You may be a little shocky. Pretty common for someone giving first aid in an accident. You don't feel it until you're off the hook." He glanced at Judy. "How 'bout you?"

"I'm okay."

Roger picked up his and Claire's coats that the EMTs had removed from Boyd and replaced with blankets. He draped Claire's around her shoulders and slid on his own.

Wondering if any of Boyd's blood was on her coat, Claire shivered.

Roger sat next to her and gathered her in his arms. "You did great, dear. I'm proud of you."

"I hope he lives. His injuries were terrible."

Roger rocked her, rubbing her arms in silence.

Young people had poured out of Sherpa & Yeti's to stand on the sidewalk, gawk, and point. Claire recognized the group of young women she had talked to, looks of whitened horror on their faces.

Siren blaring and lights flashing, a Breckenridge police Land Rover pulled up next to the ambulance. A policeman stepped out of the car and approached the ambulance crew, who had transferred Boyd to the stretcher. They pointed to Claire's family and wheeled the injured young man to the back of the ambulance.

The policeman approached the Hanovers. "Hello, I'm Officer Koch, Breckenridge police. The ambulance crew said one of you might need some help."

Impatiently, Claire waved her hand. "I'm fine. Forget about me. They need to take that poor young man to the hospital."

Officer Koch took out a notepad. "They will. Can I get your names?"

After they had identified themselves and given their contact information, the officer asked, "Did you see what happened?"

"Yes," Roger answered. "A black Range Rover hit him."

"A Range Rover? You sure?" Claire asked.

"I know my SUVs."

The officer looked up from his notepad. "Did you get a license plate number?"

"Just part of it," Roger answered. "It was definitely a Colorado plate. White mountains against a dark green background. The first two letters were A and Y."

The ambulance took off toward the medical center, sirens blaring. They all watched it leave in silence.

Roger caught the officer's attention. "The hit was deliberate. The driver waited up there"—he pointed in the direction from which the SUV had come—"and took off once Naylor stepped into the street."

The officer's brows rose. "Deliberate?"

Roger's mouth was set in an angry line. "I'm sure of it. Whoever was driving that SUV meant to kill Boyd Naylor."

Judy gasped. "No. Boyd can't die, too!"

"Too?" The officer looked even more confused. "Who else died?"

Claire sympathized with the poor man. She was still trying to sort out everything in her own mind. Something nagged at her, a detail she was missing. "I'm sure the attack on this young man is connected with the young woman who died at the ski resort yesterday."

"Why do you think that?"

Claire remembered her promise to Boyd. If he lived, she owed it to him to keep that promise. "I would rather talk to Detective Silverstone about that."

"Is he investigating the skier's death?" At Claire's nod, the officer said, "Wait here a minute," and walked to his patrol car.

After a few minutes talking on the radio, he returned. "Detective Silverstone's working an accident on Highway Nine out by Farmer's Corner. I'll take your statements and share them with him. Can you meet him at the justice center tomorrow morning?"

"Yes." Claire shivered again. She couldn't get warm.

The officer peered at her in concern. "How about the three of you get in my patrol car? We'll continue the interview there." He signaled the crepe-stand workers. "Three hot chocolates, then stick around. I need to talk to you, too."

Roger helped Claire to her feet. As she trudged to the police car, she said a silent prayer for Boyd. He needed to live, to help find out who had tried to kill him—and succeeded in killing Stephanie.

At eight-thirty the next morning, Roger pulled the car into the parking lot of the Summit County Justice Center. Claire studied the red brick building with its peaked green roof. Flanked by firs and aspens and Colorado and U.S. flags, it seemed to be just another unassuming local government building, like the public library next door.

She followed Roger and Judy through the glass doors into a quiet two-story lobby with green indoor-outdoor carpeting. The stern face of a mounted bighorn sheep stared down at them from over the entrance to the jail side of the building, as if to say, "Beware, all who enter here." The Hanovers turned in the other direction, down a hall decorated with DARE posters and drug-free pledges signed by Summit County children.

Roger held open the door to the sheriff's office, and Claire told the receptionist who they were and asked to see Detective Silverstone. As Silverstone led them to his desk, she noted the space looked like any other business office—insurance, engineering, marketing—except some of the occupants wore uniforms of black shirts and green-gray pants with black strips along the side. And their belts bristled with handcuffs, black leather cases holding who knows what, and holstered guns.

Silverstone, however, wore jeans and a work shirt. The only clothing that identified he was a member of the sheriff's office was his black fleece vest with a yellow star on the left side, emblazoned with blue letters spelling out "Summit County Sheriff's Office." He led the way into a large room divided into four gray half-cubicles open to the center, each with its own computer. Three desks were unoccupied, and a patrol officer sat typing at the last. The soulful strains of a Tab Benoit song Claire recognized from the *Voice of the Wetlands* CD came from a radio turned down low.

Silverstone motioned for the Hanovers to sit in three chairs positioned in front of one of the rear desks. "Anyone want coffee?"

Claire shook her head. Judy and Roger refused also. They had polished off a whole pot of coffee before they came, because none of them had slept much after getting home. Claire had called the Summit County Medical Center early that morning. Boyd had been flown to Denver Health Hospital's Trauma Center on the

Flight for Life helicopter. But she hadn't gotten any information out of Denver Health before they left for the justice center.

"Have you heard anything about Boyd Naylor?" she asked, as Silverstone seated himself behind his desk.

A pained expression crossed his face. "He died on the operating table. Too much damage to internal organs."

Oh, God. A wall of sadness slammed into Claire, forcing her against the back of her chair.

"Damn," Roger whispered.

Judy dug for a tissue in her purse as a tear ran down her cheek.

"I'm sorry," Silverstone said. "Did you know him well?"

"We just met him last night," Roger said.

Silverstone cocked a brow and eyed each of them. "Maybe you can explain to me why you three have been the first on the scene for not one, but two suspicious and fatal *accidents* in the last two days."

Roger gripped the arms of his chair and thrust his chin out. "You can't seriously think we had anything to do with either one."

Spreading his hands wide, Silverstone said, "I don't know what to think."

"Stephanie was my friend," Judy blurted out. "My boyfriend's sister. Why would we want to hurt her?"

"Maybe she didn't approve of the relationship."

Claire leaned forward and slapped the top of Silverstone's desk. "Look. Judy's upset enough. She's experienced more death in the last two days than in her whole lifetime up 'til now. And there's a big difference between saying a gentle goodbye to her grandfather in a nursing home and watching a young man get run down by a speeding car."

Claire glanced at Judy, who wiped her nose and stared at her mother. "I will not allow her to be upset further. We came here willingly to cooperate with your investigation, not to be accused of killing people." She sat back, crossed her arms over her chest, and narrowed her eyes at Silverstone.

A noise behind them made Claire turn around. A patrolman stood next to the one who had been typing and now sat stock still. They both stared at her.

"The crepe-stand workers can tell you," Roger said, "we not only were nowhere near Naylor when he was hit, but we provided first aid and called nine-one-one, just like we did for Stephanie."

Silverstone shooed the two officers out of the room with a wave of his hand then focused his attention on the Hanovers. "And for that massage therapist in Colorado Springs, too?"

Roger slumped in his chair and eyed Claire. "So you heard about that."

"I thought I recognized your name," Silverstone said, "and I did a little research last night. This makes three deaths you've been involved in, right?"

"Roger was totally exonerated in that murder," Claire replied, "as you should know from your research. It has nothing to do with these deaths."

"You can understand why I'd be suspicious, though."

"No, I can't."

Roger's jaw worked as he ground his teeth together. "Look, if you're going to accuse us of something, do it; then we'll sue you for false arrest."

Silverstone held up his hands, palms out. "I'm not accusing any of you of a crime. But I do need to know what's going on here, and what your connection to it is."

He rose and paced behind the desk. "We rarely get more than a few burglaries, drunk-driving arrests, maybe a domestic dispute or two in a week, and now all of a sudden, we have two deaths on our hands. The resources of our office and the Breckenridge police are being stretched damn thin to handle the investigations, let alone deal with the interference."

Could someone be hampering the investigations deliberately? Claire leaned forward. "Interference?"

Silverstone pulled a small, shiny brown object out of his pocket and rubbed it absentmindedly. "The press, who want all the lurid details. And on the opposite side, the ski resort, the chamber of commerce, and the local politicians who all want this bad news to go away fast."

He stopped and peered at the Hanovers. "Besides the timing, the only link we have between the two deaths is your presence."

"That's not the only link," Claire said, deciding that the promise she made to Boyd had died with him.

Silverstone reseated himself at his desk, his fists balled on the top. "You referring to the connection you refused to discuss with Officer Koch last night?"

"Boyd Naylor saw who killed Stephanie," Claire said. "He is, or was, the snowboarder we were looking for."

Roger nodded. "That's probably why he was killed. The SUV hit him deliberately—aimed right for him."

"And Nail-It was scared," Judy added. "The skier who hit Stephanie chased him after Nail-It saw what happened."

"Whoa, whoa." Silverstone held out his hand, palm out. "First, who is Nail-It?"

"Boyd Naylor," Claire answered. "His nickname was Nail-It."

"Okay," Silverstone said. "Now, I want to hear the whole story of what happened last night from the top, from when you first met this Naylor kid. Tell me everything he told you."

Roger laid his head on the back of his chair and looked at the ceiling. "We already did this with Officer Koch last night."

"I know." Silverstone tapped a brown file filled with papers. "And he was kind enough to stay up late and type his notes for me to read before you came in. But I want to hear it again from your mouths."

Roger rubbed his fatigue-lined face and shot Claire a baleful look.

She launched into the story.

At the end, Silverstone returned to the subject of the black Range Rover. "The Breck police have the DMV doing a license search based on the two letters you gave them. But given the popularity of those SUVs among the Denver skier population, we'll probably have to weed through quite a few. Any other features of the car stand out? A ski rack? A bent fender? Anything?"

Claire closed her eyes to visualize the SUV driving away, but the image of a different, stationary black Range Rover got in the way, sitting in a driveway. The Continos' driveway. Claire's eyelids flew open. "The Continos have a black Range Rover."

Everyone stared at her. "You can't think—" Roger began.

"What if they found out about Boyd, like Judy did?"

"But to run him down in cold blood?"

Claire's emotions churned. While she thought the possibility macabre and despicable, she couldn't help but feel some sympathy for the parents who had just lost their child. "Imagine it, Roger. Imagine how you would feel if you discovered the identity of the young man who you thought killed your daughter. If it was Judy, wouldn't you want revenge?"

Roger's hands formed claws in his lap, as if clenched around someone's neck. Then they relaxed. "For an instant, yes. But to kill someone in cold blood like that, no. I would go to the cops."

Silverstone nodded, as if in understanding, his hand massaging the hidden object.

Looking for evidence of a family, Claire searched his desk for a photo. There it was, half turned toward him. A tall, thin woman stood in a bright yellow aspen grove with her arm placed protectively on the shoulder of a little girl with black braids, about five. *Yes, he understood.*

Silverstone followed her gaze to the photo. His face softened for a moment, and he bent his head to write on his pad. "I'll get the Continos' license plate number, see if it matches, and check on their whereabouts last night."

"I can't believe it." Judy's lips pursed in a thin, disapproving line. "The Continos would never do something like that."

"You know Nick well," Claire said, "but how well do you know his parents? We think only one person was in the car. It could've been Nick's father."

Judy opened her mouth then hesitated. "True, I've only talked to Nick's dad a few times, 'cause he's always working late, but still—"

"Still, he loved his daughter, and she's just been killed."

"But Nail-It didn't do it."

"And the Continos don't know that. They still think a snowboarder crashed into Stephanie."

"Which could still be the case," Silverstone said.

Surprised, Claire said, "We told you Boyd's story about the skier dressed in black who chased him."

He nodded. "That's precisely what it could have been—a story."

"But Judy saw the skier. Not him hitting Stephanie, but getting off the lift. And I saw the tracks. And Naylor not only saw him, but drew a picture of him, too. He said the skier had black skis and thin graphite black poles and wore a black Spyder jacket and pants."

Silverstone jotted down the description. "Naylor could have seen him on the trail, too, and decided the skier would be a good unidentified fall guy in his story."

Claire's frustration rose. "So you don't believe I saw those ski tracks?"

"I'm keeping all options open right now. Maybe the tracks were there, maybe not. Maybe they were new that morning, maybe not. Since no one else saw them, I just don't know."

Claire had an idea. "It hasn't snowed since Monday, has it?"

With a quizzical look, Silverstone shook his head.

"I remember exactly where those tracks came out of the woods. The skier would've waited there for Stephanie. If we go back and take a look, we might find something useful. At the very least, if he stood there awhile, the snow would be tamped down, confirming my story."

Silverstone walked to the office door. He looked down the hall out a window facing the ski resort, then faced them, rubbing the back of his neck. "I suppose I should see where Stephanie Contino got hit, given this new information. Could be a crime scene now. We need to do it soon, though, since it looks like a snow cloud's building up. It should be ready to dump its load late this afternoon or tonight."

He studied the brown object in his cupped hand. "Logically, these deaths could still be two unrelated accidents, or an accident and the Continos' revenge. Even if Naylor's story is true, and Stephanie Contino's death wasn't an accident, that doesn't mean his wasn't."

Roger gripped the arm of his chair. "But I told you—"

Silverstone held up his hand. "I know you think it was deliberate, but we get folks speeding down Main Street all the time, especially after they've been hitting the bars."

"There's still a possibility that both of them were murders," Claire said. *If so, why? And who's next?*

Silverstone gave a grim nod. "Two murders would blow the lid off our quiet little county. That would affect the business of all four ski areas—Keystone, A-Basin, and Copper Mountain, as well as Breckenridge."

Roger squirmed in his seat. "But isn't finding a murderer, or even two, more important than the skiing business?"

"You don't understand. Every family in Summit County is tied in some way to the ski business, either directly as employees of the resorts or indirectly through jobs in the tourist industry. We're talking about a major impact on everyone's income."

Claire realized the problems related to Stephanie's death were snowballing. "I see what you're facing."

Silverstone looked at Claire. "I need to make a few calls, first, but Naylor's tale needs to be checked out. How soon can you be ready to go up on the mountain?"

Claire pressed her hand to her chest. "Just me?"

"All of you. Your daughter remembered seeing the black-suited skier when Naylor's story jogged her memory. Maybe returning to the scene will remind one of you of something else."

"Give us an hour to get our gear," Roger said grimly. "We'll meet you at the base of the Rocky Mountain Superchair."

SIX:
DOWN THE SLIPPERY SLOPE

CLAIRE STOOD WITH ROGER and Judy at the base of Breckenridge's Peak Eight and scanned the undulating mob below the side-by-side high-speed chairlifts, looking for Detective Silverstone. Skiers and snowboarders shuffled forward in fits and starts as the chairs scooped up riders in bites of four each. Late-morning was prime traffic-jam time at the mountain base. The late risers were just arriving, and the early risers had returned after their first or second run.

Voices rose in greetings or shouted into the two-way radios and cell phones that everyone seemed to carry nowadays. "I'm at the base of the Colorado chair." "Meet you in an hour at the Vista Haus." "I don't see you. Where the hell are you?"

Claire could find no sign of Silverstone in the chaotic scene. "We should've picked a less crowded place to meet."

Roger leaned on his ski poles and stretched the backs of his legs. "Don't worry. He'll find us."

Judy finished rubbing sunscreen on her nose and passed the tube to Claire. She smeared Chapstick on her lips next, then promptly nibbled it off as she glanced anxiously around the crowd.

The growing gray cloud west of the range hadn't yet blocked the sun's rays, which glinted white and sharp off the crystalline snow. Claire shaded her eyes and squinted at people streaming off the top step of the stairs from the bus stop and off the walkway from the gondola transporting skiers out of the town parking lots.

She saw Silverstone's black jacket, with the yellow sheriff's office star on the left breast. The cold had outlined his sharp cheekbones in red, making them even more prominent. Claire wondered where the man's gray-blue eyes came from, given his obvious Native American ancestry.

Silverstone turned to say something to the man next to him, and Claire recognized Hal Matthews in his red jacket with the white cross. The two men spotted Claire's group and approached, carrying skis slung over their shoulders.

"Mr. Matthews is joining us as the ski resort's representative," Silverstone said, as he and Matthews clicked into their skis.

Matthews nodded a grim greeting. "Owen filled me in on what happened to Naylor last night. A couple of my patrollers remembered him. Typical fast-riding boarder. Had to be warned a few times, but not a bad sort, really. What a waste."

"Maybe we'll find something today," Roger said, "that will help you guys figure out why two young people have lost their lives in the space of two days."

"Not sure what you hope to find up there." Matthews shot a worried glance at Silverstone's star. "I hope we don't draw a crowd.

80

At least Breckenridge police aren't coming along. Their jackets aren't as discreet as yours."

Silverstone slid on his ski goggles. "They're only interested in Naylor's case for now. But if we tie the two together, you'll be seeing a lot more of them, Hal."

Matthews managed to look even gloomier.

Silverstone clapped his hand on Matthews's shoulder. "So, you gonna get us to the head of this line? That *is* why you came, right?"

"Right," the ski patroller responded sarcastically, but he pushed ahead of them into the ski school line.

A children's instructor with desperation in her eyes herded eight young children in front of them. When she turned and spied Matthews's jacket, her face brightened in relief. "Oh, good. I need you folks to help me with these kids. Hal, can you take two?"

"Sure thing." Matthews positioned himself between two boys and skied to the chair. The instructor efficiently paired two more kids with Roger and Silverstone, and two girls with Claire and Judy, then took the last two herself.

Claire chatted up the two girls, aged eight and nine, who reminded her of Judy at that age. They were clearly apprehensive about trying Duke's Run, the advanced intermediate slope the instructor was taking them on, but tried to cover up their fear with brave claims of prowess.

Claire lifted the safety bar for them at the top. "I'm sure the instructor wouldn't take you on the run if she didn't think you could handle it. You go, girls." She gave a thumbs-up signal.

With sheepish grins, the girls returned the gesture.

"Good luck and have fun," Claire yelled as the girls skied away to join their group.

Judy raised her brow at Claire. "Always the Mother Hen, aren't you?"

"Is that such a bad thing?"

"Only if the chick you're mothering doesn't need it." Judy skied to where the men stood waiting.

Claire followed. *Where did that comment come from?*

Once joined up again, the group pushed off. Claire wound through other skiers as fast as she could to build the speed needed to crest the rise at the top of Duke's Run and maintain momentum for the traverse to the T-bar. A skier crossed her path, though, and she had to brake to a stop. She pushed herself along with her poles to skate the rest of the way. By the time she caught up to the others, she was out of breath.

Matthews signaled the T-bar lift operator and broke into the line. His ski patrol jacket and the sheriff's star bought them the approval of the waiting mob. But a few disgruntled snowboarders stared down the Hanovers as they followed, as if asking, "Why do you deserve special service?"

Unnerved by the hostile looks, Claire almost lost her footing when the T-bar jerked her and Judy forward. She caught her balance with a quick grab of the bar pushing against her rump. *Thank God.* A fall in front of all these advanced skiers and boarders—who felt obligated to guffaw when someone blew it—would have been downright humiliating.

With a deep breath, she loosened her grip. Then her poles started to slip out from where she had tucked them under her arm. When she let go of the bar to readjust, one of her skis bounced over a chunk of ice. The tip swung across Judy's skis. Before Claire could say, "watch out," the two of them fell in a tangle of arms, legs, skis and poles.

Free of their weight, the T-bar cable snapped up to its shortest length, and the bar swung off without them.

"Good one, Mom." Judy shoved Claire's leg off her own, tugged her ski out from under Claire's rump, and slid on her butt to the side of the track, barely in time to get out of the way of the next two riders.

Claire rolled and scooted off to the other side. As she retrieved her poles and struggled to stand, she heard snickers. When she looked downhill, she could see some of the skiers in the crowd pointing at her with grins on their faces. Her cheeks flamed. *Oh, God.*

Judy sat on the snow, head down and arms hanging over her knees.

"Are you hurt?" Claire called.

"No, only embarrassed to death." She shoved herself to her feet. "Are you okay?"

Claire gave herself the once-over. "I'm okay."

When Judy skied across the track, Claire could see her daughter's face was as red as her own.

"C'mon," Judy said. "We've got to get back on."

Skiing down was the last thing Claire wanted to do, but Judy was right. She pushed off and hockey-stopped beside the lift operator.

He pointed to the end of the line. "You have to get back in line."

"But we're with that ski patroller and sheriff's detective," Claire said. "We're helping with an investigation. They'll be waiting for us."

With a sigh of exasperation, the lift operator rolled his eyes. "Think you can stay on this time?"

"Don't worry, I'll kill her if she doesn't." Judy grinned at Claire and skied into place.

A snowboarder who was next in line opened his hands wide. "Hey, what gives?"

"Sorry, man," the operator said. "They're with that patroller." He waved Claire into place next to Judy and handed them the bar.

As they jerked forward, a few protests sounded from the crowd.

Claire clutched the bar with both hands, determined not to fall off again.

Judy peered at her. "How'd you fall? You've been on this lift a million times."

"I know, and I'm sorry I embarrassed you. It was a bad combination of stuff, ending with that ice chunk on the track."

It took Claire quite some time to settle into the rhythm of the uphill slide and relax her death grip on the bar. Finally feeling more confident, she glanced at Judy, who was staring pensively off toward Peak Seven.

"We haven't had a chance to really talk after Stephanie's death," Claire said. "How are you doing, honey?"

"Probably no worse than you."

"What's that mean?"

"I can't sleep, my throat's sore from holding in tears, I'm worried about Nick, and yeah, I can't help feeling a little guilty, like I could have done something to stop it." After spitting out the litany, Judy shot a wry look at her mother. "I'm sure you're feeling some of the same things, right?"

"Right." Claire relaxed a little. Judy's feistiness was a good sign. At least she wasn't giving up and letting the depression and anxiety overwhelm her. "You gonna be okay then?"

Judy threw the question right back at her. "You okay?"

"Not really, but I'm handling it."

"So am I. No need to mother me." Judy directed her gaze off to the side, away from Claire.

So she doesn't want to talk about it and probably resents me for asking. Nothing new here. Claire had received the same response many times during Judy's late teen years, but sometimes, just sometimes, a few hours after an outburst her daughter might casually bring up the touchy subject again. Then Claire could mother her, but only on the rare occasions when an invitation was offered. She studied Judy's stiff stance. *Probably not today.*

Casting about for another topic, Claire remembered something Boyd had said. "Remember Boyd mentioning Toilet Bowl? Think we can see it from here?"

Judy glanced downhill over her shoulder. "We need more altitude."

"It's strange. Here I've been skiing Breckenridge for years, and just yesterday I hear about a part of the resort I've never been in."

With a sardonic grin, Judy said, "Well, I don't think any of his gang would invite you to hang out and smoke weed with them."

"But someone might have invited you. You never heard of it before?"

"No-ope." Judy drew it out, as if she knew what was coming next.

Claire took a deep breath and decided to ask the question. The subject had been broached, and she didn't know when her next opportunity would be. "When Boyd talked about smoking weed, you nodded, to show you knew what he was talking about. I know you didn't touch the stuff in high school, but have you smoked pot since going away to college?"

Judy harrumphed. "You can't tell me you and Dad never tried it when you were in school."

"No, I can't. But we never touched anything stronger, like cocaine. Look, I won't freak out. I only want to know you're being safe."

Judy shot a glance at Claire. "Yeah, I've smoked pot a few times but I didn't really enjoy it. I haven't done it in a while, Mom, so no need to worry."

"Nothing else?"

"No."

Relief flooded over Claire, loosening the hand she had clenched around the T-bar. "I'm glad."

When they reached the top, Roger asked, "What kept you?"

A smile played at the edge of Judy's lips, but she held her tongue.

"Nothing important," Claire said. "Let's get back to the business at hand."

"Where did you first see the skier in black, Miss Hanover?" Silverstone asked.

Judy pointed to the top of the Ptarmigan run. "Over there."

"Let's go." Silverstone skied to where she pointed, followed by the others. "Okay, stand where you were when you saw him and tell me what you remember."

Judy moved over a ways, closed her eyes for a few seconds, then described the skier again.

"How was his skiing ability?" Silverstone asked.

"Real smooth, like someone who'd been doing it a long time."

Matthews leaned forward on his poles. "How close together were his skis?"

A puzzled frown creased Judy's face. "Pretty close. More like the way Dad skis than I do."

"Ah ha." Matthews turned to Silverstone. "He learned the old way, when we were told to keep our skis clamped tight together while paralleling. So, he's probably at least in his forties."

Silverstone nodded. "Good insight. Anything else you can tell us, Judy?"

She shook her head.

"We'll do the same thing at the spot where Naylor passed your group," Silverstone said. "You lead the way, and Hal and I will follow."

They made their way down the smooth upper section of Ptarmigan, through the mogul field at the bottom and over to the side. Again, Silverstone asked each of the Hanovers to recount what they saw.

As Claire finished her description of Naylor's pass, she said, "I thought he was totally out of control and was scared he would hit one of us."

Roger shook his head. "My impression was that he knew exactly what he was doing. Sure, his style was wild, but he was coming in close to check out Judy and Stephanie and make a big impression on them."

"My patrollers would probably agree with that assessment," Matthews said. "Naylor's fast . . . too fast, but he's well liked and he never hit anyone—that they know of."

But he pissed off someone enough that they hit him.

Silverstone turned to Claire. "I want you to find the place where you say the skier came out of the woods. Don't go in there. Just point it out from the slope. We'll hang back above you until you've located the spot."

Claire pushed off to ski down the slope. She shuddered when she passed the place where she had heard Judy scream, then she slowed and scanned the woods. She spied the trampled area below her where Stephanie had hit the tree. Thankfully, someone had removed the bloody snow. Or covered it up.

She stopped and searched the trees along the other side of the trail, trying to remember where the ski track had exited. She spotted a broken branch, with the end piece still attached. The same one she saw Monday? She skied closer and stared at it from a few yards away. *Yes.*

She pointed to the pine tree and yelled at Silverstone. "Over here. I remember that broken branch."

After he joined her, Silverstone clicked out of his skis and signaled Matthews to do the same. "Wait here while we search the area," he said to the Hanovers.

Matthews studied the drooping branch. "Looks recent. The ends of the break aren't dried out yet."

Silverstone trained his gaze on the ground. "Snow's trampled down about eight feet in, behind that fir. See?"

When Matthews took a step forward, Silverstone stopped him with a hand to his chest. "We don't want to step on any evidence. We'll approach from above."

He tromped uphill and pointed out a set of ski tracks entering the woods. "Here's where he probably came in."

Stepping over the tracks, Silverstone positioned himself a couple of feet on the uphill side. He followed the tracks into the woods, scanning the snow as he walked. Matthews did the same from the downhill side.

Claire watched the men's progress as they worked their way through the widely spaced trees. When they reached the trampled area, the two leaned forward, hands on their knees and scanned the ground.

A shadow swept over the slope. Claire shivered. The snow cloud that had built up during the morning loomed over the peak. A breeze ruffled her hair and blew a few snowflakes up her nose. She sneezed. "Storm's coming."

"Bless you," Roger said. "Hope these guys find something before the evidence gets all covered up."

Judy extracted a fleece neck gaiter from her pocket. She pulled it over her head, positioning it to cover her neck and face.

Feeling the temperature drop and stinging snowflakes hit her cheeks, Claire followed her daughter's lead. Soon white flakes swirled all around them. Claire tucked her gloved hands under her armpits.

Roger stamped his skis on the ground. "This standing around and waiting is damn cold."

Matthews pointed at the ground. Silverstone took a plastic bag out of his pocket and nudged something into it.

Claire took a step toward them. "What did you find?"

"A cigarette butt." Silverstone stuffed the bag into his jacket pocket, eyes still scanning the ground.

"Maybe the killer smoked it while he was waiting for us to come down."

"Maybe. Or any number of people could have stopped here and had a smoke." He straightened and motioned to Matthews. "I don't think we're going to find anything else."

When the two of them reached the Hanovers, Roger asked, "You can test for fingerprints and DNA on the butt, can't you?"

"I'll send it to CBI to be analyzed. If they can pull either prints or DNA off it, they'll run them against the FBI databases."

Claire's hopes rose. "So we might get the name of Stephanie's killer?"

"Only if he's committed a crime or been fingerprinted for a job application in the past." Silverstone clicked into his skis. "The match is best done when you have two samples—one from the crime scene and one from a suspect. We're missing the suspect here, and I'm not even sure this is a crime scene."

When Claire started to speak, he held up his hand. "I'll still send it to CBI. Even with a high priority, it'll take awhile, though. They've got quite a backlog."

Matthews studied the sky. "I suggest we get off the mountain. A mean storm is brewing. Weather service is predicting six inches."

"First, I want to take another look at where Miss Contino hit." Silverstone skied to the other side of the trail and down to the tree Stephanie hit. He leaned on his poles and peered at the scene, scanning up to the spot where the black-garbed skier had waited.

He looked at Claire. "Could you stand where you saw the ski tracks cross?"

Claire side-stepped to where she thought she remembered Stephanie's tracks and the other skier's had intersected. With all the snow swirling around, cutting down the visibility, she had a hard time pinpointing the spot. "I think it was about here."

Silverstone gazed at her, eyes unfocused as if lost in thought.

Impatiently, Matthews skied to him. "If we don't leave now, we'll be caught in a total whiteout. C'mon, everyone, I'll lead the way." He waved his arm down the hill as gusts of snow scoured its surface.

"Well?" Claire asked Silverstone. "Now that you've seen the tamped-down snow, the broken branch, and the cigarette butt, do you believe Boyd and me about the skier deliberately killing Stephanie?"

Silverstone's face was impassive. "I always believed you, Mrs. Hanover, at least to the extent of what you saw. The problem is determining what it means."

SEVEN:
ALTITUDE ADJUSTMENT

AFTER A LATE LUNCH of spicy chicken tortilla soup and hot chocolate at the townhouse, Claire mulled over the visit to the ski resort while she loaded the dishwasher. Could the cigarette butt
have come from the killer? Or was some other random person the
smoker? Even if DNA or prints on the butt matched a criminal in
the FBI database, that criminal could just be a ski enthusiast who
had made a recent trip to Breckenridge.

At least they had returned to the slope before the storm hit.
Silverstone never would have found the butt under the new snow
cover. Claire hoped he was now convinced Stephanie and Boyd
had been murdered. Or was open to the possibility.

Roger declared he was taking a nap and went upstairs.

Judy wandered around the living room, staring out the window and straightening pillows that didn't need straightening.

When Claire heard her daughter sigh, she decided action was
called for. She started up the dishwasher and walked into the living

room. "I want to make a sympathy basket for the Continos. I could use your help picking out items. Come shopping with me."

Judy rolled her eyes and plopped onto the sofa. "Mom, one of your baskets isn't going to make them feel any better about losing Stephanie."

Claire took a lot of pride in creating those gift baskets for the customers of her part-time business, but she refused to let Judy see how the flippant comment bothered her. "No, but it will let them know we're thinking of them, that we care. Maybe that'll give them some small amount of comfort."

"I guess it's something to do." Frowning, Judy picked distractedly at a sofa cushion. "I'd rather spend the afternoon with Nick, but he said he and his folks wanted to be by themselves today."

Claire sat beside her daughter. "How serious are you two?"

"I really don't know. We got pretty close before I left for France, but it's only been e-mail and phone calls since then."

Claire didn't ask how close, because she suspected she didn't want to hear the answer—that Judy had slept with Nick. "What about since you returned?"

"That's just it. This vacation was supposed to be a reunion, to see if we still felt as strongly about each other. But Stephanie's death changed everything. I've tried to talk to Nick, to help him deal with it, but he's been so distant."

Claire stilled Judy's hand. "You'll pick that sofa cushion apart. Look, Nick's probably not ready to share his grief with you yet. Men feel they have to be strong, can't show emotion. Especially young men."

"What am I supposed to do?"

"Just let him know you care, so when he's ready to open up, you can be there for him."

Judy hugged the cushion against her chest. "What if he's never ready?"

"That could happen. He may want to keep his grief private and may never feel comfortable sharing it with you."

"No, that's not what I meant." Unshed tears glimmered in Judy's eyes. "I'm afraid he'll never be ready to pick up where we left off. That he'll keep on backing away from me." She bit her lip. "I wish I knew how he really felt."

"Has he ever said he loves you?"

Judy shook her head. "He's said he cares for me, wants me, needs me, and that he loves being with me, but he's never said those three words, 'I love you.'"

"What about you?"

"I haven't said them either." Judy kneaded the pillow. "I don't know, Mom. I've never been in love before. I don't know if what I feel for him is love or not."

"What *do* you feel for him?"

"He makes me feel good, really good about myself, like I can do anything I want to, as long as he supports me. And until this happened, we could talk about anything for hours and hours. You know what I mean?"

"Oh, yeah." *You've got it bad, honey.* "Remember, I've had twenty-six years' experience loving your dear old dad. Tell me, when you're together, do you always feel the urge to touch him, stroke his hand or ruffle his hair?"

"Yes." With an excited flounce, Judy turned toward Claire. "And I always want to do things for him, which is why I wish he'd talk to

94

me now. In the fall when I was still on campus, I would bake him honey wheat bread in the dorm's kitchen and bring it to him still warm out of the oven."

Claire grinned. "I didn't know you could bake bread. I thought you were a klutz in the kitchen. When are you going to make us a loaf?"

"I don't feed people who call me a klutz." A smile cracked Judy's lips then disappeared. "But seriously, is that how you felt about Dad before you two got married?"

"I still do, though in his case, brownies are the path from his stomach to his heart."

With a jolt, Claire realized that she was Judy's age when she married Roger. Accepting that her daughter might be ready to make that big step would be difficult. Claire studied Judy's face, shining with anticipation and heartfelt emotion, and felt a rush of maternal protection. *Heaven help that young man if he breaks her heart.*

Claire stood. "Let's shop and make that basket. We'll take it over to the Continos tomorrow. Maybe Nick'll be ready to talk to you then."

"I hope so." Judy managed to look anxious and excited at the same time. She joined her mother in the hallway and donned her coat. "What are you planning to put in the basket?"

Claire threw her muffler over her shoulder. "That's part of the fun of putting a gift basket together—the thrill when I find something unique that really matches the occasion or the person who's getting the basket. I thought I'd start with a nice pen and some high-quality thank you notes or blank cards Angela can use for thank you notes."

"There's a stationery store on Main Street," Judy said. "We can walk there."

They stepped outside, and a blast of cold air peppered Claire's face with snowflakes. "We may need a hot drink before long."

While she briskly walked the two blocks into town with Judy at her side, Claire smiled to herself. She was looking forward to spending the afternoon with her daughter, sharing the hunt for those elusive items that made one of Claire Hanover's gift baskets special.

Judy turned to Claire. "Thank you cards and a pen won't fill a basket. What else do you have in mind?"

"Some soothing things, like scented candles or a book of up-lifting poems. Are the Continos religious?"

"Catholic. Nick doesn't go to church much, but his mom attends mass every Sunday."

"Okay, some religious poetry or a book about taking your grief to God, or something like that. And some soft music. A gift basket should have something for every sense—taste, smell, sight, touch, and sound. What kind of music do Nick's parents enjoy?"

Judy thought for a moment. "Classical, I think."

Claire rubbed her hands together as they turned onto Main Street. "Good, I'll ask at the stationery store where we can find some nice CDs."

An hour later, they each lugged three plastic bags of purchases, including a dyed wicker basket Claire had found for thirty percent off at an import store that carried Middle Eastern furnishings. The basket exactly matched the colors in the Continos' ski house living room and could be used to hold reading materials later.

The wind tugged at the bags, flapping the plastic edges. It tore at Claire's face, too. Her cheeks were raw, her whole body felt chilled, and her feet were killing her. She spotted a coffee and oxygen café across the street called Altitude Adjustment.

She angled her head at the café. "I need to get off my feet and have a hot drink."

"Good idea." Judy led the way.

Claire ordered a couple of vanilla lattes at the counter and searched for a place to sit. She spotted the blonde from Sherpa & Yeti's two nights before, sitting with a young man with a scraggly beard and long dark hair. Both looked distraught, their faces grim.

Claire set her packages on the seat of a booth across from the two. "There's the young woman who pointed out Boyd to us. We should talk to them."

"I think we should leave them alone," Judy said. "Can't you tell they're grieving for him?"

"Of course I can tell. That's precisely why I want to talk to them." After pushing away Judy's restraining hand, Claire walked over to the couple. She leaned down and spoke softly to the blonde, "You've heard about Boyd, I presume."

The blonde bit her lip and nodded.

"I just wanted to say how sorry I am that I couldn't have done more to save him."

The young woman's eyes widened, and she pointed at Claire. "You were the woman working on him in the street before the paramedics came!" She turned to her companion. "She was also the one looking for him at the bar."

The young man stared at Claire, narrowing his eyes with suspicion.

"May I?" Claire sat next to the blonde. "Maybe it would be helpful if I explain things. My name's Claire Hanover, and that's my daughter, Judy, over there."

She waved Judy over to join them. When Judy shook her head, Claire waved again, more insistently this time. With an exasperated toss of her head, Judy picked up her coffee and all their packages and walked over. She sat next to the young man and shoved the packages under her chair.

After she was settled, the blonde said, "I'm Mandy and this is Pete, Nail-It's roommate."

The young man's lips were drawn in a thin line, probably with teeth clenched behind them.

Of course he would be angry, Claire realized. Angry at whoever killed his friend, at the world for collapsing around him, and at the need to hide his urge to cry behind that mask of rage.

"I'm so sorry. This must be quite a shock to you."

She stifled the impulse to touch him, sensing he would resent it. Instead, she told Pete how they had figured out Naylor was the one who witnessed Stephanie's collision, the story he had told at the crepe stand, and what they did to help him after the SUV hit him.

Pete listened silently throughout, shoulders hunched and hands throttling his coffee cup. At the end, he licked his lips and said, "Thank you" in a hoarse voice.

Judy took the last sip of her coffee. She signaled to Claire with a tilt of her chin that they should leave.

Claire shook her head. She focused on Pete. "Boyd told us he drew a picture of the skier who collided with Stephanie. Have you seen it?"

"Yeah. He showed it to me the next morning then balled it up and threw it away."

"Do the police have it?"

"No. They searched the trailer last night, but they didn't ask me about the drawing."

The two young men lived in a trailer? A ski bum's life wasn't as glamorous as it seemed. "What were the police looking for?"

Pete tore a chunk from the rim of his Styrofoam cup and worried it with his fingers. "Contact information, mostly, to call his family."

"We just told Detective Silverstone about the drawing this morning. And he doesn't know it's in the trash. Do you have trash pickup at your place?"

"On Fridays."

"Can I come over and look for the drawing? I think it might help the sheriff's office find Boyd's killer."

Pete checked his watch. "I start work in a few minutes, busing tables at the brewery. But you could go in anyway. We never lock the door. Lock's busted, and we don't have anything worth stealing. We stash our snowboards at a buddy's house. Or at least we did. Nail-It won't be using his anymore." He ground his jaw.

Mandy reached over and grasped his hand.

Claire ached for Pete, wished she could hug him and give him permission to cry. She wondered where his family was. "I don't want to intrude when you aren't there. It wouldn't feel right. How about if I come by tomorrow morning?"

Pete faced her, his eyes red, and nodded.

Claire took a charge slip and pen out of her purse and passed them to him. "Boyd gave us his phone number, but not his address. Could you write it on this?"

Pete scribbled an address on the paper. "It's in Kingdom Park off Airport Road, next to the Pinewood Village ski area housing. The trailers are for those of us who weren't lucky enough to get into employee housing."

Claire put the paper and pen back in her purse and gathered up her share of the packages. "Thank you, Pete. And again, I want to say how awful we feel about Boyd. Is there anything I can do?"

Pete shook his head. "Only if you can find me a roommate. Without Nail-It's half of the rent, I'll be thrown out at the end of the month."

Oh, God. Would he take money if I offered? Claire studied the firm set of his shoulders. Probably not.

"We'll find someone," Mandy said. "The other gals are asking around."

Claire pulled out a card from her basket-making business and wrote the phone number of their townhouse on the back. "If Boyd's parents want to talk to us, or if you need anything else, you can call this number in town for the next week and a half. After that, you can reach me in Colorado Springs at the number on the front of the card."

He shoved the card in a pocket. "Thanks."

Claire rose, and Judy followed her out the door into the late afternoon dusk. They trudged up the hill to their townhouse in silence. By the time they reached the front door, Claire was breathing heavily. Once inside, she dumped the bags on the floor, shucked her boots and outerwear and made a beeline for the sofa.

When Claire plopped down beside him, Roger looked up from watching the stock reports on the business channel. "Heavy day of shopping?"

"Yes, as a matter of fact. We ran into Boyd's roommate at a coffee shop. Talking to him was almost more exhausting than shopping. The poor guy's got a lot to deal with now. Including the possibility of being thrown out on the street."

The smile faded from Roger's face. He patted Claire's thigh. "Sorry you had such a tough day. Instead of cooking dinner, do you want to go out again?"

Claire chafed her chilled arms and pulled a comforter over her. "No, thanks. I feel like a pound of hamburger that's just been taken out of the freezer. I want to stay inside and thaw out."

Judy finished hanging their coats. "How about if we order a pizza?"

Claire made a face. "I'm not a fan of pizza. Why don't you whip up some omelets instead?"

Judy sat on a stool by the kitchen counter. "Like how she says that, Dad? Just 'whip up' some omelets as if it's the easiest thing in the world." She waved her hand in the air.

Isn't it? "What are you getting at, Judy?"

"Well, duh. Remember, I don't know how to cook. You always did the cooking at home, and I ate in the cafeteria at school. This semester in France, I'm trading chores with my roommate. She cooks and I do laundry."

"It's high time you learned to cook something other than bread." With a sigh, Claire tossed off the comforter.

Before she could rise, Roger stopped her and covered her again with the comforter. "You're bushed. You stay here and relax. Between the two of us, Judy and I should be able to rustle up some omelets, maybe even some biscuits."

The blind leading the blind. But Roger used to make breakfasts on Sundays, before he started working long hours to further his career.

Gratefully, Claire sank back onto the sofa. "Can't turn down that offer."

Roger handed her the TV remote and joined Judy in the kitchen. Soon the two of them were banging cupboard doors and pots and pans. Claire tuned them out and switched the channel to the Denver news.

Within minutes, however, their voices coming from the kitchen distracted her.

"You need to stir those onions," Roger said. "They're starting to burn."

"I'm too busy chopping the peppers to keep track of the onions."

He reached over and turned a knob on the stove. "Turn the fire down, then, if you can't pay attention."

Judy waved her hand at the cutting board. "Why do we have to have all this stuff anyway? What's wrong with just cheese?"

"Your mother likes onions and green peppers in her omelets."

"Well, I don't."

"We'll leave them out of yours. Now, move out of the way so I can put these biscuits in the oven."

Judy slapped her knife down on the cutting board, backed up, and crossed her arms.

Claire decided she should intervene. She walked into the kitchen. "Why don't I finish chopping the peppers so Judy can stir the onions?"

She picked up the knife and went to work. Judy had chopped the peppers too large, so Claire re-cut the pieces without thinking about it. When she finished, she glanced over at the pan Judy was stirring in. Browned onion bits were stuck to the bottom.

"Did you oil the pan before you started?" As soon as the words were out of her mouth, Claire knew they were a mistake.

Glowering, Judy threw down the spatula. "No one told me to oil it. First you have to redo all my work, then you criticize it. If you're so picky about your omelets, make them yourself." She walked out of the kitchen and upstairs to her bedroom.

Roger's gaze followed his daughter's path. "You should've stayed on the sofa."

"I thought I was helping."

"Sometimes you help her too much. You treat her like she's still a teenager. She's an adult now. Let her make her own mistakes. We would have muddled through somehow. Now she's pissed."

Anger flared in Claire. "So now I'm a horrible mother?"

"Of course not." Roger gathered her in a hug. "Just a mother who's done a great job and is having a little trouble letting go."

Deep down, Claire knew he was right, but that still didn't make it any easier to accept her nest emptying. She worried her lip. "It's not just the cooking. Judy's under a lot of stress. And she's probably as worn out as I am."

A sizzling on the stove drew her attention. The onions had blackened and started to smoke. She shoved the frying pan to the back burner and turned off the front burner. *Damn.* They would have to start over with a new batch of onions.

Unfortunately, she couldn't start over with Judy.

EIGHT: TRAILER TRASH

CLAIRE TURNED HER CAR into the entrance to Kingdom Park mobile home village Thursday morning and checked the charge slip with Boyd and Pete's address. Someone had plowed the previous day's four inches of snow off the narrow dirt road, but Claire drove slowly to avoid slipping on the frozen mud and to scan the house numbers.

The scattered trailers squatting on cement blocks didn't look much like a kingdom—more like a slum. Though it was nine o'clock, she saw no activity except a huge slobbery Rottweiler barking at her from the window of a dingy white mobile home.

She spotted a mailbox with the right number on it, but the parking space next to the tan trailer had a rusted Subaru sitting in it. Then she noticed a row of parking spaces at the end of the short road with two vehicles, both beat-up pickup trucks, parked side by side.

She pulled in next to one of the trucks and walked to Pete and Boyd's trailer. A brown latticework skirt hung around most of the bottom, but the panel on the end was missing. The panel beside it gaped open, exposing a collection of twisted metal, possibly bike parts, and a pink plastic Big Wheel missing a pedal. Claire guessed these must have belonged to the previous tenants.

She crunched her way across frozen mud clods to the tiny wooden porch and rang the doorbell. Nothing. She rang again. Still no answer. Either Pete was sound asleep or not there.

Should I return sometime later? No, this drawing is important. She pounded on the door. That should have awakened him if he was in. And if he wasn't, he did say the door would be unlocked. And she had his permission to enter, so she wouldn't be breaking in.

She tried the doorknob. It turned easily, and the door swung open. She stepped inside and closed the door behind her. "Pete?"

The interior of the trailer was almost as cold as the outside. She stepped down the short hall into the kitchen/dining area. Dirty dishes filled the sink. An open pizza box and beer cans lay scattered across the plastic-topped table. Definitely a bachelor pad.

A few one-dollar bills and a five lay next to the pizza box. Probably change from paying the delivery person. Claire took a twenty out of her purse and slipped it under the pile. It wasn't much, but maybe Pete could buy a few groceries with it.

She quickly checked the two bedrooms and found no one. Maybe Mandy or one of her friends had offered the comfort of her arms around Pete to ease the pain of Boyd's death.

Claire studied the two bedrooms and decided the one with pen and ink drawings tacked on the walls must be Boyd's. The drawings showed boarders in action and the naked torsos of well-endowed young women with no heads. The faces must not have been as important to Boyd as what bloomed under the neck.

An overflowing trashcan stood next to a small desk beside the single bed. Claire sat on the bed, dumped the trashcan on the floor, and started unfolding crumpled wads of drawing paper. Halfway through the pile, she found the drawing.

The picture showed a few new details Boyd hadn't described. The ski poles were the bent kind for racing, not straight as Claire had presumed. The Spyder logos were clearly drawn on the jacket. Maybe Detective Silverstone could use the logos to narrow down the specific design from the manufacturer.

The crunch of tires on snow startled her. *Pete?* She peered through the mini-blinds on the window.

A black Range Rover parked sideways in front of the trailer, blocking part of the road. A man stepped out. With his back to the trailer, he scanned the area while fastening a neoprene ski mask over his lower face. When he faced the trailer, Claire saw he also wore dark sunglasses, a cap, jeans, and a black Spyder jacket with the logo on the left arm.

She checked the drawing in her hand. The jacket matched. *Oh, God.*

With shaky fingers, she stuffed the drawing into her jacket pocket. The front door was still unlocked, and she bet the man planned to do just what she was doing—search for incriminating evidence. And if he found her . . .

She stood and glanced around.

Down the hall, she spied the back door and raced toward it. As she grasped the doorknob, the front door swung in. She opened the back door, slipped out, then shut it as soon as she heard the front door shut.

Hopefully, the man heard the two sounds as one.

Her heart hammering, Claire crouched and slid down the steps from the tiny porch to the ground. Heavy footsteps along the trailer's floor indicated the man was heading for the bedrooms. She considered running to one of the other mobile homes and hiding behind it, but what if he saw her?

Spying another gap in the trailer's latticework, she crawled through. The footsteps above her approached the back door. *Damn, now what?*

Aiming for a dark section behind unbroken latticework, Claire wormed her way behind two plastic laundry baskets frozen to the ground and filled with crushed beer cans. She spied a ripped piece of brown shag carpet, lay down next to it, pulled it over herself, and listened.

Aside from her own gasps, she heard nothing. Then the back door opened. She held her breath.

The man stepped out on the porch, waited for a moment, then the door closed. Had he gone inside? Claire stared at the porch steps.

A shoe appeared on the first stair.

Oh, God! She looked around for some kind of weapon, anything to defend herself. She spotted a dark line on the frozen ground. She reached out. Her hand closed around a bent kid-sized golf club, and she slowly slid it toward her. *What good is this going to do? If he has a gun, I'm a goner.*

Both shoes were now on the ground next to the bottom step, facing away from her. Strange. The shoes were loafers, not the snow boots or hiking boots most people wore in Breckenridge.

Claire gripped the golf club, sweat beading her brow even though she shivered from the cold. Or fear. She peeked at the Range

Rover, but the license plate was too high for her to read, unless she scooted out of her hiding place. *No way in hell is that going to happen.*

A shadow appeared near the gap in the latticework. Claire held her breath.

A head bent down and peered in.

Claire shut her eyes and tensed, waiting for the bullet that would pierce her flesh.

Nothing happened.

She opened one eye. The shadow was gone. The shoes turned then stepped up to the porch. The back door opened, and the man went in.

Claire took a deep breath. *Thank God.* Now all she had to do was wait him out. Let the man do his snooping and leave, then she could get in her car and go, too.

Wait, what if he sees my car? If he had any brains, he'd realize no snowboarding bum would own a BMW. He had already shown he was smart enough to figure out who Boyd was and where he lived.

A violent shiver ran through her. She couldn't wait him out and risk him spotting her car. She had to make a run for it. *But how?* Her mind hashed through dire scenarios, none that worked, while she flinched at every step and creak above her.

The footsteps stopped in Boyd's room, and a bed creaked. Could he be sitting right where she was moments ago, looking through Boyd's things for any clue pointing to himself? Her hand closed over Boyd's drawing in her pocket.

Just leave, she prayed. *Please. Get in your car and drive away.* Her mouth went dry. *No, if I'm going to get out of this alive, I have to be the one to leave. And now's the time. Go!*

She grabbed the golf club tight and slid the carpet off herself. She eased toward the gap in the latticework, ears tuned to the slightest sound above her. As she slithered past the laundry baskets, her foot nudged the second one. The cans inside clattered.

She froze.

The bed creaked above her.

Oh, God. Claire scrambled out of the gap and took off, sprinting for the nearest trailer.

The back door slammed open on Pete's trailer. Feet landed on the ground, expelling an "Oof" from the man.

Claire rounded the back of a neighboring trailer. An attached tool shed jutted out on the other side. She ran behind it to hide.

Footsteps thudded on the frozen ground behind her.

Trying to still her heaving chest, Claire raised the golf club. As the man ran past the tool shed, she whacked his head as hard as she could.

He sprawled face-down on the ground.

Still brandishing the club, Claire took a step forward. *Is he out?*

With a groan, the man pushed himself up on his hands and knees.

Claire clubbed him again, then ran and ran, without looking back, gasping for breath, the back of her neck crawling with fear, straight to her car. She tossed the golf club aside and clawed for the car keys in her pocket while scanning the road for any sign of her pursuer. Nothing yet.

She yanked open the door and jumped in. With trembling hands, she shoved the keys in the ignition. As soon as the car started, she threw it in reverse and roared backward down the road, barely missing the Range Rover. She spun into the main road, shifted to forward, and stomped on the gas.

A check in the rearview mirror showed no one followed. Claire remembered to breathe. *Must find Detective Silverstone.*

Claire rushed into the Summit County Sheriff's Office at the justice center and leaned on the reception counter. "Is Detective Silverstone in?"

The receptionist checked a white board behind her containing names and In and Out columns. "No, he checked himself out for a long lunch."

"Do you know where he went?"

"To the Nordic Center. He snowshoes on one of their trails once a week or so. Says it helps him think. In the summer, it's fly-fishing for trout."

"When will he return?"

The receptionist glanced at the clock, which showed eleven-fifteen. "Not for a couple of hours."

"I guess I could call him on his cell phone."

The receptionist shook her head. "He never takes it with him, doesn't want to be interrupted while he's mulling over a case. You might catch him before he heads out on the trail. The note on the board says he left a few minutes ago."

Claire trotted to her car and drove up winding Ski Hill Road to the Breckenridge Nordic Center, located about a mile below the

Peak Eight base area. She parked in the crowded lot shaded by tall lodgepole pine trees and got out.

The center was a gray building with forest green trim, fronted by tall flagpoles bearing flags of a dozen or so skiing countries. Claire recognized Switzerland's flag, a white cross against a red background. A strong breeze swayed the pines and snapped the flags.

The sun was shining again after yesterday's storm. Claire walked from the shadow of the trees into the bright clearing in front of the center. Lifting her face to the warm rays, she took a deep breath of the cool, crisp air and looked around. A couple of wooden Adirondack chairs sat in the snow outside the center. Nursing a cup of hot chocolate in one of those sun-soaked chairs sure would feel good.

She shook her head and marched to the door. *I don't have time now for soaking up sun.*

Inside, a family sat on wooden benches around a black potbelly stove and munched on sandwiches. Claire's stomach growled. A woman smiled at her from behind a long counter. The woman wore a yellow fleece vest with some kind of logo on the front.

Claire approached the desk. "I'm looking for Detective Silverstone. Have you seen him?"

The woman nodded. "He left a few minutes ago, heading for the Peaks Trailhead parking lot."

"Where's that?"

The woman pulled out a trail map and showed Claire a small parking lot farther up Ski Hill Road that serviced intermediate and advanced cross-country and snowshoe trails. "You going to join him on the trail?"

"I hope to catch him before he leaves."

"Better hurry."

Claire ran to her car and drove to the lot. She pulled alongside a sheriff's car and climbed out. She didn't see the detective anywhere. She spotted the snowshoe trailhead and ran over. Seeing no one, Claire cupped her hands around her mouth and shouted, "Detective Silverstone?"

She walked a short way down the trail that was already somewhat packed down by morning snowshoers and shouted again. No answer. *Damn.*

Claire returned to the Nordic Center. This time, she noticed a snack counter off to one side. Having a little lunch by the stove while she waited for him to return seemed like a pleasant proposition.

"Will Detective Silverstone come back here?" she asked the receptionist.

"No. He usually heads out on rounds after he leaves the trail. He'll phone in sometime this afternoon so we know he made it out. He's good about checking in and out. But there's no reason for him to stop at the center. He has his own snowshoes."

Thoughts of a warm, cozy lunch faded. The prospect of sitting in her car waiting for him at the parking lot didn't thrill her. Plus, she couldn't afford a long wait. She and Roger had to deliver the gift basket to the Continos, and Roger wanted to ski that afternoon. It looked like the only way to track down the detective was to follow him on the trail.

Claire pulled out the map the woman had given her. "Okay, which trail did he take?"

"He always takes the same route." Her finger ran alongside a path marked with an expert black diamond.

"Gluteus Maximus?"

"No, that's a cross-country ski trail next to the showshoe trail, which is called Engelman. He'll take that to the Robin's Nest loop trail, eat his lunch at Hallelujah Hut here, and return." The woman ran her finger along the shorter side of the loop then studied Claire. "You ever snowshoe before?"

"No, but I need to get some information to Detective Silverstone right away."

"And he never takes his cell phone with him." The woman tapped her lips. "You could go up Engleman and the short section of Robin's Nest and try to meet him at the hut or catch him on the return trip."

"How long does each part of the trail take?"

"For an experienced snowshoer like the detective, that section of Engleman takes about thirty minutes, and the long side of Robin's Nest about forty-five minutes. He spends about fifteen minutes eating lunch at the shelter, and forty-five heading back on the short side of Robin's Nest and Engelman."

Claire did the math. Hopefully, after less than an hour, she'd be at Hallelujah Hut and she could talk to the detective on the way back. "I suppose my own gluteus maximus could use a workout."

The woman cocked an eyebrow. "Oh, it'll get one all right. You haven't come from sea level, have you?"

"No, from Colorado Springs, and I work out and downhill ski."

"I still don't recommend it, but I guess you'll survive."

Fifteen minutes later, Claire had rented snowshoes and hiking poles and gotten a lesson from the woman on how to put on the shoes and use them. She had also purchased a day pass, a couple of PowerBars, and a bottle of water. She returned to the Peaks Trailhead

114

parking lot. As she strapped on the shoes, she wondered if she was crazy.

You're not an old dog, Claire. Look at it as a chance to learn new tricks. She took a step forward, wobbled and fell sideways in the snow. *Yeah, right.*

She pushed herself up using her poles and swiped the snow from her clothes. She tried to remember what the woman at the Nordic Center had said. Walk gently, take short strides, don't lunge. Claire took a few tentative steps, shorter this time. Feeling more confident, she was soon actually enjoying herself. Striding across the snow, she puffed out her chest. Being alone on the trail made her feel as if she were an early explorer, setting out to conquer the wilderness.

A squirrel chittered at her from a tree. Claire looked up. She promptly stepped on the back of her forward snowshoe and did a face plant in a deep snowbank.

Pride goeth before a fall.

Laughing at herself, Claire sat up and spit out snow. Since she was already down, she took a swig of water from her bottle and unwrapped a PowerBar. She bit into the chocolate and peanut butter concoction. *Not bad.* She pushed herself onto her feet. The squirrel chittered again, but Claire refused to look.

You're not fooling me again, you conniving bugger.

After a few minutes, the trail sloped uphill. Soon, Claire was huffing and puffing, and her calves were screaming. She checked her watch. Thirty minutes had passed, and she hadn't reached the Robin's Nest trail marker yet.

Claire gritted her teeth and drove her head forward. She counted steps in a marching cadence. Concentrating so hard on her steps,

115

she almost missed the marker. Ahead to the right the trail flattened then rose again. At the top of the hill, Claire glimpsed a wooden structure. *The hut?* She pushed forward with renewed purpose. Too soon, the flat section ran out, and she was huffing her way uphill again.

When her throbbing legs refused to take another step, she stopped to unzip her jacket. Sweat poured down the middle of her back and between her breasts. But this wasn't a hot flash. She gulped huge breaths, her sore body crying for oxygen. Around her, stately evergreens swayed in the breeze, rocky crags jutted out behind them, and marshmallow clouds moved slowly across the brilliant blue sky.

Another glance at her watch said forty-five minutes had passed and she still wasn't to Hallelujah Hut. At this rate, she would be out here for well over two hours. *Idiot. You should have waited in the car.*

Plodding on with robotic determination, she drifted into a pain-induced haze, focusing only on putting one increasingly heavy foot in front of the other. Finally, she spied the wooden shelter ahead. On a bench on the deck out front, the detective sat and stared out over the valley.

She cupped her hands around her mouth. "Detective Silverstone!"

He turned and stood. "Mrs. Hanover. What are you doing out here?"

She slogged her way to the bench and collapsed on it. After a few deep breaths, she found her voice again. "Looking for you."

He lowered himself to the bench. "You look bushed. Have some water." He held out his water bottle.

Clare waved him off, took out her own, and drank heavily. "Give me a minute."

She rested her hands on her thighs and looked over the town of Breckenridge nestled in the valley below. "Great view."

"Yes, indeed." Silverstone's gaze followed hers, while he rubbed an object in his palm.

"What's that in your hand? You had it in the office, too, didn't you?"

"This?" Looking a little sheepish, he opened his palm to reveal a carved shape in brown-tinted onyx. "It's a Zuni fetish. Focuses my thinking when I rub it."

Claire smiled. "Is it some kind of animal?"

"A badger. It stands for the ability to reach a desired goal, being single-minded and in control."

"Appropriate, I guess, for a detective." *And me on this hellacious trek.* "You have American Indian ancestry?"

"My mother was Navajo."

"But you're so tall."

"From my father—a Swede." He stowed the fetish in his pocket. "Now what was so important that it brought you all the way out here?"

"First, I need to give you this." She dug Boyd's drawing of the black-garbed skier out of her pocket and handed it to the detective. "It's the drawing Boyd made of the skier who crashed into Stephanie Contino."

Silverstone frowned and spoke sternly. "Why didn't you give this to me yesterday?"

"I didn't have it then. I found it today."

"Where?"

"Boyd's trailer, in his trash can."

"Wait a minute—"

She held up her hand, palm out. "I wasn't breaking in. Pete, Boyd's roommate, gave me permission to look for this."

"So you knew where the drawing was and didn't tell me."

"I didn't know where it was until I talked to Pete yesterday. He told me Boyd had thrown it out." Claire felt a flash of guilt. "Sorry. I should have called you then and told you."

Silverstone raised a quizzical brow. "Now you've really got my curiosity piqued. How did you meet Pete, Mrs. Hanover?"

"Call me Claire, please."

He put out his hand. "Owen."

She pulled off her sweaty gloves and shook his hand. "Owen. Along with meeting Pete, I saw the killer this morning at the trailer, and his jacket matched the one in Boyd's drawing." She tapped the drawing.

Owen sat back and stared at her.

"He wore brown loafers. They're a common type of shoe, I know, but not really up here. I didn't get a look at his face, though." She noted Owen's confused expression. "But let me start at the beginning."

She told him everything she could remember about her meeting with Pete the day before and her experience at the trailer.

Owen's eyes grew even wider with the tale. "Do you realize how much danger you were in? You could have been killed."

"Don't you think I know that?"

"You shouldn't have gone there alone."

"Look, I thought Pete was going to be there, it was broad daylight, and all I wanted to do was get this drawing from him and give it to you. I didn't deliberately put myself in danger."

"I guess not. But from now on, leave the investigating to me." Owen rubbed his chin. "Looks like at least one of these deaths wasn't an accident if someone's looking to cover his tracks. How tall would you say the man was?"

So he believes me now. Finally. "About six feet and lean."

"Hair color?"

Claire shook her head. "He was wearing a cap and a Neoprene face mask. But he's probably got a couple of good-sized lumps on his head now."

"Your description could match either of the Contino men. I wonder what their alibis will be for today."

Claire drew in a sharp intake of breath. So Owen still suspected Nick or Anthony killed Boyd out of revenge for Stephanie's death. She tried to picture one of them running the young man down, but the image didn't fit. Then she remembered what Owen had said about alibis. He must have already asked the Contino men what they were doing when Boyd was killed.

"Did Nick and Anthony have an alibi for when Boyd was killed?"

The detective's brow furrowed as he seemed to consider how much he should tell her.

"Owen, you know my daughter's dating Nick Contino. I'm concerned about what danger she might be in. If Nick or his father is cold-blooded or crazy enough to kill someone, I don't want them anywhere near my daughter. You have a daughter. I saw her

119

picture on your desk. Put yourself in my place. Wouldn't you want to know what your daughter's getting mixed up in?"

"Yes, I would." Owen pursed his lips and sighed. "The Continos said that after Nick dropped your daughter at your place, they spent Tuesday night together alone at home, mourning Stephanie. With no visitors, no one outside the family can vouch for them."

"Did their license plate match the partial Roger saw?"

"Yes."

"Ohmigod!"

Owen held up his hand, palm out. "Wait, so do six other black Range Rovers."

"That's odd. Why so many?"

"It's not that odd. Remember your husband only gave us two letters. I've got an officer tracking down the owners and their alibis for Tuesday night." He peered at Claire. "Do you know the Continos well?"

Claire shook her head. "No. Roger and I met Nick Sunday night and his parents Monday morning after Stephanie's death. Why do you ask?"

"The Contino men's story for Monday fell through, too. Copper Mountain has no record of them being there—no ski pass sale—and none of the lift operators recognized them from photos I took out there yesterday."

"Do they have season passes for Copper?"

"If they did, and they used the passes, that would have shown up in Copper's system. But no dice."

Claire's heart started hammering. She and Roger really knew nothing about the Continos and probably couldn't count on Judy's judgment. As far as Nick was concerned, her perspective would be biased, and even Judy said she didn't know Anthony that well.

"Is Anthony your prime suspect for Stephanie's death now, too?"

Owen nodded.

"I can almost understand how Anthony might go after Boyd, but why Stephanie? She's his own flesh and blood."

"Most murder victims are killed by someone they know, many of them family."

"But what possible reason could he have?"

Owen looked away, down the valley.

"I've got to know. What if the reason involves Judy?"

He stared at her, as if measuring her ability to handle what he had to say. "Could be abuse. Or incest."

Claire stared at Owen, revulsion churning her stomach. "Oh, no, you can't mean . . ."

Owen gave a solemn nod. "There was a case in Colorado Springs a few years ago. Man killed his nineteen-year-old daughter because she threatened to reveal their incestuous relationship to her mother."

Claire shuddered. *What kind of family has Judy gotten mixed up with?* "Do you suspect Anthony of such a thing?"

"He's the right build and has the right hair color." He pointed to the drawing. "Now that I have this, I'll be taking a look at the Contino men's ski gear and clothes. Their shoes, too."

Claire gasped as an image of her daughter lying dead in the snow flashed in her mind. *Oh, God.*

Owen frowned and laid his hand on her arm. "If Judy was my daughter, I would limit her interaction with this family until we know what's going on."

Claire got a sinking feeling in the pit of her stomach. "She's out buying flower arrangements for Stephanie's memorial service with Nick right now."

NINE: SYMPATHY BASKET

AFTER AN EXHAUSTING, BUT mostly downhill, trek to her car with Detective Silverstone, Claire drove to the townhouse with her thoughts in turmoil. Anxious to talk to Roger, she called for him as she removed her coat, hat, gloves, and snow boots in the hall.

"Where have you been?" Roger clomped down the stairs. "We'll be lucky to get in a couple of hours of skiing today."

Claire collapsed on the sofa. "My legs can't take any more exercise today. I've been snowshoeing for over two hours."

"Since when did you develop a sudden interest in snowshoeing?"

"Since I found some new evidence at Boyd's trailer and had to get it to Detective Silverstone. He was out on a snowshoe trail and didn't have his cell phone with him."

"Why couldn't you wait for him to finish?"

"I probably should have, but I was trying to get back here soon enough to deliver the gift basket to the Continos and still have time to go skiing. I thought I could make the round trip on the short side of the trail in an hour and a half, but I was wrong." Claire rubbed her aching calves. "Could you get the ibuprofen?"

Roger returned with the pill bottle and a glass of water. "What was the new evidence?"

"The drawing of the skier that Boyd mentioned, plus I saw the killer in the flesh."

Roger's eyes widened. "What?"

After swallowing the pain relievers, Claire told him the whole story. Well, almost. She left out the part about the guy chasing her and having to whack him with the golf club, and only related her mad dash to the car. She couldn't lie, especially not to Roger, but she wanted to save that part for later and break it to him gently.

"Holy moley, Claire! What if he'd seen you?"

"I wish I'd been able to see his face or the license plate on his car."

"Yeah, you would have seen his face on the other side of a gun aimed straight at you! You could very well be dead yourself—a frozen corpse lying under a trailer." Roger paced, running both hands through his gray fringe of thinning hair. "Why do you keep putting yourself in danger?"

"You aren't making sense, Roger. I had no idea the man would come to the trailer. I told you where I was going this morning, and neither one of us thought visiting a trailer park in broad daylight would be a problem."

"You should have left when Pete didn't answer."

"Why? He gave me permission to enter. Look, fighting over something that's over and done with makes no sense. I'm safe, okay? What I'm really worried about is Judy, especially after what

Owen said about abuse and incest. We don't know anything about the Continos."

Roger stopped, hands on his hips. "Nick seems like a nice young man. I can't believe he would hurt Judy. You can see in the way he looks at her that he'd fight off a bear for her."

Claire stared at Roger. His perceptiveness surprised her. So her number-crunching hubby could interpret a young man's fancies for his daughter as well as he could understand his spreadsheets. "I think Judy's a good judge of character. I'm more worried about Anthony."

"He seemed normal enough."

"Yeah, seemed. Haven't you heard those interviews with neighbors of murderers after they've been apprehended? The neighbors go on about how nice and quiet the person was."

A thought struck Claire. Maybe she could at least prove to Owen that Nick wasn't the one at the trailer. "Wait a minute. What time did Nick come over to pick up Judy?"

"About eleven. He said the whole family's been having trouble sleeping and got a slow start this morning."

"Did he drive the Range Rover?"

"No. He said his father needed it, so he came in an old four-wheel-drive Subaru they keep garaged up here. I wondered why they parked the Range Rover in the driveway when they had a two-car garage. Nick said the garage is stuffed with snowmobiles as well as the Subaru."

"So Anthony could've been the man at the trailer, or Nick himself if he hustled home from Kingdom Park. Anthony may have enlisted his son's help to cover up his crimes. We need to contact Judy."

"I already tried calling her cell phone earlier, but I just got her voice mail. Either she's got it turned off or let the charge run down again." Roger shook his head. "And you refuse to carry one. I swear I don't know what to do with the two of you. If you'd taken a phone, you could have called for help while you were stashed under that trailer. Then the police might've caught the killer, and I wouldn't have been sitting here worrying about you for the past two hours."

"Sorry, honey. I never dreamed I might need to call the police. And I hadn't planned to go off snowshoeing."

He sighed. "That's precisely why you should've taken the phone. When your plans changed, you could've told me. Doesn't do much good to leave it here with me when I'm right next to the house phone." He smacked his hand on the kitchen counter by the phone.

Poor man. He has a perfect right to feel frustrated. Claire nibbled on her lip. "We might as well deliver the gift basket to Nick's parents, since we can't track down the kids. Maybe Angela knows where Nick planned to shop for flower arrangements. And I want to talk some more with Anthony, see what kind of man he is."

Or monster.

Twenty minutes later, Claire and Roger drove up the Continos' street and parked beside the driveway, which contained not one, but two black Range Rovers. As Roger hefted the large sympathy basket out of the back of their BMW, Claire walked up the driveway to look at the license plates of the two large SUVs.

Both plates started with AY. In fact, they matched in all but the last two numbers, which were less than fifty apart. Did the Continos own two Range Rovers? If so, why didn't Nick drive one of them that morning? When Roger joined her, Claire pointed out the plates. "Not just one car that matches the partial license number you saw, but two."

He studied the front bumpers. "No blood."

"They could have cleaned it up."

Roger pointed at one of the cars. "What's that?"

Claire bent down to take a look. The bumper had a two-inch dent in it. "Could that be all the damage to a car from hitting a man?"

"Could be from anything. A fender-bender, a mailbox or a parking meter. Can you really picture one of them behind the wheel of the car that ran down Naylor?"

Claire gave a theatrical shrug. "Could Jeffrey Dahmer's neighbors picture him chopping up young men in his basement?"

"Now you're getting freaky, honey."

"Just consider that we could be walking into a murderer's house."

"With a gift basket." Roger shifted the basket in his arms. "That's getting damned heavy. We'll just drop it off and leave if you want, then call Silverstone once we finish."

Feeling jittery, Claire preceded him to the front door. As she raised her hand to ring the bell, the door opened.

A great bear of a man stood in the entryway, his barrel chest straining against the seams of his leather coat. He looked to be in his fifties, with jowly cheeks and a bulbous nose, but his bushy hair and mustache were solid brown with no flecks of gray.

He scowled at Claire and Roger. "Who are you?" His accent sounded foreign, maybe East European.

Angela Contino peeked around the man. "Oh, these are the parents of Nickolas's girlfriend. Roger and Claire Hanover." She swept her hand toward the gruff-voiced stranger. "This is Gregori Ivanov, originally from Russia and a client of Anthony's."

The Russian bear stuck out his hand. Claire shook it, but Roger could only heft the basket and shrug.

Angela stepped back and pulled Ivanov with her. "I'm sorry. Please come in. You can put the basket on the bench."

Claire stepped inside with Roger, and Angela closed the door behind them. As Roger set down the basket, Claire drew Angela over to look at it. "I have a part-time gift basket business, and I put this together for you. Hopefully, some of the items will be useful in the next few days."

Angela wrapped Claire in a hug. "Thank you so much. Wasn't this thoughtful, Gregori?"

"Very much. I must go now." He laid his hand on the door-knob.

"Oh, is one of those Range Rovers outside yours?" Claire turned to Angela. "We were thinking you had two."

Angela shook her head. "We didn't even buy ours. Gregori gave it to us as a gift."

When Claire and Roger turned to him, Ivanov shrugged. "I like them so much I buy six, all in black, to give to valuable business associates like Anthony." His eyes twinkling, he thumped his chest. "But I save one for me."

Ah, so that explains the close license plate numbers. And also why so many black Range Rovers matched the partial plate Roger saw, since Ivanov probably was responsible for six of the seven.

His expression sobered. "Now I say goodbye, Angela. You watch over Anthony for me, okay?"

She nodded, escorted him out, and shut the door behind him.

Claire wondered why the Russian had asked Angela to watch over her husband. Wasn't she just as grieved? "How is Anthony?"

"Very depressed. He's spent a lot of time closed up in his study these last two days. Burying himself in work, I suspect."

"Didn't he go somewhere this morning?" Claire asked.

"No." Angela's brow furrowed. "Why do you ask?"

"Nick said when he picked up Judy that he took the Subaru because his father needed the Range Rover."

"Maybe Anthony planned to use it, but when Gregori called to say he would drive up from Denver today for a visit, he changed his plans. I thought Gregori's visit might lift Anthony's spirits. But he didn't even walk Gregori to the door. He stayed in his study and let me do it."

"So Anthony spent the morning with Gregori." *And not at a trailer park.*

"Oh, no. Gregori didn't arrive until noon." Angela smiled. "That man has a knack for showing up at mealtime. After lunch, they had a long meeting in Anthony's study."

Is she covering for her husband, or did Anthony really stay home all day?

Roger unbuttoned his coat. "What's Anthony do for work?"

"He's a financial advisor, has his own firm, and takes on only a few clients—ones with a lot of money to manage, like Gregori."

Angela wrung her hands. "I don't understand what Anthony does really, but he's always talking about money transfers and the stock market."

Claire envisioned the scene forming in Roger's mind of the former CFO and the financial advisor trading tips. "This is not the time to talk business with Anthony, dear." She turned to Angela. "Do you know which florist the kids went to?"

"They were going to a couple of different stores in Frisco and Silverthorne. Nick called about half an hour ago to say they're almost done and will be home soon." Angela lifted the basket. "Let's go in the living room so I can unpack this and see what's in it."

Claire glanced at Roger. "We might as well wait for Judy here." *And get her out of here as soon as possible.*

As they followed Angela into the living room, Roger leaned over to whisper to Claire, "Sounds like Judy's fine."

Claire nodded. "Maybe."

"And what made you think I'd want to talk business with Anthony? I'm not a total clod, you know."

The only reply Claire had time for was a curt, "Sorry."

Once in the living room, Angela insisted they should have a hot drink, coffee or tea, before she sat down. Claire assumed that, much like Anthony with his financial work, Angela took some comfort from busying herself with hostess duties. She signaled Roger that they should ask for something.

A few minutes later, Angela bustled in with a tray of cups and coffee fixings. After a sip of heavily creamed coffee, she oohed and aahed over the basket contents, lifting each of them in turn, until Claire felt thoroughly embarrassed.

"I wish we could do more," Claire said. "Do you need any help with the . . . other arrangements?"

"I've pretty much finished making plans. The service will be tomorrow morning at eleven at Saint Mary's Catholic Church here in town." Angela sucked in her trembling lip and took a moment to compose herself. "You will come, won't you?"

"Of course." Claire laid her hand on Angela's. "What about out-of-town guests? Do they need a place to stay?"

Angela shook her head. "My sister's family arrives tonight. They will stay with us. Many of Stephanie's friends are already here for spring break. Anthony was an only child, and his parents are deceased, so no one from his side of the family is coming. Gregori has a room at the Hilton. Our other friends and business associates are driving up from Denver in the morning."

She covered Claire's hand with her other one. "I'm glad you stopped by this afternoon. With the plans all made, Nickolas gone, and Anthony closeted with Gregori in his study, I was feeling lonely."

She glanced upstairs. "Maybe you can help me cheer up Anthony some. At least he should see the basket."

Claire nodded. "You want us to wait here while you bring him down?"

Angela picked up some of the gift items strewn all over the coffee table and returned them to the basket. "He might just tell me to go away. No, let's all go. We'll take the basket and some snacks to him. That way, he won't be able to refuse to see us."

Claire finished refilling the basket while Angela prepared a tray with cheese and crackers and wineglasses. When she returned, she handed Claire a large straw-wrapped wine bottle and opener. "It's almost cocktail hour. Will you join us for a glass of chianti?"

"Sure." *Maybe the alcohol will loosen the Continos' tongues, too.*

Angela asked Roger to carry the basket and preceded them up the stairs to a hallway with four doors. She knocked briefly on the first one on the right, then, without waiting for a reply, opened the study door and entered. "Anthony, the Hanovers are here, and they've brought a lovely gift basket. You have to see it."

She set the tray down on a waist-high walnut cabinet built into one wall of the study, above which matching walnut bookcases displayed leather-bound books and objets d'art. She waved Claire and Roger into the study and shut the door behind them, effectively removing any chance for Anthony to object to their company.

Anthony looked up from his desk, an imposing walnut piece that matched the bookcases. His eyes were red, and his cheeks were streaked with tears. He rotated his chair, turning his back to them, to blow his nose.

Feeling awkward catching him in such a private moment of grief, Claire whispered to Angela, "Maybe we should go."

Angela shook her head. "It's good he cried. Stay, please." She patted Claire's arm and went to her husband to say a few private words.

Claire glanced at Roger, who shrugged and placed the gift basket next to the tray. They busied themselves scanning the titles of books on the shelves to give Anthony time to compose himself.

Angela raised her voice to a normal tone. "Come see the basket, dear."

Taking this to be a signal that Anthony was presentable now, Claire faced the room.

Anthony tapped a key on his keyboard and stood, with Angela dragging on his arm. He walked over to wordlessly shake Roger's hand and accept Claire's hug. He moved as if in a trance.

Claire wondered if she was hugging a killer whose remorse was catching up with him.

While Angela pulled her husband over to look at the basket, Roger took the wine bottle from Claire and opened it. Angela seemed anxious to get Anthony to say something about the basket, asking questions like, "Isn't this nice? And the thank you notes are perfect, aren't they?"

Anthony rubbed his wife's shoulder. "Yes, the notes will be useful." He didn't show much enthusiasm, but Claire hadn't expected him to.

He looked at the bottle in Roger's hand and, with a wry smile, reached out for it. "I see Angela thinks it's cocktail hour. I'll pour." He filled the four glasses and passed them around then accepted a cracker with cheese from his wife.

Searching for something to say to break the awkward silence, Claire noticed the view out the window behind Anthony's desk. "Oh, you can see the ski area from here. How nice to be able to check the weather over the mountain before you leave the house."

She moved to the window to look out over the pines at the white ski runs etched in the sides of the mountains across the valley.

"Yes, yes." Angela seemed to desperately clutch at the line of conversation. "And we get a nice view of it from the kitchen window downstairs, too. Don't we Anthony?" She nudged her husband.

He just nodded, laid down his cheese cracker uneaten, and took a large gulp of wine.

Claire sent one of those signals to Roger that long-married couples develop between them. *Think of something to say.*

"How long have you had this place?" Roger asked Anthony.

Good. We should be able to milk the subject of the house for a while.

As Angela pattered on about the yearlong search for their second home with an increasingly impatient local real estate agent, Claire turned to walk back around the desk and accidentally bumped the keyboard perched on the edge. The computer monitor, which had been black, powered up. On it was displayed a table labeled "GI Transfers."

What does "GI" mean?

Claire remembered Anthony's most recent visitor—Gregori Ivanov. "GI" must refer to him, but the transfers confused her. Lines and lines showed dollar amounts shuffled from one bank to another, many with foreign-sounding names, in the past three months. And she was looking at page nineteen of a twenty-page chart. Why did the man need so much money moved around?

Realizing she was staring at the screen, she checked the others. Anthony stood bent over the tray, pouring himself another glass of wine. The man seemed determined to drown his sorrows. Trying to look interested, Roger nodded while Angela talked.

Claire took another surreptitious glance at the computer screen. All the amounts going in and coming out of U.S. banks were around nine thousand, right under the ten thousand reporting limit. She knew that much from Roger's work. Once the money got to banks with foreign-sounding names, the transfers grew larger.

She turned away and looked out the window again to think. Was Anthony laundering money for Ivanov? Maybe that's why Angela didn't know much about his work, because it was illegal. What if Stephanie found out and threatened to tell the police?

Lots of questions, but no answers. Where to get them? Claire thought of the connection she had made a few months ago with a drug boss named Leon in Colorado Springs. They had developed a wary mutual respect. Maybe Leon would know who Ivanov was. She made a mental note to contact him.

Anthony appeared at her elbow. "What do you find so interesting about this view?"

Claire jumped, almost dropping her wineglass, but she made a quick recovery. "Oh, my, I was so lost in my thoughts that you startled me. It's not so much the view. I was just thinking about all that's happened."

He frowned and glanced at the computer screen, but thank God, it had gone dark again. Then he gave her an appraising look.

"Sorry to bring up the subject," Claire said quickly. "Maybe we should talk about something else. I assume you and Angela aren't still planning to attend the Summit Foundation fundraiser on Sunday."

He took another drink of wine, almost emptying his glass. "Hadn't thought about it."

Angela called from across the room. "The fundraiser? We have to go. They're giving an award to Anthony."

He scowled and moved away from the desk to rejoin Angela and Roger. "How can you think of going to a public event so soon after Stephanie's service?"

With a silent sigh of relief, Claire followed Anthony.

Angela laid a beseeching hand on his arm. "The director called today to express his condolences and ask if we would still be coming. He said he could understand our reluctance to attend, but they very much want to honor you for your contributions of money and talent, especially for managing the charity's funds."

While Anthony poured another glass of wine for himself, his hand shook. "Can't you see what we'll have to endure? Everyone coming up to say how awful they feel about Stephanie and waiting to see if we'll break down in front of them." He took a swallow of wine. "I don't want to go through that. And I don't want to put you through that."

"When I asked, the director said he would spread the word that we don't want to talk about Stephanie." Angela stared at her glass and twirled it in her fingers. "Maybe we could go for a short while, for only the award ceremony, then leave."

"We'll see."

Claire decided a change of subject to a neutral topic was in order. "I'm making a gift basket for the silent auction. It will be a spa assortment with lots of relaxing items. I hope it brings in a good bid."

"I may even bid on it," Angela said. "I'm already feeling like I'm stretched as tight as an overextended Slinky."

The front door opened, and Nick shouted, "We're back."

The four adults went into the hallway and looked down the stairs. Nick and Judy stood in the doorway, arms laden with blue and purple flowers.

"Oh, they're beautiful. And in Stephanie's favorite colors, too." With tears in her eyes, Angela walked downstairs to examine the arrangements.

Anthony followed more slowly, his white-knuckled hand gripping the rail.

Claire whispered to Roger, "As soon as they finish bringing in the flowers, we should bundle up Judy and get out of here, leave the Continos alone. Plus, I've got something else to discuss with you."

"What?"

Claire shushed him. "Not here."

TEN: MAKING A DEAL

AFTER RETURNING TO THEIR townhouse, Claire didn't feel much like eating—nor did Roger or Judy, but she heated up some canned vegetable soup anyway. While stirring the pot, she debated how to broach the subject with Judy of steering clear of the Continos. And Nick. The desolate young man probably needed Judy's support now more than ever. But what if he killed Boyd, or even his sister? And if he was innocent, was it right to ask her to stay away? Would Judy even consider staying away if her parents asked?

Claire set out bowls and spoons and brought the pot to the table. For a few minutes, no one spoke as they listlessly spooned soup into their mouths. Unable to eat more than a few bites, Claire laid down her spoon. "Judy, I think there are some things you ought to know."

Judy stared at her mother. "What things?"

Claire glanced at Roger for support. "Things that will be difficult for you to hear, but they affect your relationship with Nick."

With a nod, Roger laid down his spoon.

"You're scaring me, Mom. What are you talking about?"

Reaching over to rub her daughter's shoulder, Claire said, "Before I tell you, I want you to know that Dad and I love you and are here to support you."

She clasped her hands and explained Detective Silverstone's suspicion that some dark secret within the Contino family could have resulted in Anthony killing his daughter and in Boyd Naylor becoming a witness. She left out the possibility of Nick being Boyd's killer.

Judy's eyes grew wider and wider with the telling. "I can't believe this. No way were Stephanie and her dad having…" She shuddered. "Oh, yuck, I can't imagine it, let alone say it. And Mr. Contino killing his own daughter? No. That's not possible. He would never do that—or anything criminal."

Claire kept her suspicions that Anthony was laundering money for Ivanov to herself. Without some sort of proof, Judy obviously wouldn't believe her, and this fire didn't need any more fuel at the moment. She exchanged a worried look with Roger.

Running his fingers through his hair, Roger mussed the few strands left. "The thing is, Judy, Nick and his parents are going to be busy with the memorial service and the police over the next few days."

"What are you getting at?" Judy looked from her father to her mother.

Claire sighed. "Maybe it would be best to put a little distance between ourselves and the Continos for a while."

Judy's jaw dropped. "You want me to stop seeing Nick when he needs me the most? Because of some crazy theory the police have? Are you out of your mind?"

"No, we're worried about you, dear," Claire said. "While Detective Silverstone's theory may turn out to be false, there's a chance it may be true."

Roger leaned forward. "We just don't know. And until we find out what's really going on, we think it's best that you not go over there, at least not alone."

"We'll still go to the memorial service," Claire added quickly.

Judy leapt up. "You're horrible, both of you. Nick and his parents are heartbroken and you want to stay away, to shun them, when they need all the support they can get? I damn well plan to see him." She threw down her napkin and strode out of the room.

Roger cradled his head in his hands and cast a soulful look at Claire. "That went well, didn't it?"

"Oh, shut up."

A door slammed upstairs, causing Claire to flinch. She placed her palms on the table and shoved her chair back.

"No, don't go," Roger said. "Let her sleep on it. We'll talk to her some more in the morning."

Claire remembered past arguments she'd had with her daughter. Whenever she had pushed to finish them after Judy cut off the discussion and left, she had been sorry. Letting her daughter cool down and do some thinking first always proved to be the better course of action, no matter how urgent Claire thought the issue was.

She dropped her hands in her lap. "You're right. She's too emotional now."

"As are you. A good night's sleep is what you need, too."

"I've got to make a phone call first." Claire dug in her purse for her address book.

As she flipped through the pages, Roger asked, "Who're you calling?"

"Leon." There, she found the number.

"Why him?"

"To find out what he knows about Gregori Ivanov and Anthony Contino."

Roger frowned. "Why would Leon know anything about them?"

"Because I suspect they're engaged in criminal activities." She explained what she had seen on Anthony's computer screen.

When she finished, Roger sat rubbing his chin. "Does sound suspicious, but isn't checking them out Detective Silverstone's job?"

"I doubt he can do anything based only on what I saw, and I doubt he has contacts like Leon. If Leon can back me up, I'll share whatever I learn with Owen."

"Well, I'm not comfortable with you calling up this drug boss. In fact, I find your whole relationship with him a little strange."

Claire sat back and folded her arms across her chest. "If not for Leon, you might still be in jail, dear. Remember he helped me figure out who killed Enrique."

"Only after he kidnapped you, threatened you with a knife, and bashed the side-view mirror off your car."

Claire tried to keep a straight face as she faced her grumbling, protective, grouchy, and altogether adorable husband. "You're not still mad about the mirror, are you?"

"No, I'm more concerned about the business he's in. He's a criminal, for God's sake."

"Yes, and he knows other criminals. Now, I'm calling him, so don't try to stop me."

"I can see right where Judy's stubbornness came from."

Claire stuck out her tongue.

With a harrumph, Roger picked up their bowls and carried them into the kitchen.

Claire dialed Leon's cell phone number. When she heard his familiar gravelly voice, she said, "Hello, Leon. This is Claire Hanover."

He let out a gruff belly laugh. "The lady with the iron balls, or what did your friend call it, chut-bah, or something?"

Claire grinned. "Chutzpah. How are things, Leon?"

"Can't complain, can't complain. When you gonna bring that hubby of yours down to my barbecue joint for some fine-ass ribs?"

"Soon. But we're in Breckenridge now."

"What'cha calling me from up there for?"

Claire sobered. "I need your help, Leon."

She told him about Stephanie's and Boyd's deaths, the mysterious Gregori Ivanov, and the chart on Anthony's computer.

When she mentioned Anthony's name, Leon said, "I think I've heard of him. Italian dude, right? In his fifties?"

"Yes. What do you know about him?"

"Ancient history, now. He used to be a money man for the Smaldone family in the eighties. There were three brothers, Eugene, Clyde, and Chauncey. They ran their operation out of Gaetano's in north Denver. Funny how we private entrepreneurs hang around food joints, huh?"

"I like barbecue better than Italian, though."

Leon laughed. "That's 'cause you got good taste, woman."

"You say this is ancient history. What happened to the Smaldone brothers?"

"Eugene, the boss man, died in the slammer of a heart attack in ninety-two. Clyde went in ninety-eight. Far as I know, Chauncey took over what was left of the business and is still alive and kicking. But I lost track of him in ninety-nine. He was a small player by then."

"What about Anthony Contino?"

"When Eugene got thrown in prison in the eighties, Contino saw the writing on the wall and jumped ship. Too smart to get caught in the FBI web. I suppose he's working for the Russians now, given that Ivanov guy you mentioned."

"Do you know anything about Ivanov?"

"I make a point of not dealing with the Russian mob. They're nasty. Have no honor. I could ask around. See what my other business associates know about him. It'll cost you, though."

"How much?"

"Oh, I ain't thinking 'bout money." He paused. "You prob'ly know how to do all them snow sports, like skiing, snowshoeing, and riding them snowmobiles. Now, I bet that's a hoot."

A cold chill ran down Claire's spine. "No snowmobiling for me. The son of a friend of mine crashed on one when he was only nineteen. I had to hold my friend's hand in the hospital while she received the news that her son's brilliant brain was crushed."

"That's a damn shame."

"I'll never get on one. Never. They're way too unstable." She wiped the unpleasant memory from her mind. "And after killing my leg muscles tromping through the snow on snowshoes today, I'm in no mood to get on them again anytime soon."

"Well then, all that's left on my list is skiing. I always wanted to learn to ski, but never knew anyone who could teach me. You ski good, Claire?"

"I guess you could say I'm good. I can ski down the blacks, but I take them slow."

"The blacks. What's that mean? These ski areas ain't segregated are they?"

Claire laughed. "Well they are in a way, but not the way you mean. The blacks are expert slopes. An international system ranks beginner slopes with a green circle, intermediate with a blue square, and expert with a black diamond."

"Black diamond, huh? Now that's for me." Leon chuckled. "Here's the deal. You give me a ski lesson Saturday, and I'll dig up whatever dope I can find on this Ivanov dude tomorrow."

"A ski lesson? I don't know, Leon. I'm not an instructor." She glanced at Roger, who was making crossing swipes with his arms and vigorously mouthing, "No, no, no."

Claire and Roger had taught the basics of skiing to the kids, but that was many years ago. She tried to picture the huge black man with a hefty paunch and long legs in a snowplow stance on skis. She had to stifle a giggle. This could be fun. It could also be a lot of work. But she needed the information about Anthony Contino's criminal activities, if only to convince Judy to stay away from Nick.

"I'll do it."

Roger slapped his forehead, leaned on the kitchen bar, and shook his head.

Claire gave Leon directions to the Peak Eight Base Lodge of the Breckenridge resort. "You'll need to wake up early, Leon. We should meet at the base no later than nine so we can get you outfitted with rental skis and boots before the rush starts." That meant Leon would have to leave Colorado Springs by six-thirty. "When's the last time you got up at five-thirty on a Saturday morning?"

Leon chuckled. "Many's the time I've been awake at that time, but usually 'cause I've been up all night. Hmmm. Maybe that's what I should do. Just party all night tomorrow."

"No, don't. You'll need your energy for the ski lesson. Go to bed early."

"You're hard, woman. Here our lesson ain't even started, and you're already cutting me off from the booze and the babes."

Claire shook her head. "It's your body, Leon. See you Saturday morning at nine."

After she hung up, Claire picked up the soup pot, walked into the kitchen, and dropped the pot in the sink.

Roger's gaze tracked her movements. "So, you're seriously giving that crook a ski lesson?"

Claire jammed her hand on her hip. "In exchange for information that could save our daughter's life."

"That's a bit melodramatic."

"I don't think so. Leon said Anthony worked for an Italian mob family in the eighties, handling their finances."

"You're kidding. Leon really knew something about Anthony?"

"Yes, and he's going to dig up what he can on Ivanov. You know, the more we find out about the Continos, the more afraid for Judy I get."

"There's a big difference between a money handler and a killer, Claire. Leon's probably more dangerous than Anthony is."

"Not to me. I'm going through with this, honey."

Roger blew out a disgusted breath and gathered her in a hug. "I know, Mama Bear. I know enough not to get in the way when you've bared your claws to protect one of your young."

Laying her head against his chest, Claire squeezed him. "I may be a mama bear, but you're my rock, you know that?"

He rested his chin on her head. "And you're mine." He bent down to give her a kiss that started out small but deepened into something much more. "What say we two rocks make a few sparks together?"

Good God, he wants to make love at a time like this? But that's one reason they had taken this trip. To repair their marriage. Claire realized that with all the deaths and turmoil surrounding the Continos, she and Roger hadn't made love since they arrived in Breckenridge. Her whole body sagged. Much as she wanted to show Roger she still loved and valued him, she had absolutely no energy left.

Roger kissed her nose and gazed at her. "You're awfully quiet."

"I'm sorry, Roger. I just can't." *When can I stop apologizing to him?*

ELEVEN:
THE MEMORIAL SERVICE

WHEN JUDY APPEARED WITH bleary eyes and tousled hair at the breakfast table the next morning, Claire asked her what she planned to wear to the memorial service.

"I don't know. I hadn't thought about it yet, with all the turmoil around here." She plopped a ladleful of oatmeal into a bowl and started slicing a banana.

Ignoring the barb about the previous night's argument, Claire asked, "Do you have a dark-colored dress?"

"On a ski trip?" Judy stopped her knife. "Are you kidding, Mom?"

"What about black or navy pants and a subdued top?" Most of Judy's tops could be described as lingerie, though if Judy had a dark-colored ski turtleneck, that might do.

"All I've got is ski clothes, jeans, and some strappy tops that I know you won't approve of. But why's it matter what I wear? What's important is that we're there to honor Stephanie."

147

"And part of honoring her is showing the family that you care enough to dress respectably." Claire mentally reviewed the clothes that she had brought with her. "Maybe I have something you can borrow."

Judy tossed a skeptical glance over her raised spoon at Claire. "C'mon. All your stuff would hang on me."

Ouch. Claire had to bite back a quick retort. Her internal thermostat had flashed on and off the night before, rousing her to toss the covers off or pull them up over and over again. Her fatigue shortened her patience.

She checked her watch. "Then we have no choice. Hurry up and finish breakfast. We're going clothes shopping."

Judy glanced at her father, but Roger just raised the newspaper he was reading and buried his nose deeper in it. Judy dropped her spoon. "Where are we going to find a dark dress up here in the mountains?"

"We could go to the factory outlet stores in Silverthorne. I think they have a Casual Corner or a Dress Barn. I'll put my black skirt and turtleneck on now, so if we run out of time, we can go straight to the service from the shopping area, with you wearing whatever we find. Roger, if we don't get back here by ten-thirty, we'll meet you at the church. Can you get there all right without the car?"

Roger nodded. "It's not far from here. I can walk or take the town trolley."

Claire clapped her hands at Judy. "Get moving. No time to waste."

An hour later, Claire paced outside the Dress Barn changing rooms. Her watch showed ten-fifteen. Judy had to make a choice fast if they were going to get to the memorial service on time.

Judy appeared, wearing a navy shift with a jaunty nautical bow below the bustline. Just as Claire was about to say, "That's cute," she saw the disgusted expression on her daughter's face.

"Okay, you don't like it. Put the next one on. You're going to have to pick one of the dresses you have in there with you now."

Judy ducked into the dressing room and reappeared a short time later in a forest green simple A-line. It wasn't a particularly flattering style, but the color went well with Judy's hair.

Claire took a peek at her daughter's face. Judy's expression was neutral. "Well?"

Judy shrugged. "I may never wear it again, but it's not awful. Besides, we need to go."

"Sold." Claire asked the sales clerk to cut off the tags. "She's going to wear it now. I'll pay for it while you gather up your things, Judy."

She glanced at her daughter's bare feet. "Ohmigod. Shoes. All you brought with you is sneakers, right?"

Judy bit her lip and nodded.

"There's a Nine West shoe store two doors down," the sales clerk said helpfully.

"Thank you." Claire leaned on the cash register counter. They might just make it. "Judy, dash over there now. I'll get your things after I pay for the dress."

Judy looked down. "In my bare feet?"

"Yes, it's not far. Go!"

Judy took off running.

Claire explained their predicament to the clerk while she paid and asked for a plastic bag in which to stuff Judy's discarded sneakers, coat, and clothes. Once she had everything, she hurried over to the shoe store.

With a slight wobble, Judy pirouetted on four-inch strappy black stacks. *Dear God.* But at least they were dress shoes.

With a smile, Judy said, "These are cool. What do you think, Mom?"

Claire checked her watch. No time left. "They'll do." She took out her credit card.

"Thanks, Mom. I'll get a lot of wear out of these."

She paid quickly while Judy donned her ski jacket over her dress. Claire bit her lip. Judy's get-up wasn't a great combination, but once they were inside the church, she could take off the jacket and wouldn't look too bad.

They ran for the car, or at least Claire did, in her sensible low-heeled pumps. Judy skittered along behind her with an ungainly gait.

After racing down the highway and silently cursing every red light through Frisco, Claire arrived with Judy at St. Mary's Catholic Church in Breckenridge at five minutes after eleven. She found a parking space in the lot across French Street. While waiting for traffic to clear so she and Judy could cross the street, Claire checked the church for signs that the service had already started.

A door stood open in the smaller wing built of white-painted wood with gray trim, which almost clashed with the larger, newer wing's orange-brown trim. A young couple Judy's age walked up the steps and through the doorway, above which was printed, "St. Mary's Catholic Church, founded 1881."

Good. Maybe we won't have to make an embarrassing late entrance in the middle of the opening hymn.

Claire mounted the cement steps at a smart clip while Judy held onto the metal railing to maintain her balance on the tippy heels. After taking a program from the usher, Claire looked around for Roger.

About forty people sat in the dark wooden pews. The small sanctuary probably could hold no more than a hundred. Roger signaled them from the third row.

Claire hurried down the aisle with Judy and slid into the seats he had saved beside him.

Roger looked Judy up and down as she removed her jacket. His gaze settled on her clunky shoes, and his eyes went wide. He started to speak.

Claire touched his arm and shook her head.

With a raised eyebrow, Roger flashed her a wry smile then covered the smile with his hand and looked away.

Smart man. Claire took a deep breath. Finally, she had a chance to rest after scurrying around all morning with Judy. She gazed around the sanctuary, letting its peacefulness ease into her.

The quaint room had a Scandinavian theme befitting its mountain setting. The walls were topped with a pink and blue Nordic design of flowers and bows. Red flowers accented the corners of the blue squares making up the ceiling. The blue of the ceiling continued behind an altar flanked by statues of Mother Mary and Father Joseph holding the toddler Jesus, who seemed ready to squirm away from his father's tender grasp.

In front of the altar sat a small table containing an urn and a photograph of Stephanie. Presuming the urn held Stephanie's ashes, Claire looked away as her eyes began to sting. She dug in her purse for tissues to stem the tears she knew would flow. She had never been able to attend a wedding or funeral without crying.

A movement in the front pew caught her eye. Nick nodded at Judy before facing the front. His mother sat stiffly beside him, with Anthony on her other side, his arm around her shoulders and his own slumped in sorrow.

A couple in their late forties sat in the row behind the Continos. Since the woman's hair and build matched Angela's, Claire presumed she was Angela's sister. Two young women about Judy's age sat next to them. Would Angela find it hard not to be jealous of her sister, who still had both her daughters, while Angela had lost her only one? Claire patted Judy's hand, causing her to glance at her mother.

Don't mind me, honey. Just being morbid—and frankly, thankful that I'm not Angela.

A priest in a white robe walked up the aisle to stand in front of the altar and held out his hands. "In the name of the Father and the Son and the Holy Spirit, let us pray."

Claire bowed her head. So it began—the final goodbye to a young woman whose precious life was cut off much too soon. Claire swiped at a tear running down her cheek.

The service lasted about forty-five minutes, with a quavering hymn sung by one of Stephanie's friends and a hoarse eulogy delivered by her brave brother. Some others stepped forward with remembrances: Angela's sister, friends of Stephanie's, a favorite college professor.

Claire was surprised when Judy rose to walk toward the altar.

Judy took a moment to compose herself. "I didn't know Stephanie very well—mostly through stories told by her brother, who I've been seeing for a while. From those stories, I expected to like her when we finally met on Sunday. And I did. She gave me a hug, flashed her big smile at me, and immediately I felt loved. Before the night was over, I felt as if I'd been a friend of hers for years and would be for years to come. I could see why Nick and his parents were so proud of her. And even though I only knew her a brief time, I miss her very much."

Judy's words were impromptu, brief, but heartfelt. Claire's chest swelled with pride for her very grown-up daughter as Judy returned quietly to her seat.

When Roger's hand clasped hers, Claire gave it a squeeze. She flashed a small smile at her husband and whispered, "We did good, didn't we?"

While they filed out after the service, Claire spotted Owen Silverstone standing off to the side, surveying the attendees from behind dark sunglasses. She left Roger talking to Angela's sister's husband and approached the detective. "I have some information for you."

He waved for her to follow and stepped out of earshot from a group of Stephanie's friends standing nearby. "What information?"

"When Roger and I went to the Continos yesterday to deliver a sympathy gift basket, we saw two black Range Rovers parked in their driveway, and both plates matched the two letters Roger saw on the one that hit Boyd."

Owen's brow wrinkled. "We only found one registered to the Continos."

"The other one belonged to a visitor, a Gregori Ivanov, who said he bought six. He kept one for himself, gave one to Anthony, who is his financial advisor, and gave four to other business associates."

"That explains a lot." Owen rubbed his chin and peered at her. "So you met this Ivanov? What did you think of him?"

"He's a big man, friendly, Russian, seemed to have a lot of money, obviously."

Owen stuck his hands in his pockets and rocked on his heels. He scanned the group outside the church then pointed his chin at a large man whose back was to them. "That him?"

Claire watched until the man turned to speak to someone beside him. "Yes. What did you mean when you said that explains a lot?"

"My man who was checking on the black Range Rovers ran into some interesting files." He glanced at Claire as if assessing whether he should tell her what he knew. "Files on Russian mob figures."

Claire sucked in a breath. "Oh, dear."

She told Owen about the chart she saw on Anthony Contino's computer and Roger's guess that the transfers represented money-laundering. But she didn't want to relay Leon's story of Anthony's past until she got more solid information from him and made sure it would be useful to the investigation. So far, there was no pressing reason to expose Leon, and her connection to him, to this lawman.

"This is getting stranger by the minute." Owen pulled his hands out of his pockets and opened one to reveal the badger fetish. "Not sure this bugger is helping me much on this case. Every time I seem to get a handle on some lead, the case skitters off in a new direction."

He returned the fetish to his pocket. "Thanks for the information on the cars and the money transfers, though. Knowing that six of the seven matching cars are connected to Ivanov is helpful." He tipped his hat to her and headed across the street toward the parking lot.

As Claire watched him go, she felt a hand on her arm and turned.

Angela Contino smiled up at her, but her eyes were serious. "Was that nasty detective bugging you, too?"

Flustered by the question, Claire responded with one of her own. "When was he bugging you?"

"This morning, while we were trying to get ready for Stephanie's service. He came over to the house and insisted on looking at all of Anthony's and Nickolas's ski clothes and gear. He took photos, too." Angela tensed and formed fists with her hands. "The horrible man acts like he thinks one of them killed Stephanie. That's impossible. It was an accident, an awful accident. That's all."

Her voice hoarsened on the last words, and she clamped her lips shut as if struggling for control. A tear dribbled down her cheek.

Claire dug in her purse for a tissue and handed it over. She gave Angela a moment to compose herself.

"I'm sure he's only being thorough. He has to consider all the possibilities, and sometimes people are killed by family members, as terrible as it seems." She patted Angela's arm. "Don't let his investigation ruin your remembrance of Stephanie today."

"You're right. I won't think about the detective any more to-day." Angela dabbed at her eyes. "We're having a few people over to the house for a light lunch. You'll join us, won't you?"

Claire spotted Judy talking to Nick and a few other young people. This would be an opportunity for her to spend some time with him, but still be under the watchful eye of her parents. Claire returned her gaze to Angela. "Yes, we'd love to."

TWELVE:
RECEPTION AND DECEPTION

CLAIRE STOOD WITH ROGER in a corner of the Continos' living room. They held plates of catered cucumber sandwiches, cheese puffs, crudités, and other bite-sized morsels that might have been delicious in other circumstances. With no appetite, Claire picked at her food and wondered when it would be polite to take their leave.

Obviously, the Contino family was strained to the limit, putting on a brave front for the twenty or so people who had come to the house. Angela looked like an antique china doll whose cracked face would shatter any minute. Claire had lost count of how many times Anthony had refilled his scotch glass, but instead of dulling his pain, the alcohol only made him gloomier. Nick's approach seemed to be to cloak his grief with anger. His expression was stormy as he exchanged quiet, angry words at the other side of the room with Judy.

Judy appeared to be asking him to do something, but he kept shaking his head and frowning. Finally, he turned his back on her and walked away. Her solemn gaze followed him until he disappeared into the dining room, then she surreptitiously wiped a tear from her eye.

Claire took a step toward her daughter, but Roger stopped her.

"Let her be. We'll find out what happened between them on our way home, I'm sure."

"At least we won't have to argue with her about leaving with us. Looks like he doesn't want her to stay." Claire put her plate of half-eaten food on a nearby end table. "I need to use the bathroom. After that, let's go."

When she found the powder room occupied, Claire glanced upstairs. She had been on the second floor before with the Continos, so they shouldn't mind if she used the hall bathroom up there. She climbed the stairs.

As she was drying her hands, she heard the study door open and close down the hall, followed by angry voices filtering through the heater vent—Anthony's and Ivanov's. When she heard Anthony shout "No," her curiosity overcame her manners. She knelt on her hands and knees to listen at the vent.

"The police are too close to you," Ivanov said in his brusque tone. "This morning was close call. You clean my files off your computer today."

"Yes, Gregori."

"In one week, maybe two, when heat dies down, I will bring this disk back to you. It will be good time for Nickolas to join us. His studies are almost complete. He should learn our business."

Claire stilled. *Nick is going to become involved in his father's criminal activities?*

The voices faded as footsteps clomped away from the heater vent in the study but toward the wall between the study and bathroom. Claire glanced around and spied a stack of paper cups. She snatched one, held it against the wall, punched a hole in the bottom with her finger and pressed her ear to the hole.

". . . and I don't want him involved," Anthony was saying with clipped, angry words. "I told you before. He deserves his own life in a clean business. Especially after Stephanie's death."

"An unfortunate incident, very unfortunate. I explained to you my sympathies. The idiot who killed her with his carelessness will be dealt with. I will handle it."

"No, no." Anthony's voice held an edge of desperation. "It's done and over. Can't you see? It's time to stop this, all of it. We've been hurt enough. Just leave my family alone."

"A son should follow his father's footsteps," Ivanov said in a conciliatory tone. "Who will manage our money if something happens to you? We must plan for the future, Anthony, the future of your family. And mine."

Claire heard a sound like a hand clamping down on a shoulder, followed by Ivanov's voice, firm again. "I leave you to grieve with your family. But I will meet with you and Nickolas in Denver soon."

Anthony made a strangled, unintelligible sound, but Ivanov cut him off. "You and Nickolas." He opened the study door and walked down the stairs.

A hollow thump sounded right above Claire, as if a head had hit the other side of the wall. It was followed by a stifled sob, then the study door closing. Claire waited a moment, unsure if Anthony was inside the study or in the hallway. When she heard nothing more, she cracked open the bathroom door and peeked out.

The hallway was empty.

Claire hurried downstairs, her mind churning. Ivanov, at least, seemed sure Anthony was not the one who killed Stephanie. Was the idiot he referred to Boyd, and was Ivanov offering to kill the already-dead young man? Did Anthony's statement that "it's done and over" mean he already had run Boyd down on the street three nights ago?

One thing was clear. Ivanov wanted Nick to work for him, and Anthony was resisting. If Ivanov got his way, Nick would be drawn into working for the Russian mob. And if Judy married him, she would be exposed to a lifetime of danger and deceit.

Claire clenched her fists. She would never let her daughter marry into a crime family. She would have to find a way to break up this relationship, and soon.

When she entered the living room, she searched for Judy, planning to tell her the time had come to leave. She spotted her talking to one of Angela's nieces and approached them.

Judy saw her coming, excused herself from the conversation with the niece, and met her mother in the middle of the room. With a look of concern, she gripped Claire's arm and whispered, "That man over there's been staring at me. He's giving me the creeps."

When Claire started to glance around, Judy said, "Don't be so obvious. He's by the entrance to the dining room. Act casual."

Claire slowly turned and scanned the room. Her gaze briefly fell on a thin, ferret-faced man about the same height and weight as the Contino men, but with Eastern European features. He stood talking to Ivanov, so maybe he was another Russian. He seemed to be in his mid- to late-forties.

When he looked up, as if feeling her gaze on him, Claire quickly glanced away. "The thin man with salt-and-pepper hair who's talking to that big Russian bear?"

Judy's grip tightened, and she leaned in closer. "I recognize him. I'm sure of it. But I can't figure out where I've seen him before." She drew in a quick breath. "Now they're both staring at me."

Claire looked back and saw Ivanov in an urgent, quiet conversation with the ferret man, while both stole glances at Judy. They seemed to be arguing about something, and that something involved Judy. Had Ivanov found out that Judy was dating Nick? Were the two men sizing her up as a potential mob wife? Or as leverage against Nick? *Oh, God.*

Her heart pounding, Claire pulled Judy over to Roger and politely extracted him from a conversation with Angela's brother-in-law. When the three were alone, she said to Roger, "We've got to get out of here. Now."

Roger's expression turned serious when he saw her face. He set down his plate.

"But, Mom," Judy said. "I promised Mrs. Contino that I would help clean up after everyone left."

"You don't know when . . ." A noise across the room drew Claire's attention. Ivanov and his friend were saying their goodbyes to Angela. With them gone, maybe it would be all right to stay. Claire certainly didn't want a confrontation with the two men out on the Continos' driveway. "I guess we can stay."

"You don't need to. Nick can drive me home."

"I'm sure Angela could use our help, too." *And I'm not leaving you alone in this house.*

The other guests seemed to take the departure of the two men as a signal that it was time to leave. Angela's sister gave her a long hug before leaving with her family to return to Denver. In a matter of minutes, the only people remaining were Claire, Roger, Judy, Nick, and Angela. The five of them picked up glasses and plates in the living room and carried food trays into the kitchen for Angela to put away. Judy and Claire loaded the dishwasher while the men emptied the trashcans. Anthony never put in an appearance, remaining upstairs in his study.

Angela asked Nick to carry some leftover food out to the garage freezer then resumed spooning onion dip into a plastic container. Before Claire could stop her, Judy picked up a foil-wrapped bundle and followed Nick.

After they left, a muffled bang, followed by a thump, sounded upstairs.

Angela froze, dip oozing off the end of her spoon.

"What was that?" Roger asked.

"Anthony's upstairs in the study." The hair on the back of Claire's neck stood on end.

Angela took one worried glance at Claire, then dropped the spoon and rushed up the stairs with Roger and Claire on her heels. She knocked on the study door and opened it.

"Anthony, what was that noise?" Her words ended in a choked sob.

Anthony lay slumped over the top of his desk with a revolver in his hand. A pool of blood spread out from his head and dripped over the front of the desk.

A roar of horror filled Claire's head and squeezed her chest. "Oh, God."

Angela's eyes rolled back in her head. She crumpled.

Claire and Roger lurched forward to support her before she hit the floor. They gently lowered her to her back. Claire called Angela's name, but she didn't respond. "She's out cold."

"I'll call nine-one-one again." Roger took a step toward the desk.

Claire stopped him. "Use the phone in the master bedroom. We shouldn't touch anything here."

After Roger left, Claire gingerly walked over to examine Anthony. The coppery smell of blood made her stomach clench. A large hole gaped open in the back of his skull—the exit wound. Instantly fatal. Claire tore her gaze from the gore and swallowed the bile that rose in her throat.

A wash of guilt overtook her. If she had gone to Anthony after overhearing the conversation with Ivanov, she could have stopped this, could have gotten him to snap out of his depression. *No, listen to yourself, Claire. You had no idea he was suicidal. And do you really think you could have just told someone who had lost his daughter to "look on the bright side of life"?*

A handwritten note splattered with blood lay in front of Anthony's head. Claire read it.

Dearest Angela,
I can't live with the guilt any longer. Because of me, Stephanie is dead. I hope someday you will be able to forgive me, but I could never forgive myself. You and Nick must save each other. He will know what to do.

All my love,
Anthony

163

You and Nick must save each other? What does that mean?

Angela groaned.

Claire rushed over to her. The woman's eyes were still closed.

Roger returned. "The ambulance is on its way, as well as the police."

"We need to get Angela out of here before she wakes up. We don't want her to see this again."

Roger scooted his hands under Angela's shoulders and lifted her by the armpits. "You take her legs."

They maneuvered the woman out to the hallway. While Roger closed the door, Claire found a washcloth in the bathroom, wet it, and returned.

Angela groaned again. Her eyelids fluttered.

Claire dabbed the cool washcloth on Angela's forehead. "Angela, can you hear me?"

Her eyes opened, and she stared uncomprehending at Claire. Suddenly her expression crumpled. With a keening wail, she clutched at Claire.

Claire held her tight and rocked her, feeling helpless to provide comfort any other way. What would she do if Judy and Roger were taken from her? Her eyes welled up. The grief was too horrible to imagine. And where were Judy and Nick? *How long does it take to put stuff in the freezer?*

The front doorbell rang, and Roger went to open it. He returned with two paramedics carrying a stretcher up the stairs. They stopped when they saw Claire and Angela sitting on the floor, locked arm in arm, Angela's shoulders heaving with great sobs.

"He's in there." Claire nodded toward the closed study door.

Two Breckenridge police officers followed. Claire recognized the patrolman who had interviewed them after Boyd's death. The other man introduced himself as Detective Donner. They followed the paramedics into the study.

The last man up the stairs was Owen Silverstone. With a grim face, he eyed Roger. "Officer Koch contacted me when he realized the connection this call had to both our cases. So we meet again."

"And the circumstances are just as bad." Roger laid his hand on Claire's shoulder.

Owen studied Angela. "She gonna be okay?"

Claire's pent-up emotions spilled out of her. "Of course not! She lost her husband only a few days after her daughter was killed. She may never be okay again."

Claire bit her lip and glanced down at Angela, who leaned on Claire's shoulder. *I should never say such things in front of her.*

With her eyes shut, Angela gnawed on her knuckles, lost in her misery.

Claire smoothed Angela's hair. "Roger, could you get us a box of tissues and a glass of water, please?"

After Roger left, Owen said, "What I meant was, does she need medical treatment right away, or can I leave her with you while I check out what's in there?" He pointed with his chin at the study door.

"You can leave her with me."

Claire managed to get Angela to blow her nose and swallow a drink of water while they waited for the police to return. The woman seemed to have temporarily regressed to childhood, obediently following Claire's instructions but unable to speak. Roger hovered awkwardly in the hallway, as if torn between staying available to Claire and Angela and wanting to find out what the police were doing.

Owen came out of the study first. "Can we get her into another room?"

The three of them helped Angela to her feet, then Roger and Owen supported her on either side and led her into the bedroom across the hall. Claire closed the door behind them.

Owen signaled Claire to come out into the hallway with him. After she had made sure Angela was comfortably ensconced in Roger's arms as the two sat on the bed, she and the detective stepped out.

"The coroner and forensic technician are on the way," he said. "After they do their work and formally rule it a suicide, we'll be able to remove Mr. Contino's body. I didn't want Mrs. Contino in the middle of all that."

With a nod, Claire said, "I know you're thinking of her welfare. I'm sorry about my outburst earlier."

Owen briefly laid his hand on her shoulder. "No offense taken. How are you doing?"

"I really don't know."

"If you're up to it, I need to get a statement from you and your husband. But first, I want you to check out Mr. Contino's shoes, see if you recognize any from the trailer park. The master bedroom's here." He led the way through the doorway at the end of the hall.

For a moment, Claire wondered how he knew where the bedroom was, then remembered he had been there that morning looking at the men's ski gear and clothing. She followed him into the walk-in closet. After he flipped on the light switch, she bent down to examine the men's shoes lined in a neat row on one side of the closet. Just like Roger's shoes, with all the toes equidistant from the wall. *Figures. They're both basically accountants.*

She studied the row, but the only dress shoes were black loafers. Could she have been mistaken? No, the loafers she saw at the trailer park were definitely brown. "The loafers I saw aren't here. What's Anthony wearing now?"

"Brown lace-ups."

Owen led her to Nick's room, but no dress shoes at all appeared in Nick's closet. She tried to remember what he wore at the reception. Black leather sneakers. She straightened and shook her head. "Nick's not wearing brown loafers, either."

"Where is he?"

"Good God, Nick doesn't know his father's dead yet. He's in the garage with my daughter." *How could they not have heard all of this?*

"I'll take care of telling him." Owen reached his hand into his jeans pocket to rub his beaver fetish. "I was hoping to tie up the loose end of the shoes. I don't like loose ends. Maybe the man at the trailer was someone unrelated to the case, like the landlord."

"Why would a landlord be searching the place?"

"Looking for drugs? Who knows?" He glanced at Claire. "I suppose you saw the suicide note."

"Yes."

He led her out into the hallway. "It supports the theory that something's wrong in this family. The father could've killed his own daughter, then Naylor because he witnessed it. Then he saved us the trouble of bringing him in by killing himself."

Claire wasn't so sure all three deaths could be wrapped up in such a neat, tidy package. "There's still the Russian mob aspect to the case. You need to check out Mr. Contino's computer. Hopefully he didn't delete Ivanov's files before he shot himself."

At Owen's puzzled expression, Claire described the argument she overheard between Anthony and Gregori Ivanov and Ivanov's offer to "handle it."

Frowning, Owen rubbed his fetish. "So you think there's a link between the mob money-laundering and the deaths."

"I don't know what to think. Maybe Stephanie found out her father was laundering money and threatened to go to the police. I still find it hard to believe abuse or incest was involved."

Owen nodded. "I'll have to question the son and the wife about both the mob connection and any abnormal relationship between Mr. Contino and his daughter."

At the mention of the word "son," Claire wondered again what could be keeping Judy and Nick. His mother needed him.

"Angela's very fragile right now. I'd hate to think what questions about her husband and daughter would do to her. You will be gentle with her, won't you?"

"I'll start with the son. If I can get anything out of him, I may not need to question her at all. In the meantime, we'll follow-up on this money-laundering angle. Even if Mr. Contino's work isn't related to the deaths, the information on his computer is important."

He blew out a breath. "This means bringing in yet another law enforcement office. Denver's been having problems with Russian organized crime. Since that's where the Continos and Ivanov reside, Denver PD will want to take a look at the computer."

The door to the garage opened and shut. "What's going on?" Nick yelled. "Why are an ambulance and police cars in the driveway?"

He came into view with Judy at the bottom of the stairs, their hair mussed, Judy's lipstick smeared, some of it on Nick's face. They stared up at Claire and Silverstone, eyes wide with horror and confusion.

Judy's gaze lit on her mother's face. "Mom, who's the ambulance for?"

An hour later, Claire arrived with Roger and Judy at their townhouse, exhausted from dealing with such powerful emotions. Angela had been put to bed with a sedative, and they had left Nick slouched in a chair in the living room cradling a half-empty bottle of scotch. Maybe drinking himself into oblivion was for the best.

As they entered the living room, Judy said, "I still think I should have stayed with Nick. He needs me."

Claire glanced at Roger, seeking support.

He took Judy by the arm. "Honey, sit down. Your mother and I have to talk to you."

Judy sat on the sofa and warily watched her parents take seats on either side of her. "What is this?"

"Judy," Claire began, "There's considerable evidence that Mr. Contino may very well have been a criminal working for the Russian mob."

Judy jerked back. "What, the slimy incest story didn't work, so you're trying this? Why are you two so against Nick?"

"We're not against him. He seems like a nice young man, but he's from a dangerous family." Claire told her what Detective Silverstone had said about Ivanov's connection to the Russian mob and what Leon said about Anthony's prior work for the Italian mob.

Judy's jaw dropped. "No way. Nick's father working for the mob? He seemed so quiet and normal, like a regular old boring accountant." She looked at Roger. "Sorry, Dad."

"Apparently Anthony's been doing it for years," Claire said. "Leon said he worked for the Italian mob in the eighties. That's probably where he got his start and made the connections that allowed him to join up with the Russians when the Smaldones were shut down."

Shifting in her seat, Judy frowned. "So you believe a drug dealer's lies?"

Claire laid a gentle hand on Judy's shoulder. "There's more, honey. I overheard Gregori Ivanov pressuring Anthony to groom Nick to follow in his footsteps."

Judy moved away from her mother's touch and shook her head in disbelief. "Nick would never work for organized crime."

"Hear me out." Claire explained about Ivanov buying six Range Rovers and giving one to the Continos, and Detective Silverstone's statement that many of the Range Rovers were owned by Russian mob figures. She described the chart she had seen on Anthony's computer and Roger gave his interpretation of it.

"But all this is about Nick's dad, not Nick," Judy said. "Even if his father's working for the Russian mob, which I still find hard to believe, I know Nick isn't."

"How do you know?"

"Because I know Nick. He's honest and truthful to a fault. He's never lied to me. Never."

"And how would you know if he had?" Roger asked.

Judy crossed her arms. "How do you know Mom's telling you the truth? How come you believed her when she said she didn't sleep with that massage therapist?"

Ouch. Claire grimaced.

Roger looked steadily at Claire. "Because I love her and trust her."

"Oh, sweetheart. I love you, too."

"Well, I love Nick and trust him," Judy said.

So Judy had taken the step of acknowledging her love for Nick. Claire wondered if the two had said those three little words to each other, maybe in the garage. Breaking up this relationship would seriously wound Judy. *Am I prepared to hurt her so badly?* But if Judy kept her association with the Continos, possibly even marrying Nick, then she could get hurt even worse. She could be charged as an accessory to their crimes and go to jail. Or maybe even be killed if the Russian mob feared she knew too much and might testify against them.

Licking her lips, Claire searched for the right words. "It seems likely that Nick isn't involved yet, from the argument between Anthony and Ivanov, but the Russian mob wants him. And they've got their sights on you, too."

Judy's eyes went wide. "What?"

"Remember Ivanov and that other man staring at you during the reception? They're already assessing you, wondering what kind of mob wife you would make."

Judy's hand went to her mouth, and her eyes teared up.

"Nick's family moves in dangerous circles, dear. Circles where people get killed." Claire gazed at Roger and saw her sorrow echoed in his face. *Are we breaking her heart?*

Roger put an arm around Judy's shoulders. "No matter now much we like Nick and want you to be happy, we can't allow you to put yourself in that danger. For your own safety, Judy, you're going to have to end this relationship."

Judy burst out crying, and Claire pulled her into her arms.

THIRTEEN: SKI LESSON

CLAIRE STOOD ON THE stone plaza in front of the Peak Eight Base ticket windows, shielding her eyes from the sun to scan the parking lot impatiently for Leon. Knowing him, he would pay the steep fee to park up close. Claire couldn't picture Leon and his two constant, muscle-bound companions sharing a shuttle bus or gondola ride from the free lot to the base with commoners.

She glanced at the peak—no clouds, just a wisp of snow blown by a gentle breeze off the top. The sun blazed on two inches of fresh powder that had fallen the night before, making it glitter like diamond dust under the cornflower blue sky. With a relatively warm temperature hovering right below thirty, it was a perfect day for skiing. Too bad Roger had to miss it.

But someone had to stay home to comfort Judy and prevent her from going to the Contino home to visit Nick. Before Claire left, Roger pulled out an old jigsaw puzzle and started laying pieces face-up on the dining room table. Hopefully, he could persuade Judy to put it together with him. Claire also hoped no pieces were missing. Nothing frustrated Roger more than being unable to snap that last piece into place.

She remembered him and the kids working on jigsaw puzzles during the evenings of past ski trips. She had never had the patience for the pesky puzzles. She would try to join in, pick a hole to fill, then look for the right piece, but invariably Roger, Judy, or Michael would find it first. She had to be content with solving the puzzle of putting a gift basket together.

Three large men climbed out of a bright red Cadillac Escalade. Claire caught the gleam of heavy gold rings on the fingers of the late-thirties, paunchy black man in the middle. Leon. He was flanked by his white, bald bodyguard and his tall, black driver. All three wore dark sunglasses and puffed on cigarettes as they walked toward her. She scanned their clothing—ski pants and squall jackets. Good. They had taken her advice and left the fur-lined, long leather coats at home.

She approached them and held out her hand to Leon, determined to start out on a friendly footing, because she wanted to get Leon to agree to a change in plans. "Good to see you, Leon. Any trouble on the drive up?"

Leon gave her a hearty handshake. "I slept most of the way. Woke up for Hoosier Pass, though. That's one hairy ride, but my man here can handle any road." He clapped his driver on the back, and the other man flashed a satisfied grin.

"Did you trade in your black limo for that Escalade?" Claire nodded toward the red SUV.

"Hell, no. Them's my play wheels, for when I'm going incognito, you know?" He lowered his sunglasses and winked at her over the rims.

Claire couldn't imagine Leon ever being unrecognizable. His commanding presence, gravelly voice, and boisterous laugh would always make him stand out in a crowd. She could almost feel the stares of people clambering off the shuttle bus right now. She took a deep breath. "Things have gotten worse since I called you. I was wondering if I could talk you into a slight change of plans."

Leon frowned. "What kind of change?"

"I was hoping we could talk first over some coffee, then I could buy you a lesson. I'm even more worried about Judy's association with the Continos now, and I'd like to find out what you know and get back to her right away."

"Where is she now?"

"With her father at our rented townhouse."

"As long as she's not with that family, she'll be fine," Leon replied. "I want a lesson from you, not some sorry-assed stranger. We made a deal, and I ain't changing it. Where to next?"

Claire knew from Leon's stance that he wasn't going to budge. She sighed. "To rent you some skis and boots." She led them toward the rental shop. "Did you buy a discount lift ticket at a grocery store in Colorado Springs as I recommended?"

Leon patted his jacket pocket. "Yep. Got a couple for the boys, too."

Claire stopped and stared at him. "They're coming with us?"

"Gotta have my protection."

"Do they know how to ski?"

"Whitey here says he does." Leon back-slapped his bodyguard in the chest. "But my driver don't. I figured you could teach two as well as one."

While they talked, Leon's driver had been eyeing the awkward skiers on the beginner slope, his shoulders stiff and his lips drawn in a thin frown.

Claire assessed the situation. "Two is a lot harder to teach than one. And more dangerous, because I'll have trouble watching out for you both. Let me make a recommendation." She pointed at the beginner lift. "We'll spend the whole day on that lift and the two short slopes on either side of it."

"What, no black diamonds?"

A quick glance at Leon's grin showed he was joking, thank goodness. "Your bodyguard can stay with us, and your driver can stand near the bottom of the lift. From there, he can see most of the slopes plus watch everyone getting on the lift. Unless he's really aching to learn to ski?"

Leon cocked his head at the driver. "What'cha think?"

Relief flooded the man's face. "Makes sense to me, boss."

"I doubt any of your rivals are here on the slopes today anyway," Claire added.

Leon threw back his head and guffawed. "Right you are, little lady. This ain't exactly their home turf."

With that resolved, Claire led them into the ski rental shop and watched with growing amusement as the attendant fit Leon and his bodyguard into ski boots and beginner skis. Leon wobbled in the heavy, awkward boots and cracked jokes until he had the staff and other customers in stitches. By the time he paid the bill, the staff all knew his name and had coupons for the barbecue restaurant in which he invested the profits of his criminal enterprises.

Outside the shop, Claire showed Leon how to carry his skis and they slowly made their way to the beginner chairlift. When she walked past the entrance, Leon said, "Whoa, ain't we going up this here lift?"

Claire shook her head. "You have to learn how to stop first before you go up the hill." She walked a few yards up the gentle slope.

Leon's bodyguard and driver followed close behind, but the drug boss stopped and panted. Squinting up at them, he dug in his pocket for his pack of cigarettes.

"Not a good idea, Leon," Claire said. "You need all the oxygen you can get up here. I suggest you wait until lunchtime to have a cigarette."

Shaking his head, Leon let the pack fall back in his pocket. "Damn, you are a hard woman." He trudged the rest of the way up the hill and dropped his skis on the snow.

After he caught his breath, Claire showed him how to snap his boots into his skis and explained the snowplow stance. They practiced sliding downhill a few times, then bending knees in to turn the skis on their edge and plow to a stop. Leon's bodyguard and the driver stood off to the side chatting—probably trading ribald observations on their boss's slow progress.

After half a dozen tries, she felt pretty confident Leon had gotten the concept. "Okay, let's do it once more to make sure."

"Enough, woman. I need to rest." Leon plopped down on his hip in the snow.

Claire dug out one of the two water bottles stowed in her pockets and handed it to Leon. "Have a drink of water." She looked down at Leon, who stared off over the parking lot, obviously discouraged and trying not to show it. He picked up a handful of snow and tossed it in the air.

The man needs a pep talk. "You caught on really fast, Leon. A lot quicker than my kids did. You're ready to head up the chairlift now. We can work on turns at the top."

He smiled up at her, showing his even, white teeth. "You don't say? Faster than your kids?" He yelled at his bodyguard, "Hey, Claire said I'm a fast learner."

The bodyguard flashed him a thumbs-up.

"Okay, Leon," Claire said. "Here's an opportunity for another lesson. How to stand up again when you've fallen down."

"Stand up? Don't you just—" Leon struggled to push himself up off the snow, but couldn't get his weight over his skis. "Damn, what's the secret?"

Claire laughed and picked up their poles. "These." She showed Leon how to use the poles as a lever to push himself onto his feet.

They made their way to the end of the lift line, leaving the driver behind to stand guard. Leon used the wait to repeatedly ask Claire to explain how to get on the lift. Once their turn came, he slid into place easily, angled back to grab the sidebar, and sat on the chair with a sigh.

Claire smiled at him. "Perfect form."

"I sure didn't want to mess up in front of the guys. They'd spread the word, you know. I'm getting the hang of this, ain't I?"

"Yes, you are. Now, we'll use the ride up to talk about how to get off the lift. That's where most beginners fall." When Leon's eyes went wide, Claire laughed and patted him on the knee. "Don't worry. We'll preserve your dignity."

After Leon made a successful dismount, Claire watched the bodyguard carve a few turns down the hill. He executed a hockey stop to stand and watch his boss's progress and scan the hill for potential assassins among the snaking lines of children's ski school classes. She didn't have to worry about him. He wasn't lying when he said he was proficient on skis. She returned her focus to Leon.

They worked on turns and inched their way down the hill. After another lift ride, Claire skied downhill a ways, then stopped to watch Leon work his way slowly toward the bottom of the slope. *Good control. Sweeping turns, just a tad unsteady. Better on the right side than the left. Not bad, Leon, not bad.*

He skidded to a stop in front of her, leaned on his poles to pant a couple of times, then straightened to look at her.

She flashed him a thumbs-up. "You're ready for stem christies."

"What the hell's that?"

"With my kids we called it making french fries and ice cream cones. You put your feet together in a parallel stance—the french fries—between your snowplow turns, which are the ice cream cones. And you have to keep the tips of your skis together in the turns so you don't spill any ice cream out of your cone."

Leon threw back his head and laughed. "Now food's something I can relate to. When we gonna eat?"

"Let's do one more run so you can try stem christie turns before lunch."

On the next run, Leon struggled to concentrate on opening and closing the tails of his skis as he shifted between turning and skiing straight. Claire shouted encouragement and cues, but she worried he would bite off the tip of his tongue that he kept sticking out between his clenched teeth.

When they finally reached the bottom, he announced, "I need a smoke, the john, and some chow, in that order."

Claire checked her watch and was surprised to see it was already twelve-thirty. Now she would finally get some information about Gregori Ivanov. She led Leon and the bodyguard back to his driver and waited while the three had a smoke.

She led the group to the Bergenhof restaurant, pointed out restrooms, and searched for a table. Finding a private spot in the cavernous room was impossible. Chattering people lined rows of long wooden tables covered with cafeteria trays and wet ski gear. Maybe the noise would mask the conversation Claire needed to have with Leon.

A group of skiers stood up a few tables away, and Claire rushed over to lay claim to their vacated chairs. When Leon and his henchmen appeared, she waved them over. They spread out gloves, hats, and jackets to reserve their seats, then got in the cafeteria line. Leon and his two sidekicks went for the buffalo burgers and fries. Claire chose a salad.

In the checkout line, Leon dumped a saucer-sized chocolate chip cookie on his tray and shook his head at Claire's tray. "Woman, you can't tell me that's all you're gonna eat."

"I'm watching my figure." She surveyed the calorie-laden items on his tray. "What happened to your diet?"

He sighed and looked down at his large belly. "Still got my carrots and apples in the car, but I worked hard this morning. Prob'ly sweated off two pounds." He stilled Claire's hand as she pulled a ten out of her pocket. "This one's on me."

Claire considered arguing, given that she had invited him up to pick his brain, but knew she would lose the argument. She pocketed the ten and led the men to their table.

After Leon sent his bodyguard to buy three beers at the bar, they ate silently and purposefully for a few minutes. Claire hadn't realized how hungry she was.

When the bodyguard returned with the beers, Leon took a few hefty swallows and swiped foam off his lips with the back of his hand. "Now, this part of skiing I like."

He dumped ketchup over his fries, popped a few in his mouth, then wiped his red-stained hands on a napkin. He pulled a folded piece of paper out of his pocket and spread it on the table between himself and Claire. It was a printout of a digital photo of a group of men dressed in hunting gear and standing in the woods over an elk carcass.

"This here's a photo of a hunting party from the Russian mob taken a year and a half ago." Leon pointed at the large man in the middle of the group. "That your man Ivanov?"

Claire peered at the image. "Yes, that's him."

"Damn. I was afraid of that."

"How'd you get this photo?"

"Pulled in a favor."

Claire gave Leon a worried look. "I hope it wasn't a big one."

He patted her hand. "Not your concern, lady. You got enough to worry 'bout with this man here."

"Tell me about him."

"He's nephew to the most powerful Roo-ski mobster in the good ol' U.S. of A. His uncle led the Brighton Beach gang in New Jersey in the nineties 'til he got thrown in the slammer. Still runs it from there, I hear. Gregori was a *vor* in Odessa before he came to the U.S. ten years ago."

"What's a *vor*?"

"Sorta like an illegal judge in a people's court. Decides whether people live or die. My contact told me Ivanov has tattoos on his kneecaps that mean he don't bow to nobody."

Leon leaned forward and lowered his voice as he stared at Claire. "This guy ruled in the most bad-ass city in the baddest-ass country for mobsters. He's gotta have balls of steel."

Claire sucked in a breath. Her hands had gone ice-cold. She rubbed them together, partly to warm them and partly out of nervous fear.

"If I was you, I'd stay the hell away from him." Leon took a swig of beer. "Shit, if I was *me*, I'd stay the hell away."

His bodyguard and driver nodded solemnly.

Leon jabbed his finger at the thin man next to Ivanov. "But no matter how bad Ivanov is, this rat-face is worse."

Claire stared at the photo. The man's beady eyes and salt-and-pepper hair looked familiar. With the hair bristling on the back of her neck, she remembered where she had seen the rat-faced . . . no, ferret-faced . . . man. At the Continos' home. "Who is he?"

"Viktor Petrov. Used to be Ivanov's enforcer."

The word was chilling. "Enforcer?"

"He broke people's legs, kidnapped rivals for payoffs, whatever dirty work Ivanov wanted him to do. Even killing. And he never spent a day in prison for a major crime. He just shot anyone who was a witness that he didn't trust to stay quiet."

Leon grimaced at the photo, as if he tasted bile and needed to spit it out. "Petrov's a crack shot. That gun he's holding ain't no hunting rifle. It's a sniper weapon with night scope and everything. My contact told me Petrov's the one who shot that elk. Nailed it square between the eyes from half a mile away. That fucker is bad news."

"Oh, God." Claire put her hand to her mouth. "He was at the Continos' house, for the reception after Stephanie's memorial service."

Leon looked puzzled. "You sure?"

Claire studied the photo again. "I'm sure." She wished she wasn't.

"He's supposed to be retired and living in Chile. Wonder why he's back?" Leon rubbed his chin and shot a worried look at Claire. "What was he doing? Who was he talking to?"

"He was staring at Judy, then went over to talk to Ivanov. Both of them kept looking at her. I thought they might have been sizing her up as a potential mob wife."

Leon laid his hand on Claire's. "Damn, woman. If I'd known this, I wouldn't have made you wait until now to get the dope on these two. You listen to me and listen good. Petrov don't care nothing 'bout women and wives. He's in the U.S. for one thing. To kill someone for Ivanov. I can only think of one reason for him to be staring at your daughter."

Claire felt as cold as granite. Her mouth had gone bone dry. "You think he's planning to kill her?"

Leon nodded, deep concern etched in his face.

"But why?"

Leon shrugged. "For some reason, they think she's a threat. Maybe because she's dating Contino's son. Who knows? But you gotta get that young lady of yours outta here."

Claire listened to the phone at the rental house ring and ring. After seven rings with no answer, she hung up. *Judy and Roger obviously aren't home. Maybe they went out to lunch somewhere.* Standing at the base of the beginner run, she pasted a smile on her face and waved at Leon as he took off on the chairlift with his bodyguard. He had felt confident enough to make a run without Claire while she tried to contact her family and warn them.

She tried Judy's cell phone, but it rolled over to voice mail. Again. And Roger had insisted Claire take his cell phone, so he was relying on Judy's.

Clutching the phone, Claire debated what to do next. She had promised a full day lesson to Leon, but she was sure he would understand if she cut it short. Should she go home and wait for Judy and Roger? No, that would drive her batty and leave them unwarned. Call around to local restaurants and try to find them? If there was one establishment Breckenridge had more of than T-shirt shops, it was restaurants. Maybe walking the town streets was best, so she could scan the stores as well as poke her head in restaurant doors.

They have to be found and warned. Maybe she could convince Owen to mobilize a patrol car to find Roger and Judy and provide protection. She scrolled to his number in the cell phone's address book and called it. When she asked for Owen Silverstone, the receptionist told her he had gone to Denver for the day. *Probably took Anthony's computer to Denver PD.*

Claire almost asked for the other detective in the sheriff's office, but she realized the problem right away in describing the situation to him. Convincing a stranger that her daughter was in danger based on flimsy evidence from a drug boss didn't seem likely.

What if they wanted to pick up Leon for questioning? No, she couldn't do that to him. She left her cell phone and home phone numbers with the receptionist and asked her to have Detective Silverstone call as soon as he returned.

Claire tried the townhouse again with no luck. Spotting Leon working his way slowly toward the bottom of the slope with his bodyguard, she pocketed the phone.

After making a confident hockey-stop and flashing a triumphant grin at her, he grew serious. "You make your call all right?"

She took a deep swallow to tamp down her fear. "They're out."

Worry puckered his brow. "You need to go?"

"I'm afraid I do. I think they've gone into town, and I have to find them. I'm sorry—"

"Don't be saying sorry. You make a fine ski instructor, woman. Want us to go with you to look for them?"

"No, I'm sure I'll find them soon," Claire said with more bravado than she felt. She didn't want to ruin the rest of Leon's day. He went to a lot of trouble to get the information about Ivanov and Petrov to her.

"You stay here and keep working on that stem christie," she said. "If you don't do it a few more times, you'll forget the technique. Your bodyguard should be able to help you."

She scooted her skis up next to his to give him a sideways hug. "Thanks."

He squeezed her in return. "No, thank *you*. Today's been the most fun I've had in a long time." He pulled back and patted her shoulders. "You take care of yourself and your daughter, you hear?"

"You know I will."

He shot her a thumbs-up and waved for his bodyguard to follow him to the lift.

Claire stared down the mountain toward the streets of Breckenridge below. A cloud passed overhead, throwing a shadow across the slope. She shivered.

She hoped to God that Judy was safe with Roger.

FOURTEEN: HOT WATER

EXHAUSTED AND STRUNG OUT with worry, Claire trudged up the steps of the townhouse late Saturday afternoon. She had hunted for Roger and Judy in town for over two hours and kept calling both phones, all with no luck. She was having a tough time chasing from her imagination dire scenarios that all resulted in Judy's death.

After stowing her gear in the ski closet and hanging up her outer layer garments, she entered the living room. The place was as dark and quiet as a tomb. The puzzle lay half done on the dining room table, and no note was in evidence.

Where the hell are Roger and Judy?

Her leg muscles reminded her that they had been stretched in new and painful ways that day as she crouched in the snow-plow stance with Leon. She imagined he was sore, too. Rather than numbing the pain with alcohol like he probably was doing as his driver negotiated the mountain passes on the way to Colorado Springs, she headed upstairs for the trusty ibuprofen bottle.

The shades were drawn in the master bedroom, so she turned on the light. Roger lay sprawled on his stomach on the bed, snoring quietly with one hand cupped under his face. Claire felt a flash of irritation. Here she had been worrying about him and Judy, and he had been snoozing. She shook him awake.

He rolled over, stretched, and blinked his eyes. "Oh, you're back. How was it?"

"Where's Judy?"

"Asleep in her room, I suspect. After lunch and some shopping in town, we both decided to take a nap."

"Why didn't you answer the phone all the times I called?"

"I turned off the ringer so we could sleep."

"Did Judy ever check her cell phone?"

"I don't know."

Claire rushed downstairs and peeked into Judy's darkened bedroom. Her daughter lay on the bed in the fetal position as if she felt cold, half covered by a comforter. After listening for a few reassuring slow breaths, Claire gently pulled the comforter to Judy's shoulders.

She noticed the blinds were half open and stepped over to close them. As her hand grasped the cord, she spotted movement in the bushes outside. Claire froze. Her breath caught in her throat. She peered outside, but in the twilight, she couldn't make out what lurked in the darkened woods.

A shadow swept between two sturdy pine trunks.

Oh, God.

She closed the blinds so anyone out there couldn't see in and target Judy. She rushed through the Jack-and-Jill bathroom to the unoccupied bedroom on the other side. Kneeling on the bed,

Claire clutched the windowsill above the headboard, cracked apart a couple of blinds and peered outside. Her heart hammered against her ribcage so hard it shook her, but nothing moved outside.

"What are you doing?" Roger flipped on the bedroom light.

"Turn that off. Now!"

Roger turned off the light and came to the side of the bed. He glanced out the window, then at Claire. "What're you looking at?"

Claire peered outside again, but still saw nothing. "I don't know. Something moved out there. Could be a deer or could be a mob killer with a sniper rifle getting ready to shoot Judy."

"What the hell?"

"We need to call the police."

"And tell them you're seeing bogeymen in the woods? I don't think they'd come out for that. What's made you so paranoid all of a sudden?"

Claire's eyes burned from straining to see through the dark woods. "Leon gave me some terrifying information."

Roger sat on the bed and took her arm. "Sit down and tell me about it."

"No!" She yanked her arm away. "You come up here and look with me. Hunt for anything that moves."

Roger knelt next to her, separated two blinds, and looked out. "Now tell me what's going on."

Claire glanced at him to verify he was dutifully searching the woods then returned to her own vigil. "Judy's in real danger." She related the whole lunch conversation with Leon while staring out the window.

"I don't understand. Why the hell would the Russian mob be targeting Judy? What's Detective Silverstone say?"

"Nothing yet. He went to Denver, probably with Anthony's computer. I left a message at his office, but he hasn't called."

"I think our best course of action is to have him check out Leon's story."

"But what if Petrov is stalking her right now?"

Right then, the complex's outdoor lights switched on. A stag stepped out from behind the cluster of pine trunks that Claire had been monitoring and leapt onto the spotlighted, snow-covered lawn behind the townhouse.

"There's your stalker." Roger dropped his hand from the blinds and pulled Claire down to sit on the bed next to him. "Do you think you could be drawing some hasty conclusions? I know you trust Leon, but who's to say his source is reliable?"

"Leon trusted him."

Roger ran his fingers through his hair, mussing it even more than his nap had. "This whole story doesn't make sense to me. A killer goes to a memorial service to scope out his victim—the girl-friend of the deceased's brother, his employer's accountant's son?"

Slapping her thighs in frustration, Claire said, "He could have. I don't know."

"Okay, let's say your crazy notion is true. What can we do about it? You've already alerted Silverstone."

"We could call the police and get them to protect Judy."

"They aren't going to do that, not without real proof she's a target. And Silverstone's the one to get that proof."

Claire nibbled on her lip. "We could take Judy to Colorado Springs."

"Do you really think she'd go? Leave Nick?" Roger smoothed his hand across Claire's hunched shoulders. "Look, this townhouse is in a row of four, the whole complex is lit up like Christmas, and the houses on either side of us are occupied. What was his name, Petrov? He'd be stupid to do anything here where there're so many witnesses."

Crossing her arms tight across her chest, Claire mulled over the situation. She finally had to conclude Roger was right. She blew out a breath. "Okay, we'll wait for Silverstone to call."

Roger massaged her shoulders. "You're tenser than an over-wound spring."

Claire blinked back tears. "I can't help it if I'm worried. I'm her mother."

"I know. And I'm her father." He circled his thumbs along the back of her neck and kissed the top of her head. "But worry won't solve anything. And it may not even be justified. Judy's safe and sound for the moment. All we can do is wait. The next move is Silverstone's."

Feeling her panic-tightened muscles loosen under Roger's ministrations, Claire sighed and laid her head on his shoulder. She hoped he was right, but niggling doubt knotted her stomach.

"That's better. I know what you need right now—a soak in the hot tub and a glass of wine." He gave her a pat on the behind. "Go get into your swimsuit."

The two of them went upstairs to don swimsuits, robes, and rubber flip-flops. While Roger went into the kitchen to open a bottle of wine, Claire popped a couple of ibuprofen for her sore legs. She stared at herself in the bathroom mirror, willing her anxiety to subside. When she came downstairs, Roger stood by the sliding glass door with two plastic cups and an opened bottle of Riesling.

He arched a brow at her. "Ready for our rendezvous?"

No. "You bet."

She preceded him out onto the deck into the frosty evening and quickly pulled off the hot tub cover, anxious to slip into the warm water before the below-freezing air chilled her even more. She shucked her robe and sandals and climbed into the marbled-green acrylic tub, easing into the steaming water. The temperature difference took her breath away and made her toes burn, but her body quickly adjusted as she moved to a corner seat.

After setting the bottle and cups on a built-in shelf in the corner of the tub, Roger followed her lead and slid into the tub with a loud "aahh." He poured two servings of wine, handed a cup to Claire, and tapped his against hers. "Now this is the life. Why haven't we gotten in this tub before?"

Claire sipped some wine, taking a surreptitious scan of the woods over the rim. *Cut it out, Claire. No one's there.*

She leaned her head against the side of the tub and let her feet float up in the soothing water. "Too much happening, I guess. But you were right, this is exactly what I needed."

She pushed the button for the air jets and set them to low for a gentle bubble massage. She positioned herself so a set of jets thumped against her back, loosening the tight muscles. Then she found a jet near her feet and ran her soles over it for a foot massage.

"I feel guilty," Roger said, with eyes closed and blissful smile on his face. "I didn't even ski today to deserve this."

Claire gave a little laugh. "And I snowplowed all morning. After walking the streets all afternoon looking for you two, my thighs were killing me."

"Sorry about that. I'll remind Judy to turn her phone on."

In companionable silence, they sipped their wine and gazed at the stars beyond the tall, swaying pine trees. When their cups were empty, Roger refilled them. After taking a few sips of his, he set it aside, took Claire's out of her hand, and placed the cup next to his.

He tilted her chin up and gave her a soft, lingering kiss.

She opened her eyes and saw the familiar half-lidded gaze that signaled Roger had lovemaking in mind. Feeling languid and soothed, Claire couldn't agree more. She licked her lips and parted them, inviting him in for a taste.

Slipping his tongue between her lips, Roger cupped her breast and teased the nipple with his thumb through the thin fabric of her swimsuit.

"Oh, gross."

Blinking, Claire sat up, releasing Roger from the kiss.

Judy stood on the deck with arms akimbo, staring at her father's hand on her mother's breast.

With a wry smile, Roger slipped his hand into the water and moved away to fetch his cup of wine.

Frowning, Judy said, "Should I leave you two alone?"

"No. We thought you were still asleep." Claire beckoned. "Please come in. You need to relax as much as we do."

When Judy hesitated, Roger added, "C'mon, honey, don't stand out there in the cold."

Judy hung her towel on the deck rail next to the hot tub and turned her back to her parents to sling a leg over the side of the tub. As she climbed in, her pink bikini bottom slid down.

Claire gasped. "What's that?"

Judy looked down over her shoulder. "Damn."

Claire crooked a finger over the edge of the bikini bottom fabric and slid it partway down to reveal a two-inch tattoo of a purple and blue butterfly.

Judy pushed her mother's hand away and tugged up her suit bottom to cover the tattoo. She slumped into the water, sat on the offending artwork, and glared at Claire. "I don't want Dad seeing my butt crack."

"Your father's seen your bottom many a time, Judy. I wasn't the only one who changed your diapers."

Roger grinned and Judy rolled her eyes.

"But I'm more worried about whoever tattooed you. He or she saw plenty. I hope it was a she."

From the half-guilty, half-defiant expression on Judy's face, Claire could tell the tattoo artist was not a she. "When and where did you get that done?"

"Two months ago, in Lyon."

"Are you crazy? Getting a tattoo in France? What are their safety standards? How do you know they used a clean needle? Did you research the place?"

Judy pursed her lips. "I'm not an idiot, Mom. Yes, I researched the place, and France has even stricter standards for their tattoo places than the U.S. does. They know about AIDS and hepatitis there, too. It's not a third-world country."

Claire was still having trouble digesting the fact that Judy had actually gotten a tattoo. She crossed her arms. "Well, I don't like it one bit."

Judy shrugged. "It's a little late now. It's permanent, you know."

"I wish you'd talked to us first about it, though."

"I'm an adult." Judy picked up Claire's cup of wine and took a sip. "I don't need your permission to get a tattoo."

Roger laid his hand on Claire's arm.

The touch was enough to make her pause before she blurted out a quick retort. No, Judy didn't need their permission, and she was old enough to make up her own mind about mutilating her body, but . . . Claire glanced at her daughter.

Don't push her away, Claire. You need to keep her close, especially now, when her life may be in danger. Should I tell her? No, she wouldn't believe me, would call it maternal paranoia. Better to let Owen tell her after he verifies Leon's information—and finds out if the Russian mob is really after Judy, and if so, why.

Claire let out a deep sigh. "Sorry, honey. Seeing the tattoo was such a shock. I never thought you'd . . . Never mind. Let's not let this spoil our evening, okay? At least it wasn't a belly-button ring." Claire shuddered as an image of rampant infection spreading in Judy's gut appeared in her mind.

An evil grin split Judy's face. "That's next on the agenda."

Oh, God.

The phone rang Sunday morning. Claire snatched up the receiver.

"Claire, this is Sheriff Silverstone. I'm returning your call. Hope I didn't wake you."

She rubbed the sleep out of her eyes and checked the clock. Nine-fifteen. She was amazed she had been able to sleep after hearing Leon's news. *Guess I needed the rest.*

She sat up and cupped her hand over the receiver so as not to wake Roger. "Don't worry. I'm usually wide awake by this time. I have something to show you. Can I meet you at your office?"

"I'm here now."

"I'll be right over."

Claire went in the bathroom to splash cold water on her face then threw on a pair of jeans and a sweatshirt and ran a comb through her hair. She looked like hell, but this was important. She had begged Leon to give her the photo of Ivanov and Petrov, in exchange for a promise not to leave it with the detective. Leon's source, the man who had taken the photo, felt jumpy that the Russian mob would trace it back to him if it became evidence. *I would, too, if the price of discovery was a body part, or even your life.*

Claire grabbed an energy bar, wrote a note to Roger, peeked in on Judy sleeping soundly in her dark basement room, then went out to the car, her breath fogging in the cold mountain air. When she arrived at the justice center, the door to the sheriff's office was locked. She knocked on the glass.

In a moment, Owen appeared behind the door and opened it for her. He was dressed casually in jeans and a sweatshirt. "I'm the only one in today, so I left the door locked."

"You got coffee?"

"Sure do." He glanced at her face as he led her to a small kitchenette. "Looks like you could use a cup."

Claire raised a brow.

He winced. "Sorry, shouldn't have said that. I've got the tact of a bull elephant."

Claire gave a half-hearted laugh while Owen poured coffee into a sheriff's office mug and handed it to her. She sipped the bitter slurry. *Good, it's strong enough to wake an elephant.* She took another swallow. *Just what this old elephant needs.*

"I know I look like hell. Feel like it, too. But I needed to show you a photograph. Unfortunately, I made a promise not to let you keep it."

With a puzzled look, Owen led her to his office. "What's this all about?"

"I have a source—a drug boss I met a couple of months ago."

Owen's eyes went wide, then a wry smile tugged at the corners of his lips. "You seem to have a habit of hanging around with the wrong people. If they're not the targets of criminals, they're criminals themselves."

Once again, Claire wished she could have done something to stop Stephanie or Boyd from dying. "While the dead tell no tales, criminals can be a good source of information."

"So, who's this drug boss?"

"His name is Leon and I trust him." Between sips of coffee, Claire told about her previous day's discussion with Leon and his description of Ivanov's and Petrov's backgrounds. She pulled the photo out of her pocket and pointed out the two men.

After studying the photo, Owen said, "I dug up stuff on Ivanov at Denver PD similar to what you found. His gang seems to be involved primarily in financial crimes—extortion, loan-sharking, white-collar fraud, and money-laundering for drug rings. Is that how your contact knows him?"

"No. Leon said he stays away from the Russians. Claims they're too dangerous for him. That scares me. In fact, Leon thinks Ivanov brought Petrov into the country to kill Judy."

"Your daughter? What the hell reason would he have?"

"Maybe her dating Nick Contino is somehow a threat to Ivanov's operation. Or to his plan to bring Nick into the business."

Owen nodded. "But murder seems excessive for that situation. There're lots of ways to separate couples without harming one of them."

"It's obvious your daughter hasn't reached her teen years yet. Anyway, all I know is that Ivanov and Petrov were staring at Judy and seemed to be arguing about her at the reception after Stephanie's memorial service. When I suggested to Leon that they may have been wondering about her suitability as a mob wife, which she definitely is *not* suitable for, by the way, Leon said Petrov isn't concerned with those issues, only killing or hurting people at Ivanov's command."

Claire shuddered and stared into her empty mug, afraid to broach the next subject, but knowing she had to. "I want to arrange for protection for my daughter until I can get her out of here, away from the Continos. Can your office do that?"

Owen frowned at the open case file on the desktop before him. The file was already a couple of inches thick. He rolled the beaver fetish between the fingers of his left hand and looked up at Claire, his expression grim.

"We don't have the manpower to assign twenty-four-hour guard over someone unless we've got really clear cause. And a hunch by a drug boss just doesn't cut it."

"But—"

He held up his hand. "I know these Russians are dangerous, and I sympathize with your concern. But until I have solid proof that Judy is their target, I could talk to the sheriff until I was blue in the face, and he wouldn't authorize the protection."

Claire bristled. "How can you prove she's the target, other than waiting for Petrov to actually shoot her?"

Owen checked his watch. "I'm due at the Continos in an hour to interview Nickolas and his mother. That's why I came in, to prepare questions. You've added a few more to my list. If either one of them knows anything about Anthony's business, they may have information on Petrov. I'll also ask Denver PD to send me whatever they have on the man."

Desperation constricted Claire's throat. "What do I do with Judy in the meantime?"

"How about taking her to the Springs? Getting her out of town seems to be your best option."

"She won't go, even if we can convince her she's in danger. She won't leave Nick when he's just lost both his sister and his father."

She raised her hand to rub her throbbing forehead and knocked her coffee cup into Owen's trashcan. After clattering against the side, it cracked and shattered.

"Damn. Sorry about breaking your cup."

"No problem," Owen said. "We've got two more cases of 'em, and you even got all the pieces in the trashcan. Back to Judy. First, don't panic. We don't know that she's Petrov's target. He could be here for an entirely different reason—like roughing up a rival in Denver."

"Then why were they staring at Judy?"

Owen shrugged. "Because she's pretty? Who knows? But if you're that worried about her, there are some things you can do. You and your husband should stick close to her. Keep her inside and away from open windows."

"Dear God." Claire bit her trembling lip.

"For all we know, Leon or his source could be mistaken or lying. Or Leon guessed at the wrong target." Owen gave her wrist a sympathetic squeeze. "Judy may be in no danger, and your assessment could be correct. The two men may have been debating whether she was a good match for Nickolas."

Claire rubbed her arms to banish the chill she felt. "What if Leon is right? Roger and I can't protect her from a mob killer."

"I understand how you feel. I'm a father, too, after all, and I won't rest until I figure out what's really going on. I'll call as soon as I find out anything relevant to Judy. I should have something in a few hours from either the Continos or Denver PD."

"Can I go with you to the Continos? Just to listen?"

Owen looked down his nose at her, but with a sympathetic expression, as if hating to have to chide a favorite child. "Of course not. Now go home and let the professionals do the work."

The last time Claire had heard that phrase, the professionals were determined to hang a murder rap on Roger. Letting them do their work was the worst possible decision she could have made.

FIFTEEN:
BIDDING ON BASKETS

When Claire returned to the townhouse, she found a note from Roger lying on the kitchen counter.

Judy felt blue after she called Nick, and he said he'd be busy with his mother and Detective Silverstone today. So, she and I went skiing at Keystone. No one should be looking for her there. Call my cell phone if you want to join us. Otherwise, I'll stay with her, and we'll be back by four-thirty.

Love,
Roger

So much for keeping Judy indoors and away from windows. But maybe joining the crowds at Keystone, a nearby Summit County ski resort, was relatively safe. Claire couldn't think of any way Petrov would know where Judy was. Unless he was monitoring the house and followed Roger and Judy. *And if he's the one who killed Stephanie, he's a good skier.*

Claire called Roger's cell phone. After he answered, she asked, "Do you know if anyone followed you to Keystone?"

"No, I don't. Why? Did Silverstone think someone was watching us?"

"No, but he said the police can't protect Judy until they have evidence Petrov is targeting her. She's vulnerable out there."

"We're sticking to the crowded slopes."

"I'd feel better if Judy was home behind locked doors."

"I know, but she needed this. I couldn't have kept her from going out on her own otherwise. We'll be careful. Are you joining us?"

"No, I have to finish the gift basket I promised to bring to the Summit Foundation fundraiser tonight." And keeping her hands busy while she mulled over the confusing and horrifying events of the last few days seemed like a good idea.

"I've got to get off the lift now. We'll be home in time to get ready for the fundraiser." He hung up.

Claire covered the dining room table with supplies—spa items she had purchased at post–Valentine's Day sales in Colorado Springs, a large market basket made of pale white oak, and a box of trim and packaging supplies she had brought from home. The pile of spa items included two long-handled, loofah-tipped back scrubbers, lotion, scrubs, bath oil and bubbles, scented candles, a tub pillow, a soothing CD of Indian flute music, and a pedicure kit with a gray pumice stone.

While she peeled off sales tags, she thought about a color scheme. Her gaze fell on the gray stone then picked up other neutrals in the collection. The scented items were vanilla, cinnamon, and pine in colors of ecru, tan, and green. She decided to use gray and green for the decorations.

She pulled out green tissue paper, dried Spanish moss, green raffia, brown leather strips, and pebbles with holes drilled in them to string on the leather. With the color scheme firmly planted in her mind, Claire could try to make sense of the recent deaths while her fingers worked. She started weaving leather strips around the basket.

First came Stephanie—killed by a skier wearing black Spyder clothing who used poles bent for gate racing. The quality of the gear and the skill of his pursuit of Boyd pointed to the excellence of the skier. Both Nick and his father appeared to be good skiers. Good enough that their story of skiing the back bowls of Copper made sense to Angela.

But the police found no evidence they were actually there, and Anthony matched the physical description of Stephanie's killer—tall and lean with a mix of black and gray hair. Claire wondered if Judy had ever seen Anthony ski. Maybe she could compare his form to the rude skier she spotted on the slope before Stephanie died.

Do I really believe Anthony could have killed his own daughter?

What about Boyd? Could Anthony have killed him? The license plate of Anthony's black Range Rover matched the two letters of the one she saw driving away after hitting Boyd. And Anthony seemed protective of his family. Yes, if he thought Boyd had killed his daughter, he would seek revenge.

But would he resort to murder?

Who else could have? There was one cold-blooded murderer in their midst. Viktor Petrov. And six other black Range Rovers had license plates matching the numbers Roger saw. Gregori Ivanov's did, and he bought four others besides his own and the Continos'. Did Viktor own one of those? But if he did, it should be at his home in Chile. Why would he bring it here? And why would he mow down someone with an SUV if he was a crack shot? What reason would he have to kill Boyd?

The leather fell out of Claire's hand. *If Anthony asked him to.*

Or maybe Ivanov offered Petrov's services to Anthony after hearing about Stephanie's death. But that presumed none of them killed Stephanie, pointing the finger back at Boyd, whose story rang true—and was corroborated partly by Judy.

What if Boyd accidentally hit Stephanie and constructed an elaborate lie to cover it? Somehow, Anthony would have had to find out Boyd was responsible for his daughter's death. Then he got Ivanov to fly in Petrov from Chile.

All in one day? Impossible.

But maybe Petrov was already in the U.S. for some other reason. Claire could envision Petrov killing Boyd, but the murder weapon was wrong. And Ivanov said on Friday, "The idiot who killed her with his carelessness will be dealt with." Boyd was killed on Tuesday.

If Ivanov ordered his killing, why didn't he know it was a done deal?

Claire's head throbbed. The trouble with analyzing all the possibilities was that none of them made sense, at least with the information she had. What she needed was more data on Petrov.

If he was brought to Breckenridge to kill Boyd, maybe he wasn't targeting Judy after all. Could Claire's theory about why he and Ivanov were whispering about Judy be right and Leon's be wrong? Or were they plotting some way of using Judy to pressure Nick into joining the Russian mob? Then Judy wouldn't be a murder target, but a kidnapping target—with the ransom being Nick's future.

Oh, God.

Claire looked at the rat's nest of raffia in her hands that she had knotted up while thinking. She tossed the tangled bunch on the table and dropped her head into her hands.

Stephanie. The first death. She's the key to the puzzle.

Claire was sure that once she knew who killed Stephanie and why, the other deaths would make sense, including Anthony's suicide. His note had said, "I can't live with the guilt any longer. Because of me, Stephanie is dead." So, he felt responsible for her death.

Could he be responsible without having been the one who actually killed her?

Yes, if he ordered her killing. But Claire couldn't envision Anthony doing that any more than having an incestuous relationship with his daughter. He truly seemed heartbroken by her death.

Claire's musings had hit a dead end, with no answers, only more questions. She glanced at the mess on the dining room table, then at her watch. She had to hurry and finish the basket and take her shower before Roger and Judy got home. She shoved thoughts of murder, kidnapping, and intrigue out of her mind, grabbed the raffia, and started picking out knots.

Claire stepped off the elevator at the third floor of the Beaver Run Resort and Conference Center. She felt rushed and anxious. She should have delivered the gift basket before the event began, and it was already twenty minutes after the six p.m. start time. She glanced over her shoulder to make sure Judy and Roger followed.

Judy teetered on the same shoes she had worn to Stephanie's memorial service, but she had paired them this time with a slinky purple top and a pair of dressy black jeans. Not an outfit Claire approved of for a charity benefit, but she could understand Judy's refusal to wear the same dress she had on when Anthony died. Especially with the distinct possibility of Nick showing up at the fundraiser to accept his father's award.

The opportunity to see Nick was what had persuaded Judy to leave the townhouse with them that night. Claire refused to let her stay home alone and was ready to resort to the old standby, "because I said so," when Roger remembered the Summit Foundation had planned to present an award to Anthony Contino. Then Judy said Nick had gotten a call from the foundation chair asking what he preferred they do—drop the mention of his father, eulogize him without family present, or have Nick accept his father's award. The last Judy knew, Nick had agreed to the eulogy but hadn't decided if he would attend or not.

Roger peered around the huge basket he held. "Claire, could you please find out where I can dump this thing? It's getting heavy."

Claire looked down the wide hallway encircling the Colorado ballroom. Like the ballroom, the hallway was decorated with pale olive wallpaper. Oak wainscoting separated the wallpaper from maroon wall carpeting with swirled gold and green leaves that continued down onto the floor. Windows along the west wall faced the now-dark beginner ski runs below. Linen-covered tables underneath the windows contained donated items and bid sheets.

Claire searched the tables until she found the empty space for her gift basket, then signaled Roger.

With a grateful sigh, he lowered the basket into place. "I need a drink. Either of you want one?"

Judy fingered her evening bag and glanced around, obviously searching for Nick. "White wine, I guess."

Claire wanted to keep her wits sharp, especially if any of the Continos or Russians showed up that night. "Just soda water for me."

While Roger got in line at one of the bars, Claire and Judy entered the ballroom. A string quartet played classical music in one corner. Tables of appetizers and desserts sat spaced along the walls, and smaller tables with chairs were placed in scattered groupings. Though the room was crowded, many of the chairs were empty. Most people stood and balanced drink glasses and small plates while they talked. As usual at a Colorado formal event, Claire spotted a range of outfits from tuxedos and long evening dresses to jeans and cowboy boots.

Roger returned with their drinks, handed them off, then promptly went in search of food.

Claire knew to let him forage. He was always starving after a day of skiing, and he would need quite a few platefuls of the tidbits to satisfy that hunger.

Judy saw a couple of college-aged young women across the room. "Mom, I want to talk to Anne and Chelsea over there. Remember I had dinner with them Tuesday? They're heading back to CU-Boulder tonight right after this. You mind?"

Yes, I mind. But Claire knew Judy would never agree to stick close to her or Roger's side on the off chance a Russian enforcer would try to shoot her in the crowded ballroom. The concern even sounded ridiculous to Claire. She resorted to the admonition she used when the kids were young.

"Stay where you can see me."

When Judy rolled her eyes, Claire added, "So we can find you when we're ready to leave or if we need you for something."

Roger returned with his mouth full and his plate mounded with cheese puffs, meatballs, shrimp, and other protein-packed snacks. He looked around as he finished chewing then swallowed.

"Where's Judy? I can't believe you let her go off alone."

Claire nodded her head toward the knot of three young women chatting away and gesturing wildly to punctuate every few words. "She's with friends. I told her to stay where she could see us."

Roger grinned. "I bet she liked that. Now, why was it so important to come here? Other than to drop off that damn basket and eat, that is."

"To see if anyone interesting shows up, like Detective Silverstone. He was going to talk to the Continos this afternoon and try to dig up more information on Petrov. Or the ferret man himself could show up, along with Ivanov, though I really hope we don't run into either one of them. The Continos could come—or what's left of them."

Claire grimaced at that slip. "I doubt Angela would be up to it, but Nick might have decided to accept his father's award. Plus, he hasn't seen Judy for two days. That could be incentive enough."

Roger surveyed the ballroom. "Well, none of the aforementioned seems to be here now."

Claire touched his arm. "Stay here and keep an eye on Judy. I'll check the hallway."

She exited the ballroom and joined the slowly shuffling line moving past the donated items up for auction. Between glances at bid sheets, Claire scanned the crowd for Nick, the Russians, or Owen. Especially Owen. She was anxious to find out if he had learned anything more about Petrov.

While she scanned the other gift baskets provided by local stores, she couldn't help but critique them. One was overstuffed, so not all the items could be seen. Another had no unifying color scheme, and a third, from a ski clothing shop, had no items to taste, smell, or hear—not even a Warren Miller ski film. Claire always tried to tantalize all the senses in her baskets. When she approached her own basket, she felt gratified to see the bid sheet was full of names.

A shadow of a person moved outside the window, startling Claire. She realized she had reached the portion of the hallway that looked out onto the outdoor balcony. She should check for people out there. She stepped out of the line and walked toward the door.

When she went outside, the cold air blasted her face. She clasped her arms around her. Her black skirt and shiny gold silk blouse provided little insulation from the chill.

More than a few people stood outside, many savoring cigarettes that were forbidden inside. Claire moved along the perimeter of the large balcony, trying to get a glimpse of shadowy faces in the dark. She had made almost a full circuit and was about to give up and go inside when off to her left, she heard a familiar voice— Nick's, directed away from her.

"What are you doing here?" The words were forceful, but hissed out in a low whisper, implying they were meant for only one set of ears. Those belonging to the large man standing next to him.

Ivanov! Claire turned her back to them and inched away so their view of her was mostly blocked by an outside wall angling in to artistically hide the exhausts from the kitchen below. She peeked over her shoulder to get a glimpse of Ivanov's expression, but only his eyes were visible above the glowing end of a fat cigar stub.

He took a puff and lowered his hand, shifting his face into shadow again. "I come to see you, since you no longer welcome me to your home. We must talk."

"Haven't you extracted enough blood from our family?"

"Nickolas, you are upset." Ivanov's tone was conciliatory, but firm. "You will see. We will provide good life for you and your mother."

"No, dammit. It ends with Dad. He played your game. He had to, and because of it, Stephanie's dead." Nick's voice caught, but he pressed on. "And now he's gone, too, because he couldn't live with the guilt." Nick whirled and clutched the railing.

Claire spied the movement and chanced another quick look at the two men.

When Ivanov patted Nick's shoulder, Nick flinched. The larger man let his hand drop. "I did not think he would take his own life." He sighed. "No one did."

Nick bowed his head. "What would you expect a man to do who caused his own daughter's death?"

"He did not push her."

"But he might as well have."

Ivanov's voice softened. "Do you blame him, Nickolas?"

Nick raised his head and glared at Ivanov. "No, I blame you, Gregori."

He pushed off the rail and strode across the balcony. He yanked the door open and went inside.

Ivanov watched the young man while taking another puff on the cigar. He dropped the stub on the concrete floor of the balcony and ground it out with his heel.

"We will talk again, young Nickolas. We will talk again." He shoved his hands in his pocket and moved slowly toward the door, threading through knots of people.

Claire shivered. She clenched her teeth to keep them from chattering as she waited for Ivanov to go inside. So, Anthony caused Stephanie's death somehow, but he wasn't the mysterious black-clad skier who pushed her. Nickolas didn't seem to be either, because he blamed Ivanov. But the bear of a man was too large to match Boyd's description.

Stephanie's killer must have been Petrov. The ferret-faced enforcer was the same build as the Contino men—tall and thin. And he had salt-and-pepper hair. But the nagging question still lingered. *Why?* And why would Anthony want his daughter killed, then commit suicide over it days later?

Thoroughly puzzled, Claire walked to the door, massaging her arms to rub some warmth into them. She checked that Ivanov and Nick were out of sight and slipped inside.

She hurried up to Roger in the ballroom. "Where's Judy?"

He put his arm around her then stared at her in surprise. "You're ice-cold, Claire. Did you go outside?"

Claire nodded, her teeth chattering. "Nick's here. He was talking to Ivanov on the balcony. I need to ask Judy something." She started to move away.

"Let me warm you up first." He wrapped his arms around her and rubbed her back.

About the time she stopped shivering, Claire spotted her daughter across the room. She rushed to Judy's side, with Roger close on her heels, and pulled her away from her friends.

"Judy. I found out something, and I need your help. Remember at the Continos' reception when you said you recognized a man who kept staring at you, but you didn't know where you'd seen him before? A ferret-faced man?"

"Yes, I remember."

"Close your eyes and visualize his face. Now, imagine him with some sunglasses, a black ski jacket, and pants . . ."

With her eyes shut, Judy frowned in concentration. "He took off his sunglasses to wipe them. In a lift line . . . the line to the T-bar."

Her eyes flew open, and she gasped. "He's the rude skier in black, the one who shoved past the two guys at the top of Ptarmigan." Her hand gripped Claire's arm like a claw. "The one who killed Stephanie."

Roger cleared his throat. "Gals, we've got trouble."

"What?" Claire asked. "Where?"

Roger tilted his chin over her shoulder.

She whirled and saw Ivanov pushing his way through the crowd as he made his way to the door. "Where was he? Did he hear us?"

Solemnly, Roger put his arms around his daughter's and wife's shoulders. "I saw him out of the corner of my eye right when Judy said, 'the one who killed Stephanie.' His face went white—then he took off."

At the door, Ivanov turned and stared at them. His dark eyes bored into Claire's and rooted her to the spot.

The blood drained out of her face. "Oh, God." She felt like a cornered rabbit watching death swoop down in the form of a predator hawk with talons bared.

SIXTEEN: PROTECTING JUDY

CLAIRE GRIPPED ROGER'S ARM. "Now the boss of a hired killer knows that Judy's a witness to a murder. It's no longer a question that Petrov will target Judy, it's a certainty."

"But she didn't witness the murder," Roger said, "only Petrov getting off the lift."

"That puts Petrov at the scene," Claire replied through gritted teeth. "That may be all he needs to justify killing her. Leon said Petrov never leaves a witness alive that he doesn't trust to keep quiet. And I bet that's what the two of them were arguing about at the reception. Petrov wanted to kill Judy, and Ivanov was telling him to hold off, that maybe Judy didn't see him. Now Ivanov knows she's a threat."

Judy looked confused. "What are you talking about? Who's Petrov? What do you know that you aren't telling me?" As she blurted out the questions, her expression changed to red-faced anger.

"We didn't want to worry you until we had confirmation from the sheriff's office. But now you've given us our own confirmation, and it's time you knew." Claire told her what Leon had found out about Petrov being an enforcer for Ivanov.

She laid a gentle hand on Judy's arm. "There's more, honey. I just overheard Gregori Ivanov pressuring Nick to follow in his father's footsteps."

Judy glanced around. "Nick's here? Where?"

"He was out on the balcony. I don't know where he is now. But do you hear what I'm saying? It was obvious from the conversation that Nick knew what his father was doing."

Eyes wide, Judy shook her head. "Maybe he couldn't do anything to get his father out, but Nick would never work for organized crime."

"He seems to be resisting," Claire said, "but he's boxed in, and I think it'll be hard for him to get out. The mob's already killed his sister."

"Are you sure?"

"I'm almost positive Petrov did it. I just don't know why."

While Judy gaped at her mother, Roger said, "There's Detective Silverstone. I'll go get him." He crossed the ballroom to where the detective stood with a woman in a long turquoise dress, whose face matched the photograph on Owen's desk.

"If what we discovered isn't enough for Owen to get protection for you," Claire said to Judy, "we're leaving tonight and we won't be going back to Colorado Springs."

"Isn't that a little extreme?"

"Not when a mob enforcer is gunning for my daughter," Claire said fiercely. She realized her fingernails were digging into her palms and unclenched her hands.

"I'm not leaving Breckenridge without talking to Nick first." Judy wiped her hand across her brow. "This is all too unreal for me. Here we are in the middle of a ballroom party, and you're talking about mob gunmen. I can't believe this is happening to me, to Nick's family."

The string quartet launched into the "Blue Danube" waltz, and for a surreal moment, Claire felt as if she were on a doomed ship sailing toward disaster.

Roger returned with Silverstone. The detective looked distinguished in a black Western suit coat with black suede yokes, bolo tie, and silver-banded black cowboy hat.

"I almost didn't recognize you, Owen." Claire held out her hand. "I was hoping to meet your wife."

"She doesn't like getting tangled up in police business, especially when it's one of our rare nights out."

Claire glanced over and saw his wife watching them with a slight pout on her face. The woman turned away and addressed the couple she was with. "Sorry about that, but this is a matter of life or death—Judy's."

Owen looked at Judy. "Your father told me you ID'ed the skier in black."

"Yes, I saw him at the Continos' house on Friday."

"Viktor Petrov," Claire added. "The enforcer I told you about."

"Could you pick him out of a lineup?" Owen asked Judy.

"Oh, yes."

"Would you be willing to testify to that, if this goes to trial? Remember you could be in danger from the Russian mob if you do."

Claire gasped.

Judy glanced at her mother then squared her shoulders. "If I can help put Stephanie's killer behind bars, yes I'll testify."

Anxious to know more about the man Judy might face in a courtroom—if she made it there alive—Claire asked Owen, "Did you find out anything else about Petrov?"

Owen nodded and sipped his beer. "Your contact's information checked out. Denver PD's got a two-inch file on him, mostly speculation and circumstantial evidence, a few minor convictions. They know he's done more, a lot more, but it's been impossible to get testimony against him. They were curious how I knew he was in the country, since they still had him pegged in Chile."

"You didn't tell them about Leon, did you?"

"No, I said an eyewitness spotted him at a private gathering up here in Breckenridge." He raised a brow at Claire. "The same eyewitness who spotted the illegal money transfers on Contino's computer. They're beginning to wonder what sort of witness you are."

"I hope Denver PD's not suspicious of me." Seeing Owen's smile, Claire realized he was joking. "Did they find anything on Anthony's computer?"

"Not yet. Ivanov's files had been deleted, but Contino didn't reformat his disk, so the computer geeks think they can reconstruct at least some of the contents. In the meantime, Denver PD's sending a couple of officers up here tomorrow morning to work with me. Maybe this time we can construct a solid case against him."

Claire put her hand to her chest. "Thank God. I will feel so much better with that man locked away."

"Unfortunately, we haven't the foggiest idea where he is now. No one's seen him since Friday. And the Continos don't know him. When I interviewed them today, they said he came to the memorial service with Ivanov, who they claim is only a client of Anthony's."

Roger frowned. "Angela seemed pretty friendly with Ivanov when we saw him at the house Thursday."

"She said she's politely friendly to all of Anthony's clients, which is good for business," Owen replied. "She truly seemed to know nothing about her husband's work, but I think Nickolas is holding something back. He knows more than he's telling me."

Shaking her head, Judy stepped back, but Roger stayed her with an arm around her shoulders.

"Yes, he does," Claire said. "Ivanov is pressuring him to join the mob. I told you about the conversation Ivanov and Anthony had regarding Nick on Saturday. Tonight, I overheard another one between Ivanov and Nick out on the balcony."

Claire relayed the details of the conversation to Silverstone, concluding with, "That's why Roger asked you to come over. We have proof now that Judy's a target of Petrov. We think Petrov wanted to get rid of her before, and Ivanov stopped him. Remember the argument they were having at the Continos' when they were staring at her? She needs protection, and now."

Owen studied Judy. "She may be our only means of flushing out Petrov."

Claire jammed her fists on her hips. "Oh, no. You are not using my daughter as bait to lure in a killer. I forbid it."

Judy's eyes flashed. "I can make that decision for myself."

"You can't seriously be thinking of making yourself a target. He's a crack shot." The terrifying image of her daughter lying bloody and dying clashed in Claire's mind with those of Stephanie and Boyd. She hadn't been able to save them. She couldn't bear to see her daughter die, too.

"Give me some credit, Mom." Judy placed her hands on her hips, an exact mimicry of Claire's earlier action. "I'm not stupid, and I'm not a child anymore. You can't forbid me to do anything."

Claire felt as if she had been slapped. Anger and fear warred for control of her tongue. Her mouth flapped open and closed like a fish tossed out of the water.

Owen and Roger took a step away from the battlefield and shot arched looks at each other.

Claire took a deep breath. *I will not shout at my daughter in the middle of this crowd. I will not shout . . .* Fear and reason finally won out. "Judy, I'm your mother. My instinct to protect you is natural and impossible to squelch."

Judy glared at her mother. "You can't protect me from life itself. It's time to let go. I've got to learn how to protect myself."

With tears brimming in her eyes, Claire reached out. "I don't want to lose you. Ever. Can't you see your death would break my heart?"

Judy surveyed the people nearby, some watching them surreptitiously. "You're making a scene, Mom." She hesitated then opened her arms to Claire.

Claire hugged her daughter fiercely. She murmured in Judy's hair. "Sorry, honey. Sorry for being such a mama bear."

Judy sighed. "Put your claws away. This cub'll be all right."

"Oh, God, I hope so." Claire glanced at Owen. "What do we do now?"

He rubbed his chin. "I'll get the evening patrols busy looking for Petrov. I'll look for Ivanov here, and see if he'll lead us to Petrov."

"If Ivanov's not still at the party," Roger said, "you might find him at the Hilton. That's where Angela said he was staying."

"I know. She told me, too." Owen pulled out a cell phone and tapped it in his hand. "And I'll get an officer assigned to guard Judy. In the meantime, you three stay together in this ballroom. Don't even leave to use the restroom until I return."

"But I need to find Nick," Judy said.

"Let him find you." Owen shot a worried glance across the room at his wife. "Now, to break the news to Faith that I've managed to ruin another of her social evenings."

As he strode off, the master of ceremonies announced that the evening's program would begin, and people should find seats. The sounds of shuffling footsteps and scraping chairs surrounded Claire.

She motioned for Roger and Judy to follow her to a table near the back of the room. After they sat, Claire said to Judy, "If Nick's looking for you, he'll find you here. So will Petrov, but hopefully he won't risk harming you in front of hundreds of witnesses."

Roger glanced at the bar. "I'm tenser than a tax dodger being audited by the IRS. I need a drink. How about you two?"

With her head pounding and her insides twisted into knots, Claire realized she needed to release some of the pressure boiling inside her. "White wine for me this time."

Judy gave a nod. "Me, too."

While Roger went to fetch the drinks, Judy said, "I still find it hard to believe that a Russian mobster is out to gun me down. The whole story is too surreal. This isn't the wild, wild West, you know."

Claire leaned forward, anxious to convey the seriousness of the situation. "You're a witness to a mob killing. How many times have you read in the paper about a witness mysteriously disappearing before the trial of an important criminal?"

"I'm not stupid. Deep down I know there's a real danger, and that's got my stomach in knots. But you've got to admit this whole situation is freaky. And why aren't you and Dad worried about yourselves? You saw Petrov at the Continos. You know who he is, too."

"Yes, but you're the only person left alive who can put him on the ski slope when Stephanie was killed. Believe me, he'll stop at nothing to keep you from testifying against him."

Judy's gaze had left her mother's face, along with her attention. *Damn, how can I convince her to take care of herself if she's not even listening?* Claire turned to see what Judy was looking at and spotted Nick striding toward them, his lips clamped in a tight line, his eyes strained. He wore the same dark blue suit he had donned for Stephanie's funeral.

Judy rose as he approached, and the two clasped each other in a desperate hug. Wordless, they both seemed to struggle against tears as they buried their faces against each other's shoulders.

Claire tried not to stare at them. She listened while the emcee recited a long list of sponsors to thank.

Finally, Nick pulled away to look at Judy but continued to hold her in his arms. "I missed you." He gently caressed her hair. "I needed you."

"Oh, Nick. Me, too, but Mom and Dad made me stay away yesterday, and you were tied up with Detective Silverstone today."

Nick shot a sharp glance at Claire. "They made you stay away?"

Claire jumped in before Judy could reply. "We thought you and your mother should have some private time to grieve, Nick. I'm sorry if we made an error in judgment." She threw a "keep your trap shut" look at Judy.

He took Judy's hand and started to pull her from the table. "Let's go somewhere we can talk."

Judy pulled her hand out of his. "I can't."

Claire took advantage of Nick's startled paralysis to urge both of them to sit. "Judy, Roger and I need to stay here, together, until Detective Silverstone returns. You two will have to talk here."

"What?" Nick glanced at Judy, who nodded miserably. "What business does Silverstone have with you?"

Before Claire could respond, Judy said, "He's arranging for me to have a cop babysitter."

Nick looked from one of them to the other. "What the hell are you talking about?"

"Petrov," Judy replied. "I saw him on the ski slope before Stephanie was killed."

"Who's Petrov, and what does he have to do with Stephanie's death?"

"He's that ferret-faced man who was with Ivanov at the reception at your house. I saw him get off the T-bar and ski down right before Stephanie was hit."

Seeing a frown of disbelief cross Nick's face, Claire added, "Silverstone has positive information that Petrov is Ivanov's enforcer." She laid a sympathetic hand on Nick's arm.

"That scum brought Stephanie's killer to our house?" Nick's face went red and his hands tightened into fists.

"We have worse things to worry about," Claire said. "Remember, Judy saw Petrov on the slope."

Nick stared at Judy. Claire could see the wheels turning in his mind, and the moment when he reached the awful conclusion that rocked him back in his chair as if he had been punched in the gut.

"Oh, shit." Eyes wide with fear, he ran his fingers through his hair. "Double shit."

The emcee's voice sounded on the speakers, "—and the most important person we have to thank is Anthony Contino, who was tragically taken from us on Friday. Here in his place to accept his award for outstanding volunteer of the year is his son, Nickolas Contino."

A round of hearty applause broke out. The emcee spotted Nick and signaled for him to come forward. People began to stare at him as he sat immobile.

Judy shook his arm. "You need to go up there, Nick."

He grabbed Judy's hand. "I have to talk to you."

With tears glistening in her eyes, Judy said, "I know. But right now, you've got to accept your father's award. Go."

Nick finally seemed to notice the people applauding around him. He flushed and stood, wiping his hands on his pants. He approached the stage, fumbling for an index card in his jacket pocket. He dropped it, then picked it up again, moving slowly as if still dazed.

Roger returned with the drinks and handed them out before he took his seat. He watched Nick's awkward progress toward the stage. "Is he going to make it through this ceremony? He looks kind of shaky."

Claire took a hefty gulp of her wine. "He's got more than grief working against him. Judy just told him she saw Petrov on the ski slope the day Stephanie was killed. He's still absorbing the impact."

"Shit." Roger glanced at Judy, but she was focused solely on Nick, as if willing him from afar to make it through the emcee's praise of his now-dead father and the short speech Nick would be obliged to give. "Double shit."

Claire couldn't help her wry grin. "Precisely what Nick had to say on the subject."

Owen returned to their table and leaned over to whisper to them. "I've got two patrolmen scouring the premises for Petrov and Ivanov. No sign of either yet. As soon as the patrolmen finish, they'll report to me here."

He slid into the chair Nick had vacated. "One of them, Officer Ramstead, will take the first watch over Judy. There're a few things I should go over with you three."

He glanced at Judy then followed her gaze to Nick on the stage. With hands tightly clasped, the young man stood next to the emcee rattling off his father's contributions, in time and money, to the Summit Foundation.

"We won't be able to tear her attention from Nick," Claire said. "Tell us, and we'll make sure she hears it later."

Owen cleared his throat meaningfully then looked at the two of them. "Ramstead, and whoever takes his place in the morning, should stay in the same room with Judy at all times. We can make an exception when she's in the bathroom. No windows in there, I presume?"

"Not in hers," Roger said.

"Good. I plan to sit outside your place in my cruiser tonight, after I check for Ivanov at the Hilton."

"I hope your wife's not too upset about that," Claire said.

Owen rolled his shoulders, as if his jacket was binding him. "She'll get over it. This kinda stuff comes with being a cop's wife. I've arranged for someone else to drive her home. I need to be at your place. If Petrov makes a move for Judy, I think it'll be tonight."

Claire sucked in a breath.

"Keep her inside and away from the Continos' house." Owen glanced at Judy. "I know I'm asking a lot."

"Yes, you are," Claire replied, "but we'll do whatever it takes to keep her alive. What will you do if you can't find Petrov?"

"We've already got an APB out for him. I hope we flush him before he escapes back to Chile."

"At least in Chile, he'd be away from Judy," Claire said.

Judy leaned forward, her shoulders tense. Nick had started his acceptance speech.

A Summit County patrolman in the familiar black and green-gray uniform approached Owen and whispered in his ear.

"No luck yet." Owen stood. "Let's go."

Claire stood with him. "Judy won't want to leave before talking to Nick."

Owen frowned. "Tell her to call him later. With Petrov on the loose, I'm nervous about leaving her out in an exposed area any longer."

Roger went over to Judy and whispered in her ear. When she shook her head vigorously, he pulled her up out of her chair with a firm hand on her arm. "You can call him after we get home."

"But—" Judy's gaze remained on Nick as they escorted her out of the ballroom.

He stumbled on his words as he watched them go.

Claire caught his attention and mimicked putting a phone to her ear while mouthing, "She'll call you."

When they reached the parking lot of their townhouse, Claire scanned the area, nervously checking for any signs of a lurking Russian hit man. As if there would be any.

Owen pulled his cruiser into the space next to theirs, and Officer Ramstead parked his at the end of the block. The two men got out of their vehicles and approached Roger's car.

"Stay here until I can check the place out." Owen held out his hand to Roger. "House key?"

Roger handed Owen his keychain and showed him which key was for the door.

Owen turned to Ramstead. "You watch the front door and the Hanovers." Owen drew his gun out of a holster hidden under his suit coat and entered the townhouse silently.

Claire, Roger, and Judy huddled together in the cooling car, with Ramstead standing guard and puffing clouds of condensation in the brisk night air. A few minutes later, Owen waved to them from the doorway. They climbed the steps and went inside.

Before Claire could say anything to her, Judy grabbed the phone and punched in a phone number, tossing her coat on the floor as she waited for the rings.

"Mrs. Contino, this is Judy. Please ask Nick to call me as soon as he gets home. It's important. And, Mrs. Contino, I'm so sorry about everything that's happened. I want to help—" She listened for a while, as tears came to her eyes. "Yes, I understand. Goodbye."

She grabbed a tissue to wipe her eyes. "Mrs. Contino can barely talk, she's so choked up. I wish I could do something."

Claire rubbed Judy's back. "So do I, honey, but grieving is a long and difficult process. We can't go through that for her. Or for Nick."

"But I could be there when he needs to talk. If you'd let me." She ground out the last four words.

"We feel for Nick, too," Claire said. "But our first concern is your safety. How do you think Nick would feel if something happened to you?"

And if keeping Judy safe means breaking up her relationship with Nick, then by God, I'll do it, no matter how much it hurts her.

Judy eyed her mother suspiciously, as if she had heard Claire's thought. "I need to go to the bathroom." She frowned at Officer Ramstead. "So you're to be my shadow, right?"

He cleared his throat and glanced at Owen. "Yes, ma'am."

"I'm going downstairs." She turned and walked to the staircase.

"She's not mad at you," Claire said to the officer, "just that you need to watch her."

"I understand." Ramstead hurried down the stairs after Judy.

"If you're all set here, I'll head over to the Hilton," Owen said. "I'll keep Ramstead posted via his police radio and be back as soon as I finish there." He opened the door, made sure the lock was set, then closed it behind him.

Claire collapsed on the couch, too wrung out with tension to even remove her coat. She just unzipped it and threw it open. Her stomach growled, notifying her that one glass of wine did not constitute dinner. She glanced at her watch. A few minutes after eight o'clock. "Have we got anything to eat?"

Roger shot her a surprised glance from the kitchen where he had been pouring himself a glass of water. "You didn't get enough to eat at the party?"

"I didn't get anything to eat there, and I don't think Judy did either."

Roger opened the cupboard doors. "Raisin bran, tortilla chips, microwave popcorn, baked beans—"

Ugh. Beans. "How about popcorn?"

He put a bag in the microwave oven and brought Claire a glass of water and the ibuprofen bottle.

"Thanks, honey, for knowing exactly what I needed." *One of the benefits of being married for twenty-six years.* Claire downed the pills, then dug into the popcorn when Roger brought over the bowl.

A few minutes later, the doorbell rang, making Claire jump and spill the remaining popcorn.

Roger went to the door. "Who is it?" He waited then opened the door.

Nick stepped inside, his eyes dark wells of sadness, and nodded at Claire and Roger. "Mrs. Hanover, Mr. Hanover. I can't tell you how sorry I am that Judy got involved in our troubles. I'll do everything I can to protect her."

Even if it means leaving her? "We need to have a long talk, Nick. It's our right to know exactly what's going on, for Judy's sake."

Looking even more miserable, Nick jammed his hands in his pockets. "Can I talk to Judy first? There are some things I need to say to her in private."

So, maybe he does realize he has to leave her.

"She's downstairs," Roger said. "But a policeman's with her. Unfortunately, he has to stay in the same room."

Nick grimaced.

Claire's heart went out to the young man. "I'm sure he'll keep whatever he overhears to himself, Nick. Go on. She's anxious to see you, too."

Head bowed, he clumped down the stairs.

Claire knelt on the floor to pick up the spilled popcorn.

Roger bent down to join her. "Actually, he seems like a nice young man."

"Stuck in lousy circumstances, unfortunately." Claire tossed a handful of kernels into the bowl. "Circumstances I don't want Judy involved in."

Roger glanced down the stairs, a thoughtful expression on his face. "If only there was some way . . ."

Claire sat back on her heels. "I don't see how it's possible. The Russian mob is worldwide. If they want Nick, they can reach out and grab him wherever he goes. He's stuck. His father made damn sure of that."

She pursed her lips. "But Judy isn't stuck. Not yet. No way is she going to be the wife of a criminal."

Shaking his head, Roger dropped the last popcorn kernels into the bowl and brushed off his hands. "It's a damn shame."

As Claire rose with the bowl, a whooshing sound downstairs froze her in place. "What was that?"

His brow furrowed, Roger said, "I don't know."

Claire stood and called, "Judy!"

No answer.

"Nick? Officer Ramstead?"

Nothing.

Roger's gaze darted around the room, then he dashed for the fireplace and grabbed the poker. "All I could think of," he whispered to Claire.

He motioned her to get behind him as he slowly made his way down the stairs, hugging the wall.

Claire followed. When they reached the bottom step and turned, she craned her neck to see around Roger's head and shoulders.

The back sliding glass door stood wide open. A frigid breeze slapped the vertical blinds against each other.

"Did they go outside?" Claire asked. "Where's Officer Ramstead?"

A toilet flushed and the two turned toward the bathroom. The door opened and the policeman stepped out. He looked around. "Where'd they go?" Then he spied the gaping sliding glass door. "Crap."

He ran out and around the side of the townhouse. The roar of an engine turning over filtered in through the open doorway. Soon Ramstead returned, chest heaving.

"That was a Range Rover with the two of them in it. I couldn't catch them." He bent over and leaned his hands on his knees to catch his breath.

"Why'd you let them out of your sight?" Roger asked.

"The two lovebirds were so engrossed in whispering to each other, I decided to take a leak. Never thought they'd bail on me. I was supposed to keep someone from getting in, not her from getting out." He groaned and stared at Claire. "What the hell do they think they're doing?"

"How should I know? I can't believe they would do something this stupid. All we can hope is that they went to Nick's house." *And that no one followed them.*

Anxious to get Judy back under police protection, Claire pointed to the radio on Ramstead's belt. "Can you contact Detective Silverstone on that?"

He keyed the radio. "Ramstead calling Silverstone."

"Silverstone here. I'm almost there. Hold a couple of minutes."

Ramstead tried to raise him again, but got no response.

Claire shivered. "Roger, could you close that door?"

As Roger slid the sliding glass door shut, the front doorbell rang.

"That must be Owen." Claire ran upstairs, fear gnawing at her brain and jumbling her thoughts. *What if the kids didn't go to Nick's house? What if they couldn't be found until it was too late?*

"Check first before you open it," Roger called as he and Ramstead clomped up the stairs behind her.

"That you, Owen?" she asked through the door.

"Yes."

Claire opened it and ushered him in. "Thank God you're here."

Owen's eyes went wide. "Why? What happened?" When he saw Ramstead climbing the stairs, Owen repeated, "What the hell happened?"

"The gal and her boyfriend took off." Ramstead slumped onto a kitchen stool.

"We think they're on the way to Nick's house," Roger added.

Owen slapped the kitchen counter, startling Claire. "Damn idiots. Petrov's even more likely to find her there."

SEVENTEEN:
OVER THE RIVER AND
THROUGH THE WOODS

OWEN WENT INTO COMMAND mode. "Ramstead, get in your cruiser and head back to the station. Round up some backup and some more weapons and meet me at the Contino house."

Ramstead nodded and loped out the front door.

Owen pointed a finger at Claire and Roger. "You two stay put while I head over there."

"No way." Claire grabbed her coat. "You can't keep us here when our daughter's in danger."

She didn't have to say anything to Roger, who had already shrugged on his coat. *Good man.*

Owen glared at them then blew out a breath. "All right. But I don't want you speeding after my cruiser and putting yourself in danger once we get there. Ride with me."

The four of them rushed out of the townhouse. Claire and Roger climbed into the back seat of Owen's cruiser while Ramstead loped to his cruiser. Owen reversed with a jerk, and Claire scrambled to buckle her seat belt as he accelerated out of the parking lot.

"You got any idea why the two of them took off like that?" Owen shouted over his shoulder.

"I can't understand it," Claire said. "We told Nick about Petrov, so he knew how much danger Judy was in. I can't believe he would expose her to more risk like this."

Owen frowned into the rearview mirror. "Maybe he's in cahoots with the Russians."

Leaning forward, Roger gripped the back of the front seat. "If so, he's a great actor. Even when he didn't realize Claire was listening, he told off Ivanov. Maybe he thinks he can protect Judy better at his house. They probably have an alarm system and guns."

Owen slapped the steering wheel. "Why the hell do private citizens think a gun in their hand makes them more competent than a trained cop?" He made a fast turn that threw Claire against Roger.

She worried her lip while staring out the window at the darkened landscape whooshing by. *Is Roger right? Is Nick that stupid? Or have we seriously misjudged him, and has he really given in to the Russian mob?*

Owen turned onto the Continos' street and passed a black Range Rover parked in a snowplow turnout. He slid to a halt, backed up, and directed the patrol car's headlights at the back of the Range Rover.

"Damn."

Claire craned her neck to see the license plate. "Damn what?"

"The plate's Ivanov's. That means he or Petrov or both are here. And they don't want the Continos to know. The vehicle looks empty, but I need to check it anyway. Stay here."

Owen unholstered his gun, snatched a flashlight out of his glove compartment, and climbed out of the cruiser.

Claire's throat constricted with fear. She grabbed Roger's hand.

His gaze was grim as he covered her hand with his other hand. "Don't panic yet, honey. Judy and Nick may not even be in the neighborhood."

"That's another reason to panic," Claire answered. "If they aren't here and Petrov followed them, there's no way we'll be able to find them before he kills Judy. How will we know where to look?"

Hunkered down, Owen approached the Range Rover from the rear, then stood with gun drawn and shone the flashlight through a window. After running the beam over the whole car, he laid his hand for a moment on the hood. He flashed the light around the car, across snow being swirled and shifted by the wind. He seemed to pick up a trail and followed it for a few feet.

He stopped, aimed the flashlight off in the direction the trail took, and panned the light over the area. With a shake of his head, he holstered his gun, turned the flashlight off, and returned. He got in and drove away.

Claire gripped the edge of her seat. "What did you see?"

"The car was empty, but the hood was still warm. They must have arrived a few minutes ago. Two sets of footsteps led off in the direction of the Contino house."

A few moments later, Owen pulled into the Continos' driveway and parked behind a black Range Rover—probably the same one Nick and Judy rode away in.

So much for not panicking.

As Owen opened his car door, Claire tried to open hers, but it wouldn't budge. "Why won't my door open?"

"That's the way police cars work, so the criminals in the back won't bolt on us." Owen got a thoughtful expression. "Maybe you two should stay here until Ramstead and my backup arrive."

"With two Russian mobsters prowling the neighborhood?" Roger asked. "We'd be sitting ducks in here."

"You won't be any safer outside."

"At least we could run or hide behind something." Roger slapped the seat. "Let us out!"

"On one condition." Owen stared them down. "I don't want you going in the Contino house until backup arrives. You'll find a place to hide and stay put until I say so. Understand?"

Claire nodded and Roger said, "Yes."

Owen pressed a button on the dash of his cruiser, and the locks on the back doors released. Claire and Roger quietly exited the car and crouched between it and the Range Rover while Owen reconnoitered. He waved his hand, and they all ran toward the front door. Claire slipped on the ice and fell hard.

"You hurt?" Roger offered an arm.

"I bashed my knee." She struggled to her feet, gritting her teeth against the pain.

"Let me help you back to the car."

"No! I'm fine." She pushed off his arm and limped after Owen.

Upon reaching the porch, Owen pointed to a rack of stacked firewood under the living room window. "Get behind that."

While Claire and Roger sequestered themselves between the scratchy logs and the house wall, Owen rang the doorbell and pounded on the door. "Police. Open up."

After getting no answer, he tested the doorknob. When it turned, he pushed the door open. He made a quick scan inside and held his hand up, palm out, to Claire and Roger. "Stay here, ready to run if you have to. I doubt those Russians have made it here yet on foot, but they could be in the house."

He pointed a finger at Claire. "No buts this time."

Seeing the firm set of the lawman's jaw, Claire swallowed her "But" and nodded.

"If Ramstead and the backup arrive before I return," Owen continued, "tell them I went in the front door. They should take the rear."

Roger put his arm around Claire's shoulder. "Sure."

She held her breath while Owen slipped through the front doorway.

Claire waited with Roger, crouched uncomfortably behind the musty firewood. Her calves cramped, and she started shivering from the biting cold wind. After a few minutes, she stood. "Enough of this. I'm going in."

Roger rose. "But we promised—"

"The Russians are more likely to be outside than inside. Remember, they're on foot out there in the snow. And Owen said we should be ready to run if we have to. Well, I've decided I have to run inside."

"Makes sense to me." Roger followed Claire to the front door.

After easing through the doorway, Roger opened the door to the hall closet and started rummaging inside.

"What are you doing?" Claire whispered.

"Looking for weapons." Roger whispered back as he pulled out a rolled, cane-shaped umbrella with a metal tip and handed it to her then shoved the coats aside.

"Bingo." He brandished an ice hockey stick.

Claire glanced at her umbrella then the hockey stick gripped in his hands. "Neither one of these is much use against a gun."

"They're better than nothing."

"Probably the smartest thing to do is to hide inside that closet."

"I'm not going to stand around twiddling my thumbs when Judy's in danger. And if I know you, neither are you." He inched his way along the wall.

"I'm just pointing out that what we're doing isn't very smart." *When have we ever chosen prudence over protecting one of our kids?* Claire gripped her umbrella and limped behind Roger.

They made their way down the hall, turned the corner, and scanned the empty living room, lit only by a soft glow coming from the kitchen doorway on the far side.

Angela shrieked in the kitchen.

Roger shot a worried glance at Claire then rushed forward.

Claire gimped along and almost slammed into Roger's back when she entered the kitchen. She peered around him.

Angela stood next to the sink, a smashed teacup and a spreading pool of steaming tea on the floor in front of her. Her hands clasped her cheeks, and her mouth hung open in a perfect imitation of Edvard Munch's painting *The Scream*.

Owen stood before her, his gun pointed to the floor. His other hand moved downward in a reassuring, "be calm" motion.

When Angela's gaze slid to Roger, Owen looked over his shoulder and scowled at them. "I told you to stay put."

Roger stared straight back at him. "We decided it was safer inside."

Owen gave the hockey stick and umbrella a disdainful once-over. "And you came well-armed, I see." He returned his attention to Angela. "Have you seen your son and Judy Hanover tonight?"

Licking her lips, Angela hesitated.

Claire stepped forward. "Angela, we know they came here. We need to find them. Now."

"Are they in trouble?"

"Yes," Owen answered, "but not with the law. We're trying to protect them from the Russian mob."

Angela's jaw dropped again. "The Russian mob? What are you talking about?"

Sighing in frustration, Owen rubbed his brow.

Claire laid her hand on Angela's arm. "I'll fill you in on everything if you'll just tell us where Judy and Nick are."

"But I promised Nick."

Claire's grip on Angela's arm tightened. "They could be shot any minute. You've got to tell Detective Silverstone where they are."

Angela glanced at their anxious faces then nodded.

"Nick said he wanted to take Judy to a remote place where they could talk. He said they needed to be alone. It sounded so romantic. From the way they were holding onto each other, I thought—" Her gaze softened. "I thought he might be ready to propose, you know, in a secluded spot in the moonlight. That's what Anthony did, waited for a full moon, took me outside in my parents' garden and went down on his knee. I can still smell the gardenias. I hope there's a full moon tonight."

She could drive a person mad with her talking. Claire shook Angela's arm. "Where did they go?"

"Nick didn't say exactly, but he took some supplies into the garage—blankets, food, a lantern, some of this hot tea in a thermos." She paused. "I think I know what he has in mind. There's an old, abandoned miner's cabin a few miles up the trail that goes through our backyard. Hikers and cross-country skiers sometimes use the cabin as an overnight shelter."

"When did they leave?" Owen asked.

"Oh, they haven't—"

An engine sputtered to life in the garage.

Roger whirled. "What was that?"

"Snowmobile," Claire said. "Remember when Nick said they kept four in the garage?" *Oh, God. He's not taking Judy out on one of those deathtraps is he?* Her heart started pounding.

The throaty howl of the machine roared out of the garage and around the back of the house.

"We've got to stop them!" Owen sprinted to the door leading from the kitchen into the garage. He yanked on the handle, but nothing happened.

While he fumbled with the doorknob, Angela said, "Let me. There's a key bolt." She reached for a key hanging on a hook on the side of a nearby cabinet and unlocked the door while Owen almost danced with impatience.

He slammed open the door just as another snowmobile roared to life.

Claire peered out the kitchen door into the garage, dimly lit by moonlight from outside the open garage door. A dark figure dressed all in black hunched over the handlebars of a snowmobile pointed toward the driveway, a rifle with a lump on one side slung over his shoulder. He gunned the engine and took off.

Petrov! He must have reached the house right after Nick and Judy left. If the kids were in range, he surely would have shot them. Thank God they still have a chance.

"Stop, police!" Owen fired his gun at Petrov.

Petrov had leaned into a turn and the bullet whizzed past his ear. He jerked his head to glance back at the house. But he didn't hesitate. His machine zoomed toward the young couple's trail, the headlight knifing a path of light through the trees while he leaned from side to side, making the snowmobile weave an erratic path.

Owen fired again, but Petrov kept going, disappearing around a hill.

Owen holstered his gun, jumped on one of the two remaining snowmobiles, and cranked the key. "When my backup arrives," he shouted, "tell them to follow our tracks." He roared out of the garage.

"I'm going, too." Roger said. "He'll need all the help he can get. But I need a gun."

Claire turned to Angela, whose mouth was hanging open again. *The woman would make a damn good flycatcher.* "Do you have any guns in the house?"

Angela pointed to the opposite wall of the garage, where a gun rack sporting three hunting rifles hung on the wall.

Roger ran over to the rack, grabbed a rifle and a box of ammunition, and popped the magazine out of the gun to load it. "This isn't a match for Petrov's semiautomatic, with its night scope, but it'll have to do."

"So that's what that lump was," Claire said. "How're you going to drive a snowmobile and fire that rifle at the same time?"

Roger looked at her. "Could you . . . ? No, I guess you couldn't."

Claire realized he was remembering the death of her friend's son. Her hands clenched and unclenched with fear and indecision. She was terrified of the idea of getting on one of those dangerous machines, let alone driving one, but Roger needed his hands free to fire the rifle at Petrov. Though Claire had shot a handgun in a range class before, Roger was the only one in the family who knew how to shoot a rifle. He had learned as a teenager and had bagged an elk on two of his hunting trips.

She took a deep breath. "Oh, God. I'll drive it."

Roger's eyes widened. "You sure?"

"Hell no, but for Judy's life, I'll do anything."

He gave a firm nod. "Let's go, then."

"Angela, you'll need to direct the cops up the trail when they arrive." Claire peered at the woman. "Can you do it?"

"Yes, yes I can do that," Angela answered breathlessly. "Who was the man on the snowmobile that Detective Silverstone went after?"

Claire didn't have time to break the news to Angela gently. "A Russian mobster. He plans to kill Judy, maybe even Nick, and we've got to stop him."

"But—"

Claire didn't wait to hear the next question. She ran for the last snowmobile and straddled it.

Roger hopped on the back seat behind her, cradling the rifle. "It's an Arctic Cat, the same type I rode on a backcountry tour two years ago." He reached around her and cranked the key.

The engine roared to life and the headlight blazed on. Roger showed her where the throttle and brake were. "It drives a lot like an ATV. You remember riding one awhile back on that vacation in Utah?"

"Yeah. Here goes nothing." Claire sucked in a deep breath, squeezed the throttle, and took off. She found the tracks of the other machines and followed them into the woods. Approaching the first turn, she leaned into the turn as she would have on an ATV. The snowmobile skidded, and Claire's throat constricted. Gritting her teeth, she goosed the gas, and the machine righted itself.

"That's it. You're getting the hang of it," Roger shouted in her ear.

Swallowing hard, Claire nodded. She gripped the handlebars and hugged the gas tank with her thighs. Leaning forward, she squeezed the throttle tighter and shot across the lumpy snow. *Oh, God.*

Every bounce jostled her throbbing knee. She grimaced. Maybe the pain would help her banish the raw fear wrapping around her throat and staring her in the eyes, like an anaconda about to swallow its victim.

She scanned the narrow trail arching uphill between black tree trunks. She would need every ounce of concentration to negotiate the turns on this trail, especially in the dark. The last thing she wanted to do was crash.

Don't even think it!

She hooked a tight right turn around a huge lodgepole pine, then increased speed when the trail straightened out.

243

The snowmobile's right ski hit a rock and launched the sled into the air. It slammed down into the snow, rattling Claire's teeth and shooting a knifing pain through her knee. She managed to hang on until the center tread got a grip on the snow.

Roger bounced behind her and muttered a curse.

When they crested a rise, Claire heard the distant roar of snowmobiles ahead of her. She hunkered down and accelerated to her maximum comfort range, then exceeded it. She and Roger whipped back and forth as she leaned the machine into turns around the trees. *No time for fear now.*

The trail headed downhill, and Claire had to let off on the gas. Other snowmobiles roared below her and off to the left. They sounded closer.

She spied a black surface in a low hollow in front of her and realized one of the other machines had broken through the ice covering a large puddle. "Hold on," she shouted to Roger.

The snowmobile splashed in, soaking their legs with ice-cold water, but the machine managed to grind its way out on the other side.

Below her the trail opened up into a wide meadow. Two snowmobiles lurched across the middle of the expanse. Probably Petrov followed closely by Owen. The two men hunched over their machines, snow rooster-tailing behind them. Hopefully, Nick and Judy were far ahead.

Owen raised his right hand. A shot rang out. Then another.

Claire slowed her machine, staying hidden in the trees.

Petrov's sled skidded to a stop.

Did Owen get him? Claire held her breath.

The wind stirred up a snow devil that arced and twisted between the men before heading for Petrov.

The Russian raised his rifle and fired a burst of rounds.

Owen's snowmobile veered out of control, up a hummock, and tipped over onto its back. The detective lay trapped underneath. And he wasn't moving.

"Shit," Roger hissed in her ear.

God, no! Is Owen dead? If he isn't, will Petrov finish him off?

Petrov spun off again, disappearing into the trees on the far side.

"Go!" Roger hollered.

Claire squeezed her throttle all the way and raced her snowmobile out of the woods and across the weeds poking through the snow. The machine bucked and jerked like a wild rodeo bronco, but Claire clamped her legs tight and willed herself to stay upright.

She skidded to a stop beside Owen's sled.

Before she finished braking, Roger leapt off and ran to the other machine. He pushed it over, righting it, so it came off of Owen's legs, and Claire saw they had been in a safe hollow under the snowmobile.

Owen scrambled backward on his left elbow and butt, leaving a trail of bright red blood in the snow.

Claire ran over and knelt beside him. "Where are you hurt?"

His face a deathly white, Owen panted. "You shouldn't be here, but I'm damn glad you are. Petrov's shot grazed my right forearm. No crash injuries, though. Thank God he left. I thought for sure he would try to finish me off."

"Maybe he thought you were already finished." Claire helped Owen remove his jacket from that arm.

"That's why I kept still. My only chance, really." Owen awkwardly pulled a handkerchief out of his hip pocket and pressed it against his bleeding arm. "Where's my gun? It fell out of my hand in the crash."

"I'll look for it." Roger started searching the ground.

Claire took the ends of Owen's handkerchief, wrapped them tightly around his forearm then knotted them. "Sorry if I'm hurting you."

"It's not bad," Owen said through gritted teeth. He tried to make a fist with his right hand, but failed. "I can't drive a snowmobile with this arm. Or shoot."

"Found it." Roger returned with Owen's gun.

Owen held out his left hand for the gun. "I never could get the hang of left-handed shooting, but I'll do my best to protect us until my backup arrives. I'll radio in an update and see how close the backup is."

Instead of handing over the weapon, Roger pulled Claire to her feet. "We've got to go on. We're the only ones left who can get Petrov before he kills the kids."

Owen looked up at Roger. "You'll only succeed in getting yourselves killed, too."

"Do you think we'd be able to keep on living," Claire asked, "if Petrov killed Judy and we didn't do everything in our power to save her?"

"Take this." Roger handed her Owen's gun.

"Give me that," Owen shouted.

Claire stepped back. "Sorry, Owen. One rifle won't cut it against Petrov."

A shadow passed over Owen's face, no doubt as he imagined his own daughter in such danger. He scowled and his shoulders sagged. "Damn it! I know I can't stop you. Hell, I don't want to stop you."

Claire glanced at Roger, who gave a grim nod, then the two of them dashed to their machine. "Should we take both snowmobiles?" Claire shouted.

"No." Roger straddled the back seat. "If you drive, maybe I can get a clear shot off while we're still moving."

Claire shoved Owen's gun into the side pocket of her jacket and zipped it shut. As soon as she reseated herself, she roared off again after Petrov.

At the other side of the meadow, they plunged into pine and fir forest again. Claire followed the trail as it wound up another ridge, then cut across the hill.

How far had Angela said the miner's cabin was? A few miles? Do Nick and Judy know Petrov's behind them? Do they have any weapons?

There were too many unknowns to make any kind of plan. All Claire could do was drive as fast as she could, hope they closed the distance between themselves and Petrov before he reached the kids, and hope Roger could get a clear shot off before the expert marksman returned fire.

The odds didn't look good.

The machine screamed around a turn and, before Claire could react, slammed into a pile of loose snow clods and rocks—the aftermath of a small avalanche slide down a chute between the trees. She and Roger were launched out of their seats into the pile.

She landed on her side. All her breath came out in a whoosh. Stabbing pains shot through her shoulder and thigh. She rolled onto her back and spied two boulders where the pains had begun. After a few pants through gritted teeth, the pain dulled. She sat up.

"You all right?" Roger called out.

Claire rotated her shoulder and moved her thigh. "I think so. Just bruised." And big ones at that.

She saw Roger stumbling toward her. "What about you?"

"No broken bones, I think." He gave her a hand up.

They hurried over to the snowmobile idling on its side. One side of the windshield had torn free, and it hung loosely from the bolt on the other side. Roger ripped the windshield the rest of the way off and flung it to the side of the trail. "Let's get back on the horse."

They righted the snowmobile and pushed it across the pile, with Claire squeezing the throttle some to help get the sled over. She searched the slide for signs someone else had fallen there, but the snow was too jumbled.

Had Judy and Nick or Petrov hit the pile, too, and fallen? If Judy and Nick didn't know they were being followed, then they wouldn't have been in a hurry and probably avoided the slide. Petrov, however, was in a hurry.

Claire hoped he had tumbled. Otherwise, he had a big lead on them and would reach the kids before Claire and Roger could catch him. Her mouth went dry as an image popped into her mind of Petrov pointing that semiautomatic rifle at Judy. *God, no.*

Once on the other side of the slide, she and Roger quickly mounted the machine and took off again. Now three parts of her body complained at every bump and jangle, but Claire told them to shut up.

She gripped the handlebars, her palms sweating inside her gloves, and wished she had taken shooting lessons. She was hopelessly outmatched by the Russian enforcer. And Roger wasn't much better, with just some rusty hunting practice. Their only hope was surprise and the fact that it was two of them against one of him. So, if he shot at one, the other might be able to shoot back. But that meant the one he shot could—

Claire shouted over her shoulder. "I love you."

Roger squeezed her shoulder. "We'll get him, Claire." He paused. "Love you, too."

So he's reached the same conclusion.

EIGHTEEN: THE CAPTIVE

CLAIRE MOTORED ON WITHOUT speaking for another half mile, with only her desperate thoughts and an occasional "oof" from Roger for company.

The forest opened before her. A small, dilapidated log cabin squatted in the right side of a small clearing, its windows tar-papered over and a square of blue plastic tarp nailed onto a portion of the roof. One snowmobile sat parked alongside. A dark shape in the woods to the left of the clearing transformed into a figure hunched over a second snowmobile, its motor still running.

"Kill the engine," Roger hissed into her ear.

Claire cut the ignition, which turned off the headlight, and coasted toward the edge of the clearing.

As they watched, Petrov turned off his engine and clambered off his machine.

Roger bumped Claire's back as he readied his rifle. She leaned to one side, unzipping her pocket to retrieve Owen's handgun with a shaky, slippery hand. She prayed that if she had to use the gun, she could, and would hit her target.

Because if I don't, Petrov will surely kill Roger or Judy. Or both.

Crouching with his rifle at the ready, Petrov duck-walked to the cabin, seemingly unaware of Claire and Roger's presence.

Claire gripped Owen's handgun, the cold metal pressing against her palm. *Give me courage.*

"Get down," Roger whispered.

Keeping watch on Petrov, she slid off the snowmobile seat into deep snow.

Roger aimed his rifle and fired.

Missed!

Petrov pivoted. Ducking and weaving, he began a steady fusillade of fire.

Claire rolled onto her stomach, raised her handgun, and thumbed off the safety.

Roger fell off the snowmobile on the opposite side.

He's been shot! Anger and fear pumping her full of adrenaline, she aimed at Petrov's bobbing chest and squeezed the trigger. The handgun recoiled, threatening to leap out of her fingers, but she held tight.

She squeezed again. And again.

Finally, Petrov reeled back.

A shot rang out from the other side of their snowmobile, but the bullet plowed into the tree next to the Russian.

Roger's alive!

Petrov fell with a thud.

Roger ran over to the gunman, post-holing in the knee-deep snow.

Petrov rolled and reached behind him as Claire tromped up, panting with the exertion of pushing through the snow.

"Look out," Roger yelled.

Petrov pulled out a handgun, but before he could raise his arm to fire, Roger stomped on his wrist.

The man sucked in a breath between clenched teeth, and the gun fell out of his hand.

Claire grabbed the handgun and tossed it into the woods, then aimed Owen's gun at Petrov's chest.

Nick came running around the corner of the cabin, buttoning his jeans. "We heard the snowmobiles, then shots, but we were afraid to come out until the shooting stopped. What's going on?"

"Get back," Claire shouted. "Wait until we disarm him, and keep Judy inside."

At the same time, Roger shoved his rifle into the struggling man's face. "Don't move!" He kicked the scoped rifle out of Petrov's reach.

With two guns pointed at him, the mob enforcer seemed to finally concede defeat. He writhed on the packed snow, moaning and clutching his shot knee with his free hand, while a spreading pool of steaming red blood stained the pristine snow by his leg. A string of what must have been Russian curses erupted with clouds of condensed breath from his clenched jaw.

Roger eyed Claire. "You okay?"

Keeping her gaze on Petrov's hands, Claire tried to steady her own. "Yeah. What about you? I thought he'd shot you."

Roger handed her his rifle, then yanked Petrov's jacket down to his elbows to immobilize the man's arms. He ran his hands over

Petrov's body, dug a cell phone out of the Russian's coat and pocketed it. He glanced up at Claire. "I thought the same thing about you."

A silent message passed between them before she returned her attention to Petrov.

Roger jerked off the man's boots, eliciting a howl of pain, and dumped a knife out of one of them. "Thank God you got him before he could draw a good bead on us. Why'd you aim for his knee?"

"I didn't. I aimed all three shots at his chest." Struggling to focus over Petrov's unnerving moans and her own jangly nerves, Claire kept her handgun trained on the enforcer while she laid Roger's rifle on the snow next to her. "Check his back, too."

Roger stuffed the knife he found into one of his coat pockets. He rolled Petrov onto his side and patted his back. With a triumphant grin, Roger extracted another knife and held it up. "Aren't you smart."

Petrov lunged for the knife in Roger's pocket, but Roger slammed his knee down on that arm, unsheathed the knife he held, and shoved it against Petrov's throat. Another string of garbled curses erupted from the Russian.

"Shut up." Claire yelled. "What other weapons are you hiding?"

When she got no response, she pushed the muzzle of her handgun against his forehead. One very dangerous part of her wanted to shoot him then and there, get it over with. She willed her trigger finger to stay right where it was and took a deep breath through flared nostrils.

As if sensing how close she was to losing it, Petrov stilled. He slowly opened his right hand, his left still clutching his bloody knee.

Roger pushed up Petrov's sleeve, exposing a wrist harness with a third knife. He extracted that knife as well.

Claire glared at Petrov. "Anything else?"

He shook his head.

"Okay, Nick," Claire shouted.

Nick ran over and skidded to a halt beside Claire. He looked down at Petrov, his eyes wide. "Ohmigod, was he after Judy?"

"Goddamn right." Claire's fury at the young man's stupidity boiled over. "You idiot! How could you expose her to him like this? She was safe with us before you two ran off."

"No, she wasn't," Nick shot back. "Ivanov asked Mom where your family was staying, and not knowing what he was, she told him. I had to get Judy out of there before this guy came around. Nothing stops a Russian enforcer. He would've picked off that rookie cop, no problem."

Roger pushed himself off his knees to stand. "How the hell is a deserted cabin in the woods any better?"

"If they don't know about it, infinitely better. And we weren't going to stay here longer than tonight. I was going to keep us moving until I knew Petrov had been captured." Nick's face sobered as he stared down at Petrov. "But he was a lot closer on her trail than I thought."

He looked at Roger and Claire. "I'm sorry. I was trying to protect Judy. If anything had happened to her, I never would've forgiven myself."

Claire could see the young man's love for her daughter in that look. She shivered.

"We wouldn't have forgiven you either," Roger snapped.

"I understand, sir," Nick said solemnly.

"And what about your mother?" Roger asked. "You led the Russians to your house, then left her alone in there."

Nick bristled. "I didn't *know* I was leading them there. Besides, she serves Ivanov lunch and tea all the time. When he visits, he brings her flowers. And she doesn't know anything. He has no reason to hurt her."

"Just like he had no reason to hurt Stephanie?"

"He wasn't trying to hurt Stephanie, just to scare her, to send a warning to Dad, so Dad would relent and bring me into the business. But this idiot botched the assignment. Instead of just bumping into her and giving her a message for Dad, he sent her careening off into the woods and killed her instead. When you met Ivanov Thursday, he was leaving after apologizing to Dad. Fat lot of good that did."

Nick distractedly ran his hand through his hair, mussing it, and scanned the weapons on the ground. "How'd you do this?"

"Believe me, it wasn't easy." Roger handed Petrov's third knife to Claire, picked up the man's rifle and handgun, and joined her in aiming the handgun at the Russian. "You got any rope in that cabin?"

"Yeah, I do." Nick hurried back around the cabin.

When he returned with a coil of rope, Judy came with him, her hair disheveled and her coat open and flapping as if she had just thrown it on. She ran over to her mother and gripped Claire in a tight hug.

"Careful, honey, I'm holding a loaded gun." Claire put the safety on, slid it into her pocket then clamped her arms around Judy. Tears sprang to her eyes as she thought of how easily the situation could have ended in disaster.

Nick began looping the rope around Petrov's wrists.

Judy stepped back. She eyed the handgun Roger still held trained on the injured Russian. "Did you shoot him?"

"Your mother did."

With her mouth hanging open, Judy stared at Claire.

To hide her flustered state, Claire knelt on the icy ground to assess Petrov's knee. She used his knife to cut away the pants material. A shard of shattered kneecap poked out of the wound, which was bleeding profusely. The bleeding would have to be stopped if he was going to live long enough to give the police any information.

Claire turned to Judy. "Fetch some cloth from the cabin. Rags, anything."

As Judy raced away, Claire studied the tortured Russian's face closely for the first time. She couldn't feel sorry she had shot him, but she had to stifle an instinctive jolt of sympathy for the man's pain.

"Cooperate and I'll bind this wound. Otherwise, you'll bleed to death. Understand?"

He muttered something in Russian and looked away.

Returning from the cabin, Judy gave a handful of rags to Claire. Nick rose and took Judy into his arms.

Claire picked through the rags, searching for the cleanest one, then peered at Petrov. "Prepare yourself. This will hurt."

Petrov gritted his teeth.

Working as quickly as she could, she wrapped the rag tightly around Petrov's knee as he moaned with pain. She grabbed another rag and wrapped it over the first then leaned back to check her work. She cinched a tight knot in the second rag, eliciting a howl of pain from the man.

She quickly tied two more rags around the wound then glanced up at Roger. "We need to get him to a hospital fast."

Roger scooped up his rifle, trotted over to Petrov's snowmobile, fired it up, and drove it into the clearing. He and Claire lifted the injured man into the passenger seat then tied his bound hands to the rear safety bar. From his slumped shoulders, dejected expression, and pain-whitened face, the Russian looked like he would offer little resistance, but Claire wasn't going to take any chances.

"We have to get Petrov out of here," Claire said to Judy and Nick. "And Detective Silverstone's been hurt. We need to pick him up on the way back." She peered at Judy. "You feel confident driving one of these?"

"I think so. Nick taught me how before, and I drove one on an easy trail."

"Good. You ride with Nick until we get to Owen. Then Nick should take Owen as a passenger. You can drive Owen's snowmobile back."

Roger straddled Petrov's snowmobile, Claire ran to hers, and Judy and Nick climbed aboard theirs. Now that Claire's adrenaline rush was dissipating, the cold was seeping into her bones. With a violent shiver, she slapped her gloved hands together to get the blood moving in them, then started the engine.

The return trip to where Owen lay wounded was slower and less bumpy, but Petrov still moaned each time his snowmobile was jostled. By the time they reached the detective, Petrov's head was nodding with exhaustion from fighting the pain.

Owen struggled to his feet when he heard them approach. "You got him. Good work!"

"Did you reach anyone on your radio?" Claire shouted over the roar of the engines.

"Yes, an ambulance should be at the house by the time we get there." Owen pointed his chin at the injured Russian. "Looks like he'll need it more than me. I'll call on the way back to tell them not to send someone out here for me. Now, about my gun . . ."

"Oh, sorry." Claire fished it out of her pocket and handed it to Owen.

Owen opened the magazine. "Hell, it's been fired. That means paperwork, and I'll be the laughingstock of the station for letting you take it."

"You really had no choice," Roger said.

Owen scanned Petrov. "Whose bullet is in his leg?"

"Yours," Claire replied. "I mean from your gun. The rest of the bullets I fired missed."

Owen holstered the weapon. "I'm impressed, but I'll have to get the full story later. We need to get back." He pointed a finger at Nick. "And you, young man, are in a heap of trouble."

"Well, he'll be driving you back," Claire said, "so you can yell at him on the way."

Judy leapt off the seat behind Nick, ran to Owen's snowmobile and started it up. Roger and Nick helped Owen to the back of Nick's sled, then they all roared off again.

When they pulled into the Continos' backyard, Claire spotted Officer Ramstead pacing the patio, shoulders hunched against the cold. As they cut the engines, Ramstead hurried over to Owen.

Nick and Judy ran inside the house, presumably to find Angela.

Two ambulance crewmen lugging a stretcher followed Ramstead, but Owen pointed them toward Petrov.

Two other police officers, presumably Owen's backup, stepped out of a cruiser and joined them. The taller one said, "Sorry we didn't get here sooner, sir. We were in the middle of breaking up a drunken brawl when we got the call. We had to drop the combatants at the jail first."

Owen clamped his gloved hand on the officer's shoulder. "It's okay. These civilians did your job for you. But I'll need one of you to accompany this guy to the hospital. He's being charged with murder."

Ramstead helped Owen over to Petrov's side while the crewmen loaded the Russian onto the stretcher and started an IV. Claire gave details of how she had treated Petrov in answer to one of the crewmen's questions while Roger stood with his arm around her.

Owen waited for the ambulance crew to finish readying Petrov, then told him he was being arrested for murder and attempted murder. After reciting his rights, Owen asked, "Now, where's your boss?"

Claire hadn't thought it was possible for the Russian's face to get any whiter, but it did. Petrov clamped his lips tight and shook his head.

Owen leaned in close. "You're facing two murder raps and attempted murder of a law officer, these folks here, and those two young people. You cooperate with us, and you might get life in prison. You don't . . ." Owen shrugged meaningfully.

"Ivanov can get me in prison," Petrov said. "He will order someone to kill me."

"Not if we get to him first." Owen laid his hand on Petrov's shoulder. "We'll protect you."

Petrov looked doubtful. "No, I must say nothing."

"All right," Owen said. "I'll talk. First, we saw the black Range Rover parked down the street. You and Ivanov rode in it together." He stared at the Russian.

Petrov stared back.

"The car was empty when we saw it, so Ivanov must have come with you to the Continos' house."

Claire gasped.

Owen shot her a silencing look. "He hid somewhere when you went off on your chase," he continued, "and waited for you to notify him that the deed was done."

Owen turned to Ramstead. "Search his pockets for a cell phone."

"I already found it." Roger handed the phone to Ramstead.

Owen rubbed his chin as he stared at Petrov. "I bet you had a time limit in which to contact Ivanov, and that limit's been exceeded. So, he's left, and the Range Rover's gone now."

Petrov ground his teeth and looked away.

Owen turned again to Ramstead. "Put out an APB on the Range Rover." He gave him the license plate number.

As Ramstead made the call on his police radio, Owen refocused on Petrov. "Now, we need to figure out what direction he's traveling in. I'm guessing back to Denver. Right?"

Petrov looked away and winced. "I must go to hospital now." The additional wrapping the technicians had placed around his knee was soaked in blood.

Claire pondered the problem of tracking Ivanov, then had an idea.

"What about the Eagle County Airport? A lot of rich skiers, even from as close as Denver, fly their small planes into Eagle to avoid the traffic on I-70. From the amount of money transfers we saw on Anthony's computer, I bet Ivanov can afford to lease a private jet."

Petrov sucked in a breath, confirming Claire's guess.

"Eagle Airport it is." Owen waved his hand at the ambulance technicians. "You can take him now."

He signaled the taller backup cop to go with them.

While the technicians pushed Petrov's wheeled stretcher toward the ambulance, Nick and Judy ran out of the house.

"Where's Mom?" Nick asked Ramstead.

The police officer looked confused. "When I arrived and got no answer to my knock, I went in and searched the place. No one was in the house."

Owen frowned. "When did you get here?"

"About ten minutes after your radio call that you were hurt."

A sinking realization hit Claire in the pit of her stomach. "Oh, God. Do you suppose Ivanov took Angela with him?"

A look of horror flashed across Nick's face. "No. No! First Stephanie, then Dad, and now Mom?" He stumbled back as if he had been socked on the jaw, then he fell to his knees. A strangled howl escaped his lips.

Judy dropped to her knees beside him and threw her arms around him. She shot a beseeching look at her mother, as if asking, "What do I say to him?"

Claire opened her palms wide, signaling that she had no idea. What could you possibly say to someone threatened with the deaths of his whole family? The loss was too devastating to comprehend.

The ambulance left with its sirens wailing.

As the sound diminished in the distance, Owen spoke to Ramstead and the remaining backup cop. "We've got a Russian mob boss to chase, who is most likely holding this man's mother hostage." He indicated Nick, whose face was buried against Judy's shoulder. "We've got to notify all the jurisdictions on the way to the Eagle Airport—Frisco, state police for I-70, and Eagle County."

The backup cop's eyes went wide. Claire surmised this was the most exciting call this small-county cop had responded to in ages. Drunken brawls were more the standard fare in Summit County.

"Ramstead will drive me in his cruiser," Owen continued, "and you follow."

Ramstead glanced at the wounded arm Owen was cradling against his chest. "Shouldn't you go the hospital?"

"It's already stopped bleeding. I'm sticking with this until we've got Ivanov. C'mon." Owen stepped toward the driveway.

Nick scrambled to his feet and scrubbed his cheeks dry. "I'm going with you."

"No, you're not," Owen said, his jaw firm. "We're not taking civilians along on a high-speed chase."

"Then I'll follow in the Range Rover," Nick said. "My mother's in danger. She's the last member of my family left alive. You can't stop me from following unless you arrest me."

Owen paused, as if weighing the options. "Okay, arrest you, we will. Ramstead, I'll let you do the honors."

In the process of wiping away her tears, Judy said, "What? You're charging him with a crime? How can you be so cruel?"

Ramstead recited Nick's rights then listed the charges of kidnapping and obstruction of justice. He pulled out his handcuffs, but Owen stayed his hand.

"I think he'll cooperate. He's getting what he wants—to come with us. Just put him in the back of the cruiser."

As Ramstead led Nick to the car, Judy ran after them.

"Not her," Owen shouted.

Judy whirled and faced him, feet planted and hands on her hips. "Where Nick goes, I go."

"Oh no, you don't."

Ramstead opened the cruiser's rear door, and Nick slid onto the seat. As Ramstead started to close the door, Judy yanked his free arm, throwing him off balance. He stumbled back. Judy leapt into the car next to Nick and slammed the door shut.

Owen slapped his uninjured hand against his thigh in disgust and strode toward the car. "We don't have time for this foolishness!"

Claire took off after him.

Roger caught up with her. "Where're you going?"

"Where Judy goes, I go."

"What?" Owen stopped and turned, causing Claire to smack into him.

Claire backed up and met his angry stare eye-to-eye. "You should know me by now, Owen. Nothing will stop me from protecting my daughter."

NINETEEN:
FLYING TO THE AIRPORT

"GODDAMN MOTHER BEAR," OWEN muttered. "Get her out of the car, and you won't have to protect her."

Judy scrambled to fasten her seat belt then folded her arms and glared out the window at Owen and Claire.

"I'm sure you've seen that look on your daughter's face, Owen," Claire said. "You think any of us will be able to get her out without a fight? And you know I'll fight to get in there with her."

Owen blew out a disgusted breath. "Put your claws away. I'll get my ass kicked for this, but if we don't move it, Ivanov will escape. Get in the back with them."

He glanced at Roger. "I suppose you want to come along, too."

Roger grinned and took Claire's arm. "Where she goes, I go."

Owen pounded his fist on the roof of the cruiser. "You Hanovers are an impossible family. Six of us won't fit in one vehicle. You'll have to ride in the other cruiser."

With a slamming of doors and clicking of seat belts, they climbed into the two cruisers—Roger with the backup officer in his vehicle, Owen beside Ramstead in his, and Claire in the backseat next to Judy and Nick. Sirens wailing and lights flashing, the cars took off.

Owen told Ramstead to slow down when they passed the snowplow turnout at the end of the street. As he had predicted and Petrov had confirmed, the black Range Rover was gone. Owen waved Ramstead on.

While Ramstead drove through the neighborhood streets onto Highway 9, Owen rapid-fired instructions to the radio dispatcher, who relayed replies from the other jurisdictions.

Finally, he turned to Ramstead. "With Frisco police blocking traffic for us, we should be able to sail through there onto I-70. Hopefully, the two cruisers that state patrol is scrambling will join up with us close to Copper. I hope to catch Ivanov before he gets to the airport, but dispatch is alerting airport security just in case. Drive as fast as you can, but remember we've got civilians in the back seat."

"Yes, sir."

Owen cast a deprecating look into the backseat, checked that their seat belts were fastened, then faced the front again, crossed his arms and muttered, ". . . ing, stubborn troublemakers."

Claire thought she caught a note of admiration in the curse.

While Owen strategized with Ramstead, the two police cruisers sped north on Highway 9, then eased through the intersection with Swan Mountain Road that led to Keystone. Even at ten o'clock on a Sunday night, the traffic-lighted intersection was busy, and many cars had to maneuver to the side of the road to get out of the way. After the intersection, the road curved wide around

Lake Dillon, one of the water supply reservoirs for thirsty Denver residents on the other side of the Continental Divide.

Claire noticed Nick's pensive reflection in the window as he stared out at the ice-covered lake glowing in the moonlight. While she sympathized with what he was going through, it was time to get some answers from the young man, for Judy's sake at least.

After clearing her throat to get Judy and Nick's attention, Claire asked as gently as she could, "Nick, how long have you known about your father's work for, um, criminal elements?"

Judy squeezed his hand.

That action made Claire wonder. *How long has she known?*

Nick faced Claire and rubbed his thumb against the back of Judy's hand. "Only a couple of months. Mom and Stephanie never knew, though I'm sure Mom has figured it out by now."

He squirmed, as if what he had to say next would be difficult. "And Judy didn't know until I told her tonight. I should've told her earlier. Maybe then, you all wouldn't have been involved in this mess. I'm sorry."

Judy's head shot up, an angry glint in her eyes. "You think I would've left you if you told me? Did I leave you tonight? You don't have much faith in me, do you?"

Nick ran his hand through his hair, a gesture that reminded Claire so much of Roger that her throat choked up.

"I didn't mean that. It's just, I mean, I should . . ." Nick's gaze lit on Claire, pleading for her help.

She had a good idea what he meant. He wasn't worried Judy would leave him. He planned to leave her—to protect her. Claire's estimation of this young man rose a few notches.

She nodded in silent understanding to him and laid her hand on Judy's arm. "Judy, now's not the time to get into this. You two should talk about your relationship in a more private place, and at a time when you can focus on it. Nick's too worried about his mother right now."

Judy looked at Nick, then back at Claire and pursed her lips. "You're right, Mom. As always."

That "always" sounded a little bitter. But Claire brushed it off as she returned to her original question. "So you found out a couple of months ago . . ."

"After Gregori Ivanov started pressuring Dad to bring me into the business, Dad sat down and had a long talk with me. He was in too deep to get out, but he was hoping to save me."

Owen had stopped talking to Ramstead and sat still, or as still as he could with the car rolling from side to side with Ramstead's sweeping turns. He seemed to be listening intently to Nick.

A guilty look swept across Nick's face. "In fact, the day Stephanie was killed, Dad and I weren't really snowcat skiing at Copper."

"I wondered about that," Claire said. "Your ski clothes were too dry when you arrived at the medical center."

Nick nodded. "We needed to get away from Stephanie and Mom, and Ivanov and the others, to figure out how we were going to keep me out of the business. If we hadn't been so busy planning how to save my hide, maybe we could've saved Stephanie's." Nick's voice caught, and he gazed out the window again.

His reflected face showed a despondent frown.

Another victim of survivor's guilt. "But you said that Ivanov said Stephanie's death was an accident."

Owen turned at this news and raised his eyebrows at Claire.

Nick wheeled around, his eyes black pools of guilt and anger. "But if I'd said yes to Ivanov, she'd be alive today."

"Oh, Nick." Judy's gaze overflowed with love and sympathy. She put her arms around him and drew him into a hug.

Claire quickly filled Owen in on what Nick had said about Petrov's botched scare-job. As she was finishing, Ramstead made a screeching left turn that threw her against Judy and Nick. He barreled down Frisco's Main Street. Flashing lights signaled police roadblocks at each of the stop signs, allowing Ramstead to race through the town. Another screeching left turn directed the cruiser onto I-70.

Claire checked out the back window. The cruiser Roger rode in was right behind them. *What can I say to Nick to assuage his guilt?*

"Nick, you can't beat yourself up about Stephanie's death. It wasn't your fault. Ivanov's the one who ordered Petrov to run into her. The blame rests fully on his shoulders."

"Or Dad's." Nick glared at Claire as if daring her to deny him.

Claire stared right back at Nick. "That's what your Dad thought, what he tried to convey in the suicide note, but he's not to blame either. As you said, he was caught in a situation that he couldn't get out of."

Claire wasn't sure she believed that. If Anthony had ratted on Ivanov years ago, maybe none of this would've happened. Or maybe Anthony would've been killed then, instead of committing suicide two days ago. And if Ivanov hired expensive lawyers and wiggled out of the charges, or most of them, he could've been back on the street in a few years. With Anthony out of the way, Ivanov would have had a clear shot at recruiting Nick—probably using the same tactics of threatening his family.

Even if the police caught the wily Russian tonight, the man could weasel out of prison in a few years and target the Continos again. And if Judy married Nick, she would be threatened, too. Claire nibbled her lip. *I've got to get her away from this family.*

She glanced at Nick and realized he had been studying her.

"I know what you're thinking," he said. "And you're right. Ivanov seems to be willing to kill my whole family to get his hands on me. A family he's supposedly been friends with for years. For all I know, Mom could be dead right now."

"I doubt that, Nick," Owen said. "He's not thinking of you right now. With your father dead, he doesn't need you as a pawn. He's just trying to save his own skin. I'm sure he suspects we're closing in on him. So, he'll keep your mother alive as a hostage, take her with him out of the country. Which we'll try our best to prevent."

Nick's eyes widened as he sucked in a breath between clenched teeth. "I surrender. Ivanov can have me. As long as he lets my mother go."

"No!"

Before Judy could say more, everyone was thrown to the left as the cruiser followed the wide, sweeping right turn the highway made past Copper Mountain. The lights of two state patrol cars winked in the distance before them.

Owen got on the radio to talk to them while Ramstead pushed the accelerator in an attempt to catch up. Claire craned her neck to see the speedometer—then was sorry she had. The needle wavered past ninety.

She tried to make sense of what Owen was saying into the radio. He seemed to be talking to the Eagle County Sheriff's Office, but instead of talking about the Eagle Airport, they kept referring to the Vail Valley Jet Center.

What the heck is that?

Judy and Nick had lapsed into silence and sat clutching each other. Claire decided they needed a respite, and not wanting to interrupt Owen's important conferencing, she sat back and waited for a break in the conversation.

The cruiser accelerated down the incline coming out of Vail Pass, gaining on the two state patrol cars in front of them.

Finally, Owen put down the radio mike and checked the speedometer. "Keep it under eighty. We've got things under control for now."

Ramstead nodded and squeezed the brakes gently. Down at the bottom of a steep decline, the lights of East Vail winked into view.

Owen faced the occupants in the backseat. "Okay, here's what's going on. Eagle County cops have searched the Vail Valley Jet Center—"

"What's that?" Claire asked.

"The private jet facility at the airport," Owen answered. "The cops searched that parking lot and the public airport lots. No black Range Rover matching our description. They're working with airport security now to get into the locked car garages at the Jet Center so they can check those."

"How many are there?" Claire asked.

"Fifty. A valet's supposed to take all the cars in and out of the garages, but if Ivanov knows the airport, he might've been able to get into a garage unobserved. But we think he's on the highway somewhere between us and the airport. State patrol's got a couple of squad cars coming the other way from Eagle, searching for a black Range Rover on this side of the highway."

"What if he manages to get on the plane with Mom?" Nick asked. "Can we stop them from taking off? Shut down the airport?"

"The airport can't shut down flight operations yet. One more commercial flight's coming in. It's an American Airlines flight from Los Angeles due to arrive at ten, but it's running late. The airport authorities tried to divert it, but it's already past Salt Lake City, it doesn't have enough fuel for DIA, and the other regional mountain airports are either closed for the night or the pilot has no experience landing at them." Owen paused. "Nick, do you know if Ivanov's got a pilot's license?"

"I don't think he does."

Owen rubbed his chin. "Okay, if he doesn't, and he's contacted his pilot to get his jet ready, and that pilot's not crooked, he'll file a flight plan. Then we can figure out which jet is Ivanov's."

"Smart," Claire said. "Then airport security can hold that pilot and plane."

"Precisely."

"Black Range Rover near mile marker one fifty-eight," a voice reported from the radio.

"Gotcha!" Owen whirled and grabbed the radio. "Let me know when you've got a plate ID."

He faced the backseat again. "One of those two cruisers will pull a U-turn at the next exit, catch up to the Range Rover, and read the license plate. The other will keep coming our way to make sure we don't miss another black Range Rover."

"Won't the appearance of a police car alert Ivanov that we're chasing him?" Claire asked.

"The cruiser will pass him and keep on going, as if it's after someone else."

A highway sign appeared in front of their car, advertising the upcoming Dowds Junction exit at mile marker one seventy-one. Claire figured they were about ten minutes behind Ivanov—if the Range Rover was his. She leaned forward, anxious to hear the license plate report.

Owen tapped Ramstead's shoulder and pointed at the two state patrol cars in front, which were pulling away from them. Ramstead accelerated.

The radio crackled. "Got him. The plate matches."

Owen keyed the mike. "How many occupants in the car?"

"Only one spotted, who seems to match your description."

Judy squeezed Nick's hand. "What about Mrs. Contino?"

"She could still be in the car," Owen said. "Maybe tied up and lying down on the back seat."

Nick's eyes went wide. "She'll be terrified."

Another voice reported in, and added, "…in quiet pursuit. Should spot him soon."

"That's the other state cruiser that was traveling east. He turned and is following Ivanov now. We aren't going to approach until he gets off the highway and through Eagle. That cruiser in front and a couple of airport security vehicles will set up a blockade on the airport access road."

Nick's forehead furrowed. "If he tries to crash through the blockade, my mother could be hurt."

Owen tapped the mike against his chin. "There's that risk. But we think he'll be too smart for that. Most likely, when he sees the

272

blockade, he'll pull a U-turn. By then, we'll have set up our own blockade behind him. He'll have nowhere to go."

It seemed like a smart plan to Claire. Hopefully it would work—and result in Ivanov peacefully surrendering, so no one would get hurt. But that was asking for a lot.

Judy and Nick looked drained, faces drawn with worry. The knuckles of the hands they held clutched together had gone white.

They probably didn't have any feeling left in their fingers, Claire thought and wished she had Roger nearby so she could hold his hand. She glanced at the Summit County cruiser behind them. How much had that officer told Roger about what was going on?

Owen chattered on the radio, making plans for the two blockades and getting status reports on Ivanov's location from the two state patrol cars that now had Ivanov's black SUV sandwiched between them. They each were staying about a quarter mile away to keep his suspicions from being aroused.

Ramstead eased up on the accelerator.

"What's happening?" Claire asked. "Why are we slowing down?"

"We're about three miles behind him now," Owen said. "We'll stay that far back to give us time to set up the blockade behind him after we all get off the highway. The exit's coming up soon.

"Now, I need you three to cooperate once we stop. There's no time for arguments. This car won't be part of the blockade. We'll swap Mr. Hanover for myself, and Ramstead here will drive you four out of shooting range. And you'll stay put and do whatever he says, right?" He peered at each of them in turn.

Nick and Judy nodded, and Claire said, "Yes, sir."

Owen stared at Claire a little longer. When she didn't flinch, he seemed satisfied and turned around.

He pointed out the Eagle exit to Ramstead. "We'll go through the roundabout then turn right on Highway 6. Right outside of town there's a mile stretch with no side streets. Airport security and the first state cruiser will set up on the other side. We'll stop at this end, do the swap, then you take these civilians up the nearest side road. I'll radio you when it's over."

Ramstead nodded as he exited the interstate. The expression on his face reflected in the rearview mirror showed disappointment that he would miss out on the action.

In a way, Claire was disappointed, too, but felt glad Judy would be out of harm's way. And Roger. Her lips twitched. Of course, he was probably thinking the same thing about her.

As Ramstead drove through the roundabout, then headed west, the streets of the dark town were deserted, though lights showed in some of the condo and hotel windows. Claire checked her watch. Almost eleven. Sunday night in the small mountain town was dead.

She cringed. *Bad word choice.*

After they left town, Owen pointed to a lone side street on the left. "Pull over there."

The other Summit County cruiser pulled in behind them, and Roger hopped out.

The state patrol car that had been in front of them positioned itself across the two-lane highway, past the point where the side street intersected.

With a last "stay put," Owen got out and ran to the cruiser behind them. He gave Roger a pat on the shoulder as the two passed each other.

As soon as Roger closed the door, Ramstead took off down the side road then turned around about a mile away. He put the car in park and turned off the lights but left the engine running and the heater going. His fingers began a nervous staccato on the steering wheel.

Roger turned to Claire. "So, as I understand it, Ivanov's between the two blockades, but we don't know if Angela's with him."

"Right, but—"

"He spotted us and made a U-turn," a voice on the radio said. "He's headed your way. We're in pursuit."

The two cruisers at their end must have turned on their lights. Red and blue flashed in the distance in front of them.

Everyone strained forward to hear the radio.

Owen's voice came on. "We see him. He's coming straight at us. He's not slowing down . . . Shoot at the tires, not the vehicle! We don't want to harm the hostage."

Three shots rang out. Tires screeched.

Claire held her breath, hoping she wouldn't hear the sound of a crash next.

"He drove off the highway, went around us," Owen said. "One tire's out. Ramstead, he's headed your way!"

"Shit!" Ramstead flipped on the lights and positioned the cruiser across the road. He slammed on the brake, unlocked the doors, and pulled out his gun. "Everyone out. There's a flashlight in the glovebox. Get in the ditch."

Nick jumped out, letting cold air blast into the car, and pulled on Judy's arm. "C'mon!"

Claire and Roger ran to catch up with the young couple. Roger beamed the flashlight into the ditch beside the road. About three feet deep, the bottom looked to be a jumbled mix of weeds, rocks, ice and snow.

Nick slid into the ditch with a clatter of loose gravel and frozen snow clods, and helped Judy down. He offered his hand to Claire.

Holding on, she scooted down on her bottom then stood. One foot slipped on an ice puddle, and her sore knee buckled. A white hot flash of pain shot up her leg.

Nick steadied her, then pulled her and Judy beside him.

Roger slipped down the embankment next to Claire, scattering his own little avalanche of dirt and snow.

Claire popped her head up over the rim of the ditch. When Roger tried to pull her down again, she pushed him away. "I need to see what happens."

"If shooting starts, I'll knock you down." Gritting his teeth, Roger turned off the flashlight.

Owen's voice sounded from the radio in Ramstead's cruiser, "You in position, Ramstead?"

Legs planted, Ramstead stood behind the cruiser, licking his lips and aiming his service pistol down the road. He keyed his shoulder radio. "Yes, sir. Civilians are in the ditch."

A rough, lumbering rattle made Claire whip her head around. The black Range Rover barreled down the road with a flat front tire flopping against the rim. Three cruisers followed close behind with lights flashing and sirens blaring.

As the SUV neared and its headlights lit up Ramstead, he held up an arm. "Stop!"

Ivanov kept coming.

Claire clenched her fists.

Ramstead fired a slug through the Range Rover's front grill, then leapt to one side, rolled, and came up on one knee, gun still pointed at the SUV.

Steam poured out of the punctured radiator. The Range Rover skidded and swerved. Its speed slowed, but it still slammed into the side of Ramstead's cruiser.

Owen's voice came out of Ramstead's car radio. "Good work, Ramstead. Stay put and cover us."

Ramstead kept his gun aimed at Ivanov.

Owen's cruiser and the state patrol car screeched to a halt behind the Range Rover. The three officers ran out, all but Owen with pistols drawn. They crept along either side of the Range Rover.

Claire could see Ivanov's head resting on the steering wheel. *Has he given up? Is he injured? Or only pretending and hiding a weapon?* She held her breath.

The state patrolman and the officer who drove Owen opened the driver and passenger front doors simultaneously, yelling, "Freeze!" then, "Hands up!"

Ivanov slowly raised his hands. They were empty.

With a whoosh, Claire let out the breath she had been holding.

Nick lurched forward, but Roger pulled him back. "Wait, Nick, until they've got him cuffed."

"But Mom—"

"A few seconds won't make a difference."

Within those seconds, the police cuffed Ivanov, searched him, and laid him out on the road with Ramstead's boot on Ivanov's back and his gun aimed at the Russian's head. A cocky grin played across the man's lips.

Owen opened the far back door of the Range Rover and looked in. He called out, "Nickolas Contino," then leaned into the vehicle.

Nick bolted out of the ditch, followed by Judy, Claire, and Roger. They ran over to the car, and Nick wrenched open the near back door.

Angela Contino sat up, rubbing her wrists, where Owen had just finished cutting off a rope. She held out her arms for Nick.

Nick gathered her in a fierce hug. "You all right, Mom?"

"I am now, honey."

They looked at each other, tears running down their cheeks, then clutched each other again.

Claire pulled Roger and Judy away. "Let's give them a moment of privacy."

She walked over to Owen, who was reciting rights to Ivanov. The man lay in the road cursing his fate, Petrov, and the Continos. At least that's what she assumed he was doing, since the names were all she could make out among the angry Russian words.

When Ivanov saw her, he spat at her and resumed his cursing.

Claire kicked dirt over the glob of already-freezing spittle in front of her shoe. For a second, she was tempted to do the same to Ivanov but realized the impotent Russian mob boss wasn't worth the effort.

She put her hand on Owen's shoulder. "You did it. You caught him."

Owen shot her a wry grin. "Yep, and Ramstead will be impossible to live with for a couple of weeks."

He turned serious. "But we wouldn't have figured out who killed Stephanie Contino and Boyd Naylor—or why—without your help." He offered his hand.

A warm glow of pride suffused Claire while she shook hands. "Thanks."

She turned to the Range Rover, and saw that Nick and Angela had climbed out. Judy wrapped her arms around the two of them. Claire frowned. *Now, on to problem number two.*

TWENTY:
WHAT'S BEST FOR JUDY

CLAIRE AWOKE MONDAY MORNING to a ringing in her ears and a muzzy, thick tongue. She glanced at the clock. Almost ten. *Boy, we slept in.* Of course, after the drive back from Eagle and giving statements to Owen, they hadn't gotten back to the townhouse until well past two a.m. She still felt bushed. *What woke me up?*

The doorbell rang.

Ah, ha. She crawled out of bed and limped into the closet to fetch her robe.

Roger shifted then opened one eye to peer at her. "Why're you up?"

"Someone's at the front door." She gave him a kiss. "I'm going to answer it."

With a groan, Roger sat up. "I'll go with you."

They padded down the stairs in their slippers and opened the door.

Nick stood on the stoop. Wearing a sheepish expression, he looked them over. "Sorry to get you out of bed. May I come in?"

Roger waved him in and took his coat while Claire loaded the coffeepot.

Nick ran his hand through his already-mussed hair. "Mom and I have been up all night talking. We decided we need to get away for a while, where Ivanov's mob can't reach us."

"Isn't the Russian mob worldwide?" Claire asked.

"They're not in Sicily," Nick said. "Mom has cousins there who said they'd put us up."

"Don't you have charges pending?" Roger asked. "Kidnapping and obstruction of justice, if I remember correctly."

Nick nodded. "I talked to the DA this morning. Detective Silverstone lobbied to drop the kidnapping charge, said Judy went along willingly and he probably would have done the same thing if she were his girlfriend. And I agreed to community service in exchange for dropping the obstruction charge. I'll be contacting Dad's business associates to ask them for donations to the Summit Foundation, and I'll put in some hours doing hands-on work, too."

Claire set out coffee cups. "How can you leave, then?"

"I have a year to fulfill my obligation, and the work doesn't have to be done here. The DA agreed that it's probably a good idea for Mom and me to disappear for a while."

"What about your classes?"

Shoving his hands in his pockets, Nick frowned. "I'll have to wash out this semester. If I explain what happened to the dean of the business school, he should allow me to maintain my active student status even if I drop all my spring classes. Hopefully I can pick up my studies again in the fall somewhere else, maybe even Italy."

Roger quirked an eyebrow at Claire then asked Nick, "So you plan to stay in Italy?"

Nick's returning stare was both defiant and desolate. "If we have to."

Claire leaned on the counter, bolstering her confidence to ask the question they had all been tiptoeing around. "What about you and Judy?"

"That's why I'm here," Nick replied. "I need to talk to her."

Roger gave a nod, his face serious, as if anticipating Judy's reaction to Nick's news. "I'll wake her up."

While Roger headed downstairs, Claire poured herself a cup of coffee. "You want coffee, Nick?"

"No, thank you. I've already drunk a whole pot of Mom's tea."

Claire sat on a stool by the counter. "I want you to know that Roger and I think you're a fine young man, and we know you and Judy care a great deal about each other."

She paused. *How should I phrase what I need to say next?*

Nick's dark eyes were wells of sadness. "But—"

Claire's heart went out to the miserable young man. "Judy is our daughter, and we worry about her safety." She laid her hand on his arm. "As I know you do, too."

"Yes," Nick whispered.

Footsteps signaled that Roger and Judy were ascending the stairs. Claire picked up her coffee cup. "I know you'll do the right thing.

And if it helps you to know, we'll provide whatever comfort and support Judy needs to get through this."

With a gulp, Nick said, "That does help. Thank you."

Judy entered the room, sleepy-eyed, barefoot, and wearing her sheep-print flannel pajamas. As Nick's gaze swept toward her, it was obvious that everyone else in the room was forgotten by the couple.

While Judy walked over to hug Nick, Claire poured Roger a cup of coffee. "Let's go watch some TV." She pointed with her chin toward their bedroom door.

Claire followed Roger up the stairs. When she turned to close the door, she saw Nick pulling Judy down to sit on the sofa, his lips drawn into a determined line. She wished she could protect Judy from what she was about to hear, that she could stop her daughter's heart from breaking.

She sighed and shut the door.

Roger had turned on CNN. The two of them sat on the bed and quietly sipped coffee, until Claire lost patience with the depressing stories of war, terrorism, and disasters and switched the channel to a game show.

"You think he's breaking up with her?" Roger asked.

Claire nodded. "And it'll make them both miserable."

"I wonder . . ."

"Wonder what?" Claire scanned his face.

"If they really need to break up. After all, Ivanov's in jail."

"But what about the rest of his gang? And the whole Russian mob? Somebody's bound to target Nick. He's smart to get out of the country and to put some distance between himself and Judy."

"I suppose." But Roger didn't sound convinced.

Raised voices filtered up from downstairs. Though Claire ached to know what the love-struck couple was saying, she bumped up the volume on the TV to drown them out. Soon the front door slammed.

Judy burst through their doorway moments later, with tears running down her cheeks. She collapsed on the bed, sobbing.

Roger turned off the TV and retrieved a box of tissues from the bathroom.

Claire stroked her daughter's hair and waited for the storm to abate. Finally, as the sobs diminished, she asked, "Want to talk about it, dear?"

Judy sat up and swiped at her nose. "Nick's being totally unreasonable. He said he's going to Sicily and I shouldn't wait for him to return. He said I should date other people."

She shoved herself off the bed and paced the room. "He has no right to tell me that. I love him! I told him I'd wait as long as it takes. Or go to Sicily, if I have to. But he refuses to tell me where he's staying or how to contact him."

Claire shot a worried glance at Roger. The conversation between Nick and Judy hadn't gone exactly as she thought it would. "Did he try to break up with you?"

"Yes, but I refused. I said I'd break off the relationship only if he looked me in the eye and told me he didn't love me." She stopped and stood with hands on her hips.

"And—" Claire prompted.

A triumphant gleam lit Judy's eyes. "He couldn't do it. He loves me and I love him. We belong together. It's as simple as that."

Oh, God. "What did Nick say to that?"

Judy waved her hand in the air. "Said Ivanov's organization will go after him, that I wouldn't be safe with him."

"He's right, you know."

"I'll take my chances."

Claire hated to do it, but it was time to sink the knife in deep. "Will you take chances with his life, honey, with the life of the man you love?"

Judy stared at her. "What do you mean?"

"If the Russian mob gets its hands on either you or his mother, kidnaps you, and threatens to kill you, what will he do?"

Judy opened her mouth then hesitated.

"He said it in the car last night," Claire continued, "in reference to his mother, but he would do the same for you. He'd buckle under and go to work for the mob to save your life. Do you want that for him, Judy? A life of crime?"

The realization slapped Judy in the face, wiping clean her look of defiance and replacing it with horror. "No. God, no."

Knife set, time to twist it. Claire swallowed back tears. Once again, the old adage of "this will hurt me more than it hurts you" applied.

"Then if you love him, you have to let him go."

Judy's face crumpled as the tears began flowing again.

Roger gathered her in his arms.

She stared at Claire over his shoulder. "Dammit, Mom, why does doing the right thing have to hurt so much?"

Claire walked into the family room that afternoon, where Judy lay under an afghan on the sofa, staring blankly at a black-and-white movie on cable TV and clutching a pillow to her chest. A pile of used tissues sat next to the box on the coffee table.

I knew she would just sit around and mope. Claire hadn't wanted to leave Judy alone to go skiing with Roger, but he insisted, saying Judy needed some time alone to accept her situation. Busy brushing snow and ice off their ski equipment in the garage, he couldn't see how miserable Judy had made herself while they were gone.

Claire sat on the sofa arm and swept a lock of Judy's hair off her forehead, then left her arm resting on her daughter's shoulder. "I'm going to buy some things to make a thank you basket for Owen Silverstone."

"Why?"

"If not for him and his office catching Ivanov, you or Angela Contino could be hostages or dead right now. I want him to know we appreciate having our daughter safe in our arms again."

"Okay, I'll be here when you get back."

"You're going with me."

Judy shot Claire a "what-are-you-kidding?" look.

"You need to get up and do something to take your mind off this situation with Nick, and I want some help picking out stuff."

Judy returned her gaze to the TV. "I'd rather stay here."

"I know. But I'd rather you didn't." Claire stood and offered her hand. "C'mon. I'll keep bugging you, and you won't be able to hear the rest of the movie anyway."

Judy let out a monumental sigh, then threw off the afghan and sat up. "All right, already. Give me half an hour to shower and dress."

An hour later, the two of them were downtown in a sporting goods store. Claire picked up a boxed set of double-walled plastic beer mugs with trout flies embedded between the walls. *Perfect.*

She walked over to Judy, who was studying the small gifts in a glass display case by the cash register.

"Owen's receptionist said he likes fly fishing, so I'll build the basket around that theme," Claire said. "He was drinking a beer at the fundraiser, so we'll get these and a twelve-pack of assorted Breckenridge Brewery beers."

Judy pointed at a pewter keychain in the display case with two pewter trout hanging off it. "What about this, too?"

"Great idea." Claire waved over a store employee and asked her to get out the keychain.

When the clerk saw their purchases, she picked up a bag of candy hanging on a rack on the other side of the register. "Giving a gift to a fisherman? How about these chocolate river rocks?"

"You are a smart saleswoman," Claire said with a smile. "Add them in."

They stopped at the brewery next to buy the beer, then Claire said to Judy, "Now, if we could find some fishing-related music that he could listen to while he's having a drink, the basket would be complete."

Judy raised a skeptical brow. "Fishing music? Good luck."

They walked into a music store, and Claire waved over a long-haired clerk with a ski-goggle tan. "I've got an unusual request. I'm putting together a gift basket for a fisherman, and I was wondering if you had any CDs with the word 'fish' in their titles, or by bands with 'fish' in their names, or even with a fish on the cover."

"That is unusual," the clerk replied. "Let me do a computer search." He typed "fish" into his computer, scanned the results, then flashed Claire a goofy grin. "I've got the perfect CD. *Ask the Fish* by Leftover Salmon."

He walked to a rack, flipped through a tray, and pulled out a CD with a large orange salmon on the cover. "It's even on sale because it was cut in 2001."

Claire took the CD. "What kind of music is it?"

"Cajun slamgrass."

"What the heck is that?"

"Sort of a mix of blues, Southern rock, and bluegrass."

Judy pursed her lips. "I doubt he'd like that kind of music, Mom."

Claire thought back to the times she had visited Silverstone in his office. "I remember hearing Tab Benoit playing in his office once. That's Southern blues, right?"

The clerk gave a nod. "Pretty close match to Leftover Salmon."

"And it matches the basket's theme," Claire said. "At least it's not punk rock or that stuff they were playing in Sherpa & Yeti's."

The music clerk's eyes widened in surprise, and he gave Claire the once-over, as if he couldn't believe she had been in the nightclub.

Claire handed him the CD. "We'll take it."

Claire and Judy returned to the house, where Claire dug through the supplies she had brought with her to find a suitably sized basket and packaging materials. After constructing the gift, she dragged an unwilling Judy with her to visit Owen at the Summit County Justice Center.

He looked up from his computer when they walked in and watched Claire place the basket on the center of his desk. "What's this?"

"A small appreciation gift from us." Claire waved Judy into Owen's visitor chair and borrowed the other detective's visitor chair for herself. "Go ahead. Open it."

Rubbing his chin, Owen said, "We're not supposed to accept gifts over fifty dollars from private citizens. It could be misconstrued as a bribe by defense attorneys."

Claire did some quick mental calculations, leaving out the basket. That was packaging, after all. "You're safe. It's under the limit."

Owen untied the brown raffia bow and opened up the dark green cellophane. As his gaze swept over the contents of the basket, he started to chuckle. "You've got me pegged. How did you find out I was a fly fisherman?"

"Your receptionist told me." Claire glowed with the delight she always felt when a basket recipient obviously appreciated the contents. "So you like it?"

"You bet. Thanks. I've got fishing gear, clothes, and books up the wazoo, but no one's thought to give me fish glasses or a keychain. And what's this?" He read the CD cover and laughed. "Should be interesting. I like bluegrass."

Claire flashed a triumphant grin to Judy.

Judy rolled her eyes and sank deeper into her chair.

Owen moved the basket to the side of his desk and rubbed his hands together. "And I've got some interesting news for you. We took a DNA sample from Petrov and put a rush analysis on it." He leaned back in his chair and laced his hands behind his head. "Perfect match with the DNA on the cigarette butt we found on the ski slope."

Claire flashed him a thumbs-up. "Aren't you glad we went back to search the slope?"

"Yep." He reached behind him and pulled a large plastic bag off the floor that contained a pair of brown loafers. "Recognize these? We found them among Petrov's belongings when we searched his hotel room."

Claire studied them. "They sure look like the pair I saw on the intruder at Boyd's trailer."

Owen nodded and returned the shoes to the floor. "That little piece of evidence, Judy's eyewitness account, the DNA match, and the fact that Petrov's ski clothes match Boyd Naylor's drawing are enough to put the final nails in Petrov's coffin. And he knows it. We're charging him with murder one for Stephanie's death, which is a capital crime. And we're analyzing fibers, prints, and other evidence from Ivanov's Range Rover, even found some blood under the hood grill. We're sure Petrov used it to murder Boyd Naylor. Once we've got a solid case for that one, we'll file the second murder one charge. When we told him all that this morning, he started squirming."

He leaned forward, elbows on his desk. "Here's a bit of information you'll find interesting. When we told Petrov that the list of charges against him would include attempted murder of Judy and Nick, he insisted he never intended to kill either one of them."

"Then why the hell was he following them to the cabin with a rifle strapped to his back?" Claire asked.

"He also had a flask of ether and some rags, as we discovered later. He intended to sneak up on them and knock them out or use the gun to force them to administer the ether to themselves, so he could kidnap Judy and hand her over to Ivanov."

"What did Ivanov want with me?" Judy asked.

"He was going to hold you at his place until Petrov got out of the country. Then he was going to release you to Nick. As Petrov said, they didn't want to piss off Nick. They were trying to recruit him, after all."

Judy frowned. "Kidnapping me would piss him off."

A wry smile cracked Owen's lips. "Ivanov's home in Denver is palatial, with an indoor swimming pool and sauna and a massage therapist and gourmet chef on staff. Petrov said you would have been well taken care of."

"Darn, Mom," Judy said to Claire, "look what you made me miss."
Claire snorted.

"What Petrov said made a lot of sense," Owen continued, "and our cases for those two attempted murder charges were weak. However, the charge for the attempt on my life, yours, Claire, and your husband's will definitely stick, with all of us as eyewitnesses. A jury would have no problem recommending the death penalty for a murderer who also tried to kill a cop. Petrov's sweating, knows even a passel of high-priced mob lawyers would have a hard time seeding doubt in a jury with all the evidence we've got. He says he wants to cut a deal with the DA in exchange for fingering Ivanov as the one who ordered him to do it."

"Wasn't Petrov afraid Ivanov would have him killed in prison?" Claire asked.

Silverstone nodded. "I explained how we could protect him, with a new identity, even in prison, and transfer him to a facility out-of-state, among other things. By the time I finished, I was able to convince Petrov his chances of living were higher by cooperating with us than by keeping his mouth shut."

Judy sat up straighter. "So that means Ivanov will be in prison for a long time."

"Maybe, maybe not. We're going after bigger fish"—Owen pointed at the gift basket and grinned—"than Ivanov. Between Petrov fingering Ivanov for murder and what Denver PD will reconstruct about Ivanov's mob activities from Anthony Contino's computer disk, it won't be long before good old Gregori knows he's screwed, too. The Russian mob will be a lot more worried about him and what he knows about the organization than they will be about a semiretired hit man. They'll be trying their darnedest to kill him before he talks. We're hoping that over time, we can convince him to cut a deal himself."

"A deal for what?" Claire asked.

"To rat out his bosses—the ringleaders of the Russian mob nationwide, maybe even worldwide—in exchange for saving his own hide."

"My God," Claire said. "I didn't realize this case would have such huge repercussions."

"And repercussions here, too." Owen said. "Think of all the publicity this will generate for us." He swept his hand in the air as if defining a newspaper headline. "Small Summit County Sheriff's Office Cracks Open Nationwide Russian Mob. We may even get those salary raises that have been on hold for two years." A satisfied smile brightened his face.

"I hope so, Owen," Claire said. "You deserve a raise."

"Are you saying this may mean the end of the Russian mob," Judy asked, "at least in the United States?"

"Very likely," Owen said. "At the least, we'll drive whatever fragments remain into hiding."

"Is Judy in any danger still?" Claire asked. "From these fragments, for instance?"

"I can't imagine why the mob would bother with her. Petrov only went after her because she could place him in the area when Stephanie Contino was killed. But he knows we've got him cold even without her testimony. Ivanov's main interest was keeping Anthony Contino's lips sealed by using Nick for leverage. But Contino's computer will do the talking for him."

Judy scooted forward to the edge of her seat, hope blooming in her face. "So, what about their threat to Nick?"

"Judy, they'll be too busy trying to save their own skins to go after him." Owen held up a finger. "However, this will all take time. Months, in fact. Nickolas Contino called me a bit ago and said he and his mother were leaving the country. That's probably a smart thing to do, until we can convince Ivanov to spill the beans and we round up his associates."

"Will Nick be able to return in time for fall semester?" Judy's hands gripped the arms of her chair.

Owen thought for a moment. "Possibly."

Judy sucked in a breath and whipped her head around to look at Claire, eyes bright with joy. "Do you know what this means?"

With sudden clarity, Claire realized this was the moment. The moment her daughter became lost to her, or to her influence, at least. Judy would go to Nick and convince him she would be safe with him. She would wait for him to return from Sicily, then they would marry and start a life of their own. She was perched on the edge of the nest, ready for her final long flight away to her chosen mate.

But Claire wasn't ready. She would never be ready to release her only daughter. What mother is? With her heart breaking, Claire answered, "Yes, dear. I know."

Judy leapt up from her chair. "We've got to drive over to the Continos now, before they leave for Denver." She held out her hand to Owen. "Thanks, Detective Silverstone." Without a glance back to her mother, she headed down the hallway.

Claire got up more slowly to offer her hand to Owen.

He pointed his chin down the hallway. "What was that all about?"

"Nick tried to break up with Judy, afraid he'd always be in danger from the Russian mob, and he didn't want to put her in danger. But from what you said, that won't be a problem anymore. So, there's no reason for them not to marry now."

Owen's gaze slid to the photo of his own young daughter, then to Claire. "You'll miss her, won't you?"

Claire offered him a sad smile. "That's a parent's job, isn't it? To raise a child strong enough to leave and break our hearts."

Claire walked in the front door of the townhouse alone.

Roger looked up from a mystery book. Claire had brought it to Breckenridge to read but hadn't had time to crack it open. "Where's Judy?"

"I left her at the Continos' house."

Roger raised his eyebrows in surprise. "I thought she and Nick broke up."

Claire sank onto the sofa next to him. "The reason they broke up is gone now." She explained what Owen had told her and Judy. "So Judy and Nick can get together again."

She sighed, laid her head back against the sofa, and closed her eyes. She felt the soft pressure of Roger's lips against hers and returned the kiss automatically. She opened her eyes.

Roger's expression was serious. "How do you feel about that?"

"I feel like she's being ripped out of my arms. But, I know it's right. I can see the love flowing between those two. They're perfect for each other." Claire opened her hands and looked down at her empty palms. "It's time for me to let go. I can't protect her anymore."

Roger leaned back. "She'll be all right. Nick will make sure she's safe."

Images of Judy rushed through Claire's mind—getting on the plane to go off to France alone, coming in exhausted after helping the Continos plan Stephanie's funeral, driving her own snowmobile back from the miner's cabin where she had almost been killed.

"You know, Judy's pretty damn competent. She can protect herself."

Roger turned and flashed a grin. "I was wondering when you would realize that." He patted her hand. "You raised her up right."

"I just wish she wasn't so all-fired independent. Like that tattoo!"

"It's not so bad—small, and kinda pretty."

Claire sat up, folded her arms, and tilted her head. "Pretty, huh? Think I should get one? Maybe a little rose, right here?" She tapped the top of her right breast.

Roger reached over and unbuttoned the top button of her shirt. He planted a kiss on the soft skin of her left breast. "No, here."

Claire burst out laughing and threw her arms around Roger. *God, I love this man.* She reveled in the familiar feel of his hands roaming her back under her shirt as they got down to some serious necking.

The front door swung open and Judy stepped in.

Claire drew away from Roger and hastily buttoned her blouse. *Judy sure has a knack for throwing water on the flame.*

Judy didn't seem to notice, though. Eyes bright with excitement, she literally bounced into the room. "Nick and I are officially engaged." She let out a little whoop and twirled.

Claire jumped up and hugged Judy. "I'm excited for you."

Roger added his hug then asked, "When's the wedding?"

"Not until next summer. I knew you and Mom wouldn't want me to get married until I finished college. If Nick takes a couple of extra courses, he might be able to finish his MBA by then, too. Assuming he's back in school this fall."

Thoughts of flowers, venues, menus, and invitations whirled in Claire's head. "We can start planning the wedding now, though. We have all of this week left before you leave."

Judy's smile faded. "I'm afraid we don't. I've got less than an hour to pack my bags before Nick and his Mom pick me up. We changed my flight so I can fly with them to Sicily tonight and spend a few days with them before I go back to France."

Claire frowned. "I wish you'd consulted with us first."

Roger put his arm around Claire and squeezed her shoulder. "We would've agreed, though."

We would've? Claire shot a look at Roger. His calm, answering gaze made her stop and think a moment. *I just finished saying it was time to let her go, didn't I?*

She turned to Judy. "Yes, we would've. How can I help?"

Judy threw her arms around Claire and Roger. "You two are the greatest."

An hour later, Claire stood with Roger on the front stoop of the townhouse, waving goodbye to Judy as Nick backed the Continos' Range Rover out of the driveway. Claire felt wistful as they drove out of sight. Judy would be so far away and wouldn't return until June. But then she would spend the whole summer with her parents, planning her wedding.

Roger pulled Claire inside out of the cold air and shut the door. He put his arms around her and stepped back to look at her, a sly grin playing on his face. "Well, we've got a whole week ahead with just the two of us. Whatever will we do with ourselves?"

Claire kissed the tip of his nose. "How about starting with a bottle of wine and a soak in the hot tub?"

Roger smiled. "My thoughts exactly. Bathing suits optional."

THE END

Neil Groundwater

ABOUT THE AUTHOR

Beth Groundwater writes two mystery series for Midnight Ink, the Claire Hanover series and the RM Outdoor Adventures series. This book is the second book in the Claire Hanover gift basket designer series. The first, *A Real Basket Case*, was nominated for the 2007 Best First Novel Agatha Award after it was published in hardcover. Beth lives in Colorado and enjoys its many outdoor activities, including skiing and whitewater rafting. Contrary to what some readers think, she does not have a gift basket business of her own, but she enjoys creating gift baskets for family, friends, and charity auctions. Beth loves speaking to book clubs about her books in-person or via speakerphone or Skype. To find out more, please visit her website at bethgroundwater.com and her blog at bethgroundwater.blogspot.com.

www.MidnightInkBooks.com

From the gritty streets of New York City to sacred tombs in the Middle East, it's always midnight somewhere. Join us online at any hour for fresh new voices in mystery fiction.

At midnightinkbooks.com you'll also find our author blog, new and upcoming books, events, book club questions, excerpts, mystery resources, and more.

MIDNIGHT INK ORDERING INFORMATION

Order Online:
• Visit our website www.midnightinkbooks.com, select your books, and order them on our secure server.

Order by Phone:
• Call toll-free within the U.S. and Canada at
  1-888-NITE-INK (1-888-648-3465)
• We accept VISA, MasterCard, and American Express

Order by Mail:
Send the full price of your order (MN residents add 6.875% sales tax) in U.S. funds, plus postage & handling to:

> Midnight Ink
> 2143 Wooddale Drive
> Woodbury, MN 55125-2989

Postage & Handling:

Standard (U.S. & Canada). If your order is:
> $25.00 and under, add $4.00
> $25.01 and over, FREE STANDARD SHIPPING

AK, HI, PR: $16.00 for one book plus $2.00 for each additional book.

International Orders (airmail only):
> $16.00 for one book plus $3.00 for each additional book

Orders are processed within 12 business days. Please allow for normal shipping time.
Postage and handling rates subject to change.